A CHILD OF ARTHUR

A CHILD OF ARTHUR

An Inspirational Novel

By
LEE KESSLER

Printed in the United States of America
ISBN: 978-0-9888408-2-9
Library of Congress Control Number: 2017917968

Brunnen
PUBLISHING

DEDICATION

This book is dedicated to William Ferris Cummings, whose life ended far too soon, just a few weeks before I went up the mountain in Brunnen, Switzerland.

I do not know if the strained relationship between the young college speech teacher and her student, who was a member of the Black Panthers, resulted in Ferris learning from me. But I certainly learned from him. Through all the years I have always remembered him, and I have often been reminded by life that victory comes out of struggle.

It was through our struggle that I gained a great deal of compassion and understanding. I never knew what happened to Ferris, but it is my understanding now that, although his life was short, he did it right.

And for that, I want to dedicate this book to him and to his memory.

AUTHOR'S NOTE

It is a given that this question will be asked, so, after some soul-searching, I decided to answer it in advance. The novel you are about to read is an auto-biographical novel. The characters are fictitious to reveal the state of mind and character of Grace Archer. However, the story did in fact happen.

The "Romantic Encounter" occurred on that mountain in Switzerland, as it is written. The year 1980 was the darkest time of my life, and after coming down from that mountain, I have gone on to live a wonderful, rich, and victorious life. So I hesitated to ever let this story be published, since the depressed and desperate woman who went up to that mountain ridge—and who wrote this story more than 30 years ago—no longer exists.

But I realized that in these dangerous and turbulent times there are many who may be in exactly the same position emotionally and psychologically as I was in 1980. And, that being true, it is my hope that this journey from desperation and discouragement to purpose and victory may shed some light, and light the way.

Truth be told, there would be no other justification for my revealing something so deeply personal, albeit long ago handled, than the expectation that you, my reader, may find some hope, some comfort here.

The following story was written in the summer of 1980—almost a fictional diary. Except for editing to correct punctuation, grammar, and clarity of sentence structure so that you can actually understand what I wrote back then, it is as it occurred, and as it was written then. For those of you who know me as a fairly sophisticated writer of political fiction, the different style of this novel—and possible immaturity of the writing—may be evident. The immaturity of my first novel, written 30 years ago, is a testimony to something, and is what this novel is about. It is a journey from one to the other.

It is a romantic novel in the fullest definition of the word "romantic": involving mystery, idealism, adventure, separateness, and heroism, as well as affection and love.

The beginning and the end have been updated to fit the story into the plausible present life of "Grace Archer." Everything in between is as it was experienced and written about long ago. The present-day conclusion of the story was shocking and affirming even to me. And it alone warranted telling the rest of the story, and bringing into daylight the admittedly embarrassing journey of a woman through potentially life-damaging devastation into a life of adventure, mystery, and, yes, "grace."

I am grateful to have emerged victorious, and it is my prayer that each of you who may be "on a mountain top" searching, descends from the mountain back into life, and that you create a great life and great adventure for yourself.

This story, which could have remained only with me and my memories, now is yours in the hope that it enlightens somehow.

CHAPTER ONE

S he had known that one day the story would have to be told. It had been more than 35 years since she had met him on the mountain in Switzerland, yet hardly a week went by without her remembering him. And now that she had publicly thanked him at the ceremony where she and her producing partners had accepted the award for Best Picture of 2020 for the adaptation of her first bestselling novel, *White King and the Doctor*—and with the other two books of the trilogy in production as well—she knew what the first question in her first post-award interview would be.

Grace, what have you done? She chastised herself for having to open those defining moments in the summer of 1980. It was momentary, however, as deep in her heart she knew she had intended to reveal this at some point in her life. Now, in the final chapters of her own life's story, Grace Archer knew it was time.

For many would wonder how the actress who had been the first woman in the world to portray the legendary diarist, Anais Nin, could possibly have transformed into a stellar businesswoman and leadership coach to a generation, a social activist whose projects were designed to present ideas which could change the world, a passionate human rights activist, and an outspoken political activist.

She smiled, realizing just how much she had, in fact, changed. The original Grace Archer who went up the mountain that day long ago bore no resemblance to the woman she had become, and her life and its full activities bore no resemblance to her life of 1980, let alone 1967—the first time she had unknowingly met him.

The front door chime rang out, and she heard Bertha quickly open it, greet her guests, and begin to escort them to her on the patio of her home. She had decided to do this outside overlooking the Pacific. Smiling now, she admitted she still had a bit of a devilish streak. Selecting three journalism majors from USC to have the honor of the exclusive interview, as compared to the usual Hollywood suspects, she knew their enthusiasm alone would carry them through, and they would not fail to ask the question that had to be asked, if the true story were to be told.

It was not their first question she dreaded; it was their last—if they were as earnest as she perceived this trio to be. *Ah, well, it'll be over in a few hours...* she thought, as Bertha led two young men and one young woman to her.

"I'm Grace Archer. Welcome to my home." She extended her hand firmly to each, looking all three in the eye to see which one seemed the most confident. To her surprise, they were all evenly matched, but she sensed they had already selected the "head of their party." His name was Doug. He was tall, clean-cut, with wavy dark hair and eyes the color of the Mediterranean. He respectfully thanked her for this great opportunity and introduced Adam and Alyssa. Though mere colleagues, the two looked like brother and sister, each sporting curly red hair and a few freckles. There seemed a natural alliance between the two, and Grace wondered whether their questions would mirror each other as well.

Seated now, with beverages and refreshments, Doug placed an mp3 recorder in the center of the patio table, and each of his colleagues opened up their notebook to commence note taking. Adam and Alyssa sat side by side. She noticed Adam was left-handed, and that Alyssa seemed more inclined to listen than to take notes. They certainly represented different styles of engagement in listening and interviewing. Grace decided she liked these young people.

"Is it all right to record?"

"Yes, definitely," Grace answered. Though her heart was pounding, she quashed her own anxiety and prepared to tell the story she had never told. She and she alone knew what happened on the mountain. Much benefit had come from it, and it was time to give credit where credit was due. It was not a secret she wished to carry to her grave.

"We know, Ms. Archer, of your noteworthy works in the last thirty years," Doug began. "But we would like to ask today about what happened that changed you so, and what led you onto the path you have been on?"

She nodded and smiled at him.

Doug continued. "And, given that you spoke of this at the Awards, I would first like to ask you, who is Klaus? And why were you thanking him?"

There it was. They had begun just as she guessed young, ambitious, self-confident journalists would start an interview, which could enhance their careers immensely. The opening question had been asked, and she was ready.

"It's best if I answer that by reading you a story. In the spring of 1980, I traveled for the third time to a small town on Lake Lucerne. It was a desperate and dangerous time in my young life, and the only haven I trusted was this little-known community..."

She could see it clearly now, as she reached into her memory to select the best point to begin. It was important for them to understand why she had been suffering, and why she had fled to Brunnen, Switzerland years ago. Pausing for a moment, she opened a manuscript she had placed on the side table. "This is my autobiographical novel. I wrote it in 1981 but never published it. Your answer lies in here." She selected the start point and began reading to them the work she intended to publish next.

CHAPTER TWO

It wasn't until she was thirty that she experienced depression. Like a Golden Girl, she had lived a previous life that seemed to be brightly illuminated, with only the occasional shadow of despair fleeting through. To her, in fact, it seemed as if she had only occasional clouds, which would block the sun for a day or two and then be gone, leaving nothing behind—no scars, no healing wounds.

But since that day in February 1978, darkness was a constant factor in her life. That is not to say she was living in a state of depression, rather that Depression was always present—waiting in the wings of activity and feeling, waiting to enter onto the stage if she were too tired, or suffering from defeat or uncertainty.

Before, she had known warmth, brightness, and an intrinsic sense that any darkness was transitory and harmless—not a part of her cosmos. It was almost like a fugitive from someone else's pain who had strayed into her story, looking for his rightful place. Recognizing his error, Depression would hastily exit, begging forgiveness for his false entrance. He would not be seen again for months.

Now, however, her life was changed. Even when she felt brightness and direction, there was a pervasive sense—an intimation if you will—of a dark and powerful force always hovering, always ready to enter. She sensed that this time the entrance would be authoritative and aggressive, with no hasty and apologetic exit. This time, the character would enter the play readily, if only she gave him the right cue.

A few times in the last three years she had thrown that cue, and Depression had indeed entered. Only through an ensuing fierce battle could she extricate herself and restore calm. And always now she was aware of the threat—the possibility of his re-entrance. Life was now light, air, and brightness in the midst of infinite darkness and clouds—a finite oasis. Depression had gone from undesired acquaintance to intimate friend. Her task was to hold him at bay.

And she thanked God—or whatever was out there responsible for the order of things—that she was in the oasis now. Three years ago it had not been so.

She hadn't heard the announcement. Only when the young man's hand lightly touched her arm did she look up.

"Madame, we are boarding now. Your boarding pass?"

Charming dialect, she thought, wondering if he were French. *Lovely eyes,* she noted. Grace opened her bag for the young man. As always, when someone's eyes gazed steadily at her, she couldn't find the boarding pass. For someone who made her living with eyes gazing at her—who relished people watching her in a role performed with remarkable control—she never could understand why it was that boarding passes, parking ticket stubs, dollar bills in her change purse, etc. seemed to elude her when she was called upon to present them. Like objects with a life of their own, they seemed intent upon causing her to fumble, to lose control, to appear clumsy. Tonight was no exception. She exhaled loudly as she told herself to relax, that it would turn up.

Voila! Right there on top. The blue eyes flickered, and the young man said, "Danke schön," as she handed over the recalcitrant card. That rush of impatience came up again. She seemed so impatient today. Grace knew why, but she did not want to take time to think it through now. If she could just get to Brunnen, there would be time enough to do that there. Everything would be all right in Brunnen.

Keep that storm front out, she coached herself. *Hold onto the oasis.*

The trip would have been so much easier had Robert, the producer/writer she was dating, been able to travel on the same flight. He, however, lived in Los Angeles, and she lived now in New York. With a recent filming schedule conflict, he was unable to make the connection into New York to fly with her. Instead, he was arriving a bit later, coming straight in from Los Angeles. It was his first trip to Europe and their first trip together.

Though Grace had some trepidation about this, and what it might portend in their volatile relationship, her thoughts were not on Robert. *Keith again! Why today? Why Keith? It must be Brunnen,* she reasoned. The last time she was there a decade ago, she was with her husband, treating him to a vacation in Bavaria before they moved to Los Angeles for him to begin law school. Ten years later she was returning, but without a husband. The husband had jettisoned at eight and one/half years.

Sitting at the window looking out at the flagman motioning the plane away from the gate, she felt a little jolt, slight really. And the trip was on.

Jettisoned after eight and one/half years. That was an appropriate way to put it. That night was very clear to her now. It was a night when she had asked a question she didn't really want to hear the answer to. The answer had been there anyway.

Grace snapped back to present time when the stewardess handed her ear phones. Along with the earphones came a Swiss chocolate bar, a magazine, the menu in French, and a pair of red and blue booties. *Now what in the hell are these for?* she thought. *With Balair written on them.* Casting a glance at her neighbor as he kicked off his shoes and put on his booties, she followed suit and settled in for a comfortable evening flight to Zurich, Switzerland.

In order not to be distracted, she plugged in the ear phones, selected a classical channel, and turned the volume to its lowest position as her gaze drifted out the window. Pretending she was sleeping, she enjoyed her little deception, her moment of stolen solitude. The fact that she had to steal solitude caused her to hesitate. These damned doubts! Why were they sneaking in like this? Why now? And why so often?

She knew they were divisive. Perhaps the trip would disperse them and bring her back to Robert again.

She acknowledged the feeling of sadness—the sense of something lost, or at the very least changing. She acknowledged a sense of malaise accompanied by fear. But, like a patient who is unwilling or unprepared to deal with certain symptoms, she denied them. *Remain in the oasis, Grace,* she coached herself. *This is no storm front, probably only scattered clouds. Just a shadow in a bright day.*

It had not always been so. Ah, pain. She was back to that night again. Keith had been away on business for two weeks. It was February 1978. The fact that February had always been disastrous for her eluded her for a while. They had had a standing joke about it. This February was to be no exception. In fact, the others were all preparatory—a training ground of thirty-one years—for the jolt she was to get that night.

She had been married when marriages were to be forever. June 22, 1969 was the only sunny day in the month of June that year. It was a good sign, a sign typical of her life to date. Actually the day had been postponed from the 14th because the country club in the nearest town couldn't handle their reception on that day. Since she was to have one of the biggest and most formal weddings in her little village of nine hundred people in an upstate New York county, the day had been changed.

Her father—a tall, severe man who looked like George Washington—had bought a new Cadillac, ostensibly to have four doors so that she could get in and out more easily in her gown. But she knew he had coveted that silver car for months and needed only an excuse. Cars were his weakness. No one minded. Despite the Vietnam War. Despite tear gas in her world at the University of Wisconsin Graduate Department of Theatre, despite Martin Luther King, she and her family lived isolated from that world—secure in their comprehension of the world but without involvement in it.

All were unscathed by the slings and arrows of the outrageous fortune of the late '60s. She herself had survived the tumultuous period of youth's revolt and confusion with remarkable clarity. She had not used drugs, did not drink, and was not part of the sexual revolution. In fact, that day in June, dressed in her white peau de soie gown with seeded pearls and lace bodice, she was a virgin—almost. Ironic that.

All her life she had done the impossible. If she had set her mind to do something, it had been accomplished. If she wished to achieve some goal, she assessed the requirements and set up the plans, the work regime, and settled in to very shortly thereafter achieve her goal. It all had come easily for her—her life and the American dream. She was graduated Summa Cum Laude from a small Presbyterian college in Western Pennsylvania whose school song was astonishingly written in a minor key, thereby making it all but impossible for anyone but music majors to sing.

Gerald Ford had given the commencement address that graduation day. Perhaps because, alphabetically, she was the first Summa Cum Laude grad to be called forth, or whether something in her sparked his interest, the future President had looked up, scanning the graduates, waiting for her to rise. As she did, he had deviated from the planned decorum by rising and personally handing her the diploma and shaking her hand. Their eyes had met and, as he firmly crunched her fingers together, he had simply said, "Well done. Keep it up." Little did she know that ten years later, she would be his spokeswoman in a very controversial California television commercial. At that moment she had flushed, probably blushed, and, above all, had felt blessed.

She was the only female Summa Cum Laude graduate that year. She was the only one, further, who had won every scholastic award presented by the college. She was the one who, with her debate partner Keith, had been debate and oratory champions. It seemed only natural then that she would be the only one who, in her senior year, would have become pregnant while technically still a virgin.

The doctors in Western Pennsylvania had had a difficult time with that one. She had been sent to three—each of whom had said, "Yes, you're pregnant, and yes, your hymen is completely intact. How did you do this?"

She remembered only that Keith and she were fooling around on a debate trip. Naked or near naked, they were in a hotel room consumed with a sense of ignorant liberation, believing that if the man came outside, no harm could be done. Grace may have had the highest IQ in her private college, but she also had never read anything regarding birth control. To add insult to injury, she had become pregnant two days after her period.

The third doctor, upon hearing that, had said, "Well, that just goes to show you the idiocy of the rhythm method." He had revealed that he had read of one or two such cases like hers, but had never experienced one. And there she was again—in the top 99th percentile!

The nurse who first apprised her of the test results had oozed warmth and an almost jealous enthusiasm for Grace's condition. "You'll be happy to know the test was positive. You are pregnant. The doctor, of course, will be happy to take care of you during your term. I've set up a schedule of visits for you and a diet..." Grace never heard the end of that sentence. She had vomited in the phone booth, dropping the phone. Keith had helped her back into an empty classroom, set her down, and let her weep. Kneeling beside her, his arm awkwardly consoling her shoulder, he had done what any young man of his era and background would have done. He asked her to marry him.

Grace was grateful, but she had no intention of having a baby. She had just received a coveted fellowship to the University of Wisconsin for four years of study with full expenses paid, and no teaching requirement. She was the sixth-ranked student at the University of Wisconsin. She was also very conservative, very insulated, very afraid, and *very* certain she did not want a baby.

An abortion was arranged. That was no small accomplishment in those times when all were still illegal. It was essential that her parents never know. Keith made the arrangements by day, and she lay in her room by night, secretly praying for the baby to be gone.

Two days before she and Keith were to have flown to New York City to have an abortion, under the guise of a special debate tournament at New York University, she had miscarried. Her prayers were answered. She was relieved. So was Keith.

The only setback to their wedding that sunny day one and one-half years later was the fact that, two days before the wedding, Keith had been called to active duty. The Draft Board had tracked him to her minister and the minister had called to tell him. Keith's particularly spicy John Birch Society mother from the North Shore of Chicago laughed as she chewed her potato salad and said, "Well, it looks as if you'll be a 'war bride' after all!"

Actually, Keith was in the Reserves. He had wanted to serve his country—within reason. He had no desire to go to Vietnam, and he did desire to go to law school. So he had compromised. He had enlisted in the Reserves.

Their honeymoon was cut short, and five days after they were married he left for four and one-half months of training in a hell-hole of mosquitoes, steam, and spinal meningitis called Fort Leonardwood in Missouri. Grace very practically used the lonely summer to write her Master's dissertation, get her degree, and move to a small Illinois college where she would teach drama, speech, direct plays, and develop a drama department. She was twenty-two.

All these pleasant anecdotes make a good story, but not necessarily a good marriage. Although they seemed to have a perfect marriage with companionship, friendship, compatibility, shared dreams, playfulness, and a beautiful home with just enough funk, she lay in bed that night, eight years later, knowing by the squeezing in her gut that something was wrong.

That February she was working at the Meredith Tandem Forum in Los Angeles. For a young actress in the L.A. theatre scene, this was the most prestigious and experimental of the theatres in Hollywood. Her career was going well. The television roles were getting larger, and her recognition among casting people and directors was running high. She was enjoying the reputation of being a "splendid actress"—that is to say a "true" artist, not just a "Hollywood" actress.

She had just performed her one-woman show on Anais Nin for the first time. Now she was understudying a major star in the West Coast premiere of "First Day." The play later moved to New York. The role was incredibly challenging, as it was the story of a released convicted killer on her first day out, trying to make a life for herself. It was tough both physically and emotionally. The demands upon the actress were especially intense, as she's on stage the entire two hours, controlling the flow and rhythm of the entire piece. The understudy's job was a tough one on this show, and was aggravated by the star's lack of concentration in a staged rape scene. She rarely played the scene as it was choreographed. The result was that either she or her male partner were likely to get hurt. Grace knew she would have to go on, and she was ready. Deep inside, she felt it would be her big break—the role that would establish her as a stage star with powerful presence.

But that night she was still angry at Keith for his stunt the week before. He had been away at a trial all week, and had left flowers in her dressing room at the Tandem with a note saying he was going to a University of Southern California basketball game, and would see her at home after the show. It was so typically sweet and thoughtful of him. Even romantic. And she had raced home, saying no to a drink with friends in order to get home to him.

He wasn't there. By midnight she knew, of course, that the game was long over. She had begun to worry and had stationed herself on their deck overlooking the San Fernando Valley and the only access street to their house in the hills. Only a few cars had driven up, but none were the Renault 17 she had given him for his 30th birthday.

At 1AM the phone had rung. Leaping at it, she had shouted, "Hello."

"Now don't worry. I'm all right." It was Keith.

"Where are you? I was so worried."

"At the police station. We were mugged."

"Oh my God…"

He had reassured her, "But I'm all right. There was a knife skirmish, but I'm okay. They got the guy, but I have to stay here to make an ID."

At first, there was relief. But then she remembered he had said "we." A question not to be asked?

"Who were you with?"

He had delayed a second—or a minute. "A couple of girls from the office."

"How'd you manage to hook up with them?"

"Well, I had given them my tickets. When I returned early, I realized I could go, too, so I joined them there," he had said smoothly.

"And you were mugged at the game?"

"No, at the Red Onion."

Grace knew that was a disco. Her mind had struggled not to piece this together. But only one picture came together, no matter how many times she shook it up, hoping another, better one would appear.

All she had said was, "You left me flowers."

"Yes."

What was in his voice? "You told me to meet you at home."

"Yes."

She knew she sounded as if she were interrogating or reading an indictment, but she couldn't stop herself. He had given the direct textbook witness answers—a simple, unembellished yes or no. So she pursued. "And you went to a disco with two girls?"

"Yes."

His courtroom delivery confused her, and there was no way to conceal the hurt. "I'm coming down to get you. Where are you?" she had demanded.

Keith jumped in. "No. I'm all right. We'll finish here soon. They're about to take my statement on the knife fight."

That brought him around, she thought, and added quickly, "I want to come."

He had shouted, "No! I don't want you to. I could have been killed tonight, Grace. Almost was. I expected you to be sympathetic, not accusatory. But no. Well, I'm not going to have a jealous wife come down here and upset these girls anymore!"

"But what about me?" She was defensive now. "I'm upset, too. I've been afraid. I'd like to be with you."

He was very angry and had started to hang up. She tried to reach into the phone with, "I won't make a jealous scene, I promise."

"I'll see you at home." And he was gone.

She had written him a long note explaining that she had not meant to accuse or to criticize. She had been angry at being stood up, angry from fear, angry at his thoughtlessness, and she had reacted to that. Fearing that her tone of voice would undermine the logic of her arguments, she had written it down. On a yellow legal pad she had poured it all out as articulately and completely as she well could. And like Martin Luther at Wittenberg, she had tacked the thesis to the front door and gone to bed.

When he pulled up in front, she had looked at the clock. It was 3AM. She had feigned sleep as he approached the door. *Why doesn't he come in? Of course,* she reminded herself, *I posted a God-damned thesis to it!* No doubt he was struggling to read it in the light of one art-deco porch light.

Their bedroom was on the same level as the entrance, and she had heard the latch turn as he entered. He had stood in the bedroom door. It seemed like an eternity. Apparently believing she was asleep, he had come over to the bed, sat beside her, embraced her, and whispered, "I love you." As he embraced her, she had heard the "thesis" fall to the floor.

That was a week ago. He had been away again on the same trial in beautiful Bakersfield and would be home soon. She had wine chilling.

When he came in, the amenities were covered in less than 45 seconds. Declining the chablis, he said he was very tired and would like to sleep. She waited in bed as he undressed, hastily covered himself with pajamas, slipped into bed, and turned off the light. Trying to engage him—lonely, needing to talk, even if only shop talk; needing to be kissed or held or even tickled—she made the grand stand play, guaranteed to bring him to his senses.

Dramatically, with shimmering conviction, she bounded out of bed, hurling the covers back, and popped on the rheostat-controlled spotlight, which was focused on their bed. Keith rolled over—caught on the illuminated stage of their California king-sized bed—costumed only in his striped pajamas. He blinked as she said, "We have to talk."

Pausing for maximum effect, and to make certain he understood her feelings, she then continued. "If we don't, we're not going to make it to number 10." She had expected the act to end with dialogue like, "Don't be silly, Grace, you're just dramatizing. I'm just tired. I'm overworked. We'll talk about it. You know I love you." Any of these would have sufficed.

Keith had center stage, however. He looked her straight in the eyes, took a deep breath, and delivered the curtain line. "I know."

Blackout. And the beginning of darkness.

CHAPTER THREE

J ust as Grace felt her left side knotting up, as if in a reflex reaction to the blow of the memory, she heard a quiet, measured voice say, "What would you like?"

The stewardess had rolled her coffee, tea, or Seagram's cart to their seats. She asked for only water. Her neighbor, who had been reading, hidden behind the *International Times*, lowered the paper and ordered a scotch and water. He spoke in perfect Oxford English with a German accent. Seizing the opportunity, he introduced himself as Rudolf Isel, an import-export executive from Zurich whose firm had offices in New York, Hong Kong, Singapore, and Tokyo. *That explains the Oxford English,* she noted.

Grace had never been good at initiating or carrying on conversations with strangers. And for a moment, she wished Robert were there. She knew he would have launched into a long conversation about Europe and the Common Market, asking questions about the Austrian and German economies, about socialism, about French President D'Estain's problems.

That was one of the things she admired most about her friend—his curiosity. Being a writer and producer, he always probed new people, opening them up and encouraging them to talk at great length about themselves. He would listen, nod, and take it all in hungrily. That was something she had great difficulty doing. Grace was basically very shy. For years she had assumed her shyness came from arrogance—that she was withdrawn in order to avoid "casting pearls among swine," as her mother used to say. She suspected now, though, that it really was fear, or worse—fear that she really held no "pearls" after all, and that someone would discover her truth.

She exited the conversation as inoffensively as she could by telling the "International Times" she was going to try to rest. Leaning back against the window, angling her body away from the man, she closed her eyes. But, having brought up Robert in her mind's eye, she now couldn't turn off the image. Like someone fixated, unable to change the channel, she was looking at him as she had when they were last together for Thanksgiving in Los Angeles.

He had changed in the three years she had known him. He now had the beginnings of a middle-aged belly. Try as he would to hold it in if he caught her looking at his stomach, it was there—a roll or two. He blamed it on her Thanksgiving dinner—cooked eighteen months earlier—and reassured her he could lose it in a minute. Why didn't he? she had asked herself. Either he couldn't lose it, or didn't want to. She wondered if he were accepting middle age.

His arms, though, were still strong and muscular, his chest still broad and firm. Although the pectorals were sagging some—not helped by the extra weight. His legs were in great condition—well-shaped and in perfect muscular tone. When she first met him, he ran ten miles a day. Now he didn't run at all. *My influence?* She hoped not.

Another critical observation crept in. He was being treated by her doctor for high blood pressure now, and had been for ten months. Although he swore he was eating no salt, and had revised his diet, she was sure he was secretly indulging. She imagined him sneaking to the Old World Deli near his Culver City studio, gorging himself with liver pate.

Pushing that thought aside, she decided to look at something she admired, his hands. When they touched her, she knew she was real and not someone's fantasy. From his touch, she always knew she was appreciated. His hands had taught her she was beautiful. Early in their relationship they had confirmed what her own eyes had always seen. At the time, though, when her vision was blurred and she was drowning in the total blackness of rejection and lost identity, his hands had shown her the way. They had restored her to her sensual self. He had done it easily and naturally. The fact that she stood in the light at all today was due largely to Robert. For this she was, at the very least, grateful.

The incipient anxiety waned, and she let her mind's eye take a closer look at Robert's features. His individual features were all irregular and far from perfect. Put together, however, she found him rather handsome, definitely distinguished, and sexy—rarely all at the same time, however. His mouth was long and narrow, his active lips thin and muscular, and his teeth were too small. When he grinned, it created the appearance of a line in his face. His eyes were small, but a beautiful blue. The skin below the eyes was pouchy and beginning to pucker with age.

That and the fact he constantly rubs his eyes, she thought. She hated herself for nagging him about it, but she knew he was destroying the delicate tissue every time he enthusiastically rubbed his tired eyes, and then pulled at the skin underneath, as if exercising it. Any woman who spends hours learning and applying the techniques of keeping the skin from breaking down and bringing on premature aging would cringe if she saw him pull at that delicate skin. *But, he works on the opposite side of the camera from me,* she reminded herself, and promised herself she would not bring it up again—certainly not on this trip.

Appraising his body further, her eyes went now to his hair. Robert hated his hair; she loved it. It was very curly and went naturally into the tight curls other men used permanents to create. It was dark brown, with gray dramatically located around the temples. And there was plenty of hair, despite the receding hair line. When left to dry naturally, it took the perfect "natural" shape. And it made him look younger and more boyish. He never trusted it, however. *He and his hair have an interesting relationship,* she thought, smiling. He was forever trying to bat it down. Using the palms of his hands, he would bang it down, as if trying to paddle it into shape. Turning his head from side to side in the mirror, he would bat first one side, and then the other, until satisfied. It was rather like watching a ping pong game, and she marveled that he had never given himself a concussion. Such was the severity of the battle until the unruly curls were forced into submission.

Apparently when he was young, his brutish Irish brother had teased him about his hair and used to call him "Little Orphan Annie." So often what is said to a child in jest, or in pique, is never forgotten. It makes an indelible imprint on the young one and affects choices made throughout their life. Robert hated being called "Little Orphan Annie," and he had grown to hate his hair. He had never forgiven his hair for providing his brother with the opportunity to ridicule. Like Faustus, he would have made a pact with the Devil to have altered his hair. To this day, he was extremely sensitive.

Grace could understand this well enough. She herself had been called a name by the kids who went to the school where her father was principal. Twenty years later, she had cosmetic surgery to change the offending area. During those twenty years, however, she had lived with, been scarred by, and had made life choices in reaction to the nickname "Little Beak." Not until after her surgery at age thirty-two did she realize that the kids were not referring to her nose. Her father had a huge nose. Derisively reacting to this stern, dictatorial principal, they called him "the Beak." Grace, by virtue of her parentage and not by virtue of the size of her own nose, was dubbed "Little Beak."

The past could not be changed, however. She decided to stop looking into that past, opened her eyes briefly, and looked out the window again. It was night now. Only the rhythmic blinking lights on the wing were visible in the darkness. So, she closed her eyes once again.

She remembered the first time she had met Keith. It was in the spring of her sophomore year in college. The campus was especially beautiful—laden with azaleas and oleander in all shades of pink and purple. The smell of lilacs was buoyant. And she, too, felt so alive, as the earth returned to life and pushed forth blossoms.

The year had been difficult between her father and her. When she had started college, she was a pre-med major, emphasizing chemistry. Her father believed she would follow in her brother's footsteps. He was seventeen years older and now a famous liver research surgeon with the government. Instead of opting for the money and fortune he would have acquired in private practice, he had opted early for the chance to change the future—to rewrite the text books. And he had done just that. He had made very little money. He seemed fulfilled. But he did drink too much. And he did yell at his daughters.

She had always admired him and felt close to his artistic temperament. They had similar patience and determined ability to achieve goals. Chemistry was her main field. She was doing brilliantly in it. Her only problems of adjustment in college had been great loneliness and great intensity—feelings of a responsibility to learn everything possible. She had solved the loneliness by participating in drama, taking the lead in plays at night. The intensity had been solved by her chemistry professor, who was also her advisor. One day in her Freshman Chemistry class she had asked a question. The entire amphitheater of three hundred students had become restless. She heard coughing, whispering, and laughter and feared she had asked a stupid question. The feeling was not ameliorated when a tall, red-headed fellow she had a severe crush on leaned forward, laughing, and said, "Grace, how many years of chemistry have you had?" Simultaneously, her professor, instead of answering, said, "I'll talk to *you* after class."

She went to the front of the theatre and waited behind the others who had last-minute questions. Dr. Nagel peered between two students and motioned for her to wait. She was afraid and embarrassed to have revealed such ignorance and disrupted the classroom. Suddenly he darted to her and said, with 1965 formality, "Miss Archer, did someone once tell you that you were a computer?" She said she didn't understand. He continued. "I know why you asked the question." He seemed impatient. "I did not answer it because the rest of the class did not even understand the question."

"Not understand?"

"Yes. It was beyond them. And I want to give you some advice. You are not a computer. You do not need to know everything there is to know in this world. No one expects you to. It will come in time. Do you understand?"

"I think so. Yes, sir." She didn't. But she never asked another question in chemistry—or any other class. Neither at Grove University, nor at the University of Wisconsin. From that moment on, she was content to hold in what she knew, and answer her own questions.

Sometimes, when he apparently felt she was backsliding, Dr. Nagel would torment her in chemistry lab. After a three-hour struggle with an "unknown" in Qualitative Analysis, she would walk to his window, beaming triumphantly as she handed in her sheet, confident she had solved the puzzle perfectly. It was then that he would look at her, look at the sheet, check his log book for the correct analysis of her sample, and place a large zero on the page. He would hand the paper back to her, watching closely from behind his wire-rimmed glasses. He seemed to enjoy watching her face fall—panic setting in, eyes tearing up. The thought of a "zero" caused her to hyperventilate.

Then, at just the right moment of her excruciation, he would jerk the paper back, saying, "Oops, almost forgot." And he would add another zero in front of the first, look at her to see if she understood, and then add a number one in front of the two zeroes. And then he would observe her face transform from despair to relief. His decision to personally supervise her obsession with perfection—her need to be best—resulted in many such tricks. Despite this, she liked him. He was full of joy. He must have read her lack of it, and therefore decided to work on her intensity.

In the midst of all this came "Hedda Gabler." She was selected to play Hedda. The head of the Drama Department sent a student emissary to her dorm to talk with her and ask her if she would play the role. She did not have to audition. He told her that the director had said, "I've been waiting all my life to direct this play, waiting for someone who could play Hedda. I've finally found her." *Now who could say no to that?* she thought. She took the part. She was just seventeen.

The night the play closed, she made the mistake of returning to the theatre during the striking of the set. As she watched the walls of the set—the substance of her life as Hedda—being dismantled, she knew that she could not let her go. As the last flat disappeared into the hold, she made her decision. The next day, she went to Dr. Nagel and changed her major from pre-med to acting.

Her father was furious when she told him. She had waited until spring vacation to tell her parents. The week was a blur of battles and threats. She vaguely remembered talk of "wasting her life, wasting her brain, being irresponsible with the gifts she had been given." Her mother was unobtrusively supportive. Being too afraid of Grace's father to defend her daughter, she remained silent. But Grace knew she approved.

Suddenly the storm stopped as quickly as it had begun. Suspecting her father had a plan, she waited. Nothing happened. Late that summer, her mother confided in her that they had driven to the college for the May Day celebrations, and while Grace was being inducted into a national sophomore honorary, her father had talked to Dr. Nagel, trying to elicit his help in dissuading his daughter from "throwing her life away."

Dr. Nagel had said, "You know, Mr. Archer, we have a great many bright girls at this college. We pride ourselves in that. But Grace is more than bright. She's brilliant. I wouldn't worry. She'll be successful at whatever she chooses to do. I know that you'll be proud of her." Her father never mentioned it, but he never argued again about her being an actress. He did become teary on occasion when things became difficult years later in Los Angeles, however.

One year later, at the beginning of "Midsummer Night's Dream," the cast was short two actors. During the first read-through on stage, the director said two young men would be coming that night to read. If they wanted, they would join the cast. As they came onstage and were introduced—both being named Keith—Grace had been overcome with a feeling that, by the end of the play, she would be dating one of them. Little did she know that both Keiths were fraternity pledges to the same fraternity and were going out for the play on a challenge by one of their brothers during Hell Week.

That first night, at the close of rehearsal, the Keith who looked vaguely like Errol Flynn had come up to her by the backstage door. Attempting to strike up a conversation, he said, "Are you going down?" To which she responded without thinking, "No. Do you think I always do?" There was an awkward pause as both tried to grasp the meaning of what the other had said. Keith flushed deeply, stuttered a bit, and disappeared back onto the stage. A moment or two later, he reappeared—this time from the audience area.

"I'm sorry. I uh, I uh, I meant…" He struggled. "Well, I thought you lived at the dorm near mine. I meant are you going downhill to the dorm?"

Then it had been her turn to blush. The double entendre became clear to her, and she stood there not knowing what to say. An amazingly articulate response came out. "Oh."

"Let me walk you to your dorm—uphill," he said, recovering.

"I'd like that."

Arriving at the dorm, they sat on the stone wall outside the entrance and chatted easily with one another. Apparently feeling more confident, Keith suddenly blurted out, "Before some other rapacious gentleman does this, would you like to go to May Day with me?"

She said she would.

"Great." He put his arm around her to give her a kiss—whether of gratitude or passion, she wasn't sure. Either way, he made the move so swiftly, and with such hard pressure on her lips, that she lost her balance and he, holding her, tumbled backward into the bushes with her.

They were married three years later.

It was curious that she would have remembered all this. That was ten-year-old history. Her mind changed channels, and she was standing now in the restroom of the Meredith Tandem Forum on opening night of a very dark play, talking to her agent Carolina. There was a distance between them in recent months. Grace didn't fully understand it. All she knew was that she hadn't worked in four months and, although she never had been particularly close to this subagent, she somehow doubted whether Carolina was working hard enough for her. She had always felt Carolina was a bit too slovenly, not classy enough to appreciate or effectively represent her. The agency owner—a principled Irish woman with natural flaming red hair—seemed to feel, however, that the girl had talent, was aggressive, and ambitious. She had personally seen to it that Carolina improved her appearance—wearing dresses rather than jeans and blousy tops.

Looking at her tonight, Grace thought she looked quite sexy in her orange dress with a deep décolletage. *My God her breasts are enormous,* she observed. Her hair was cut and styled, and her recent weight loss revealed a slender waist, still-too-round hips, but nice legs. All-in-all, she was a great improvement over last year.

Grace absently commented on a gold chain around her neck with the word Pooh carved in gold. Carolina, in her Brooklyn dialect, described where she'd received it. Grace knew she was being snobbish, but that dialect made her flinch. The girl was obviously intelligent, but that damned dialect made her sound coarse and uneducated. She reprimanded herself for criticizing something Carolina could not control, and tuned back in as Carolina cooed.

"My brother gave this to me. My family nickname is Pooh. He started calling me that years ago. Only he, and a few intimate friends, call me Pooh."

Grace smiled, thinking, *What does one say to a remark like that?* She reproached herself for not being better at small talk. That was one aspect of her business she was no good at. So all she said was, "Well, I'd better get back. Nice to see you."

Afterwards, having made their way backstage, Grace and Keith waited to congratulate her friend on the new show. Keith was seated, Grace standing, as they chatted with a friend. Grace saw a bare arm reach between several people, a gold bracelet dangling. The hand tapped Keith on the leg. He turned to see who it was. Grace turned, too, continuing her conversation with her other friend. It was Carolina. She looked only at Keith and said quietly, "Hi."

Keith smiled, said "Hi," and turned back abruptly to Grace and her friend, angling his body to exclude Carolina and include only his wife. It was a subtle move. No one would have taken notice. The whole exchange lasted only a few seconds. In that instant, however, Grace knew that her husband and her agent were lovers. She continued smiling through that Hollywood party.

That terrible night two months earlier in February when Keith had stunned her with his curtain line, they had sat up all night, picking at the truth. He told her that for some time he had had many lovers, that he was not in love with anyone else, that he was bored with everyone and everything. He found Grace more interesting than anyone else, but he felt numb and trapped.

Returning from the Meredith Tandem following this realization, however, Grace exploded. They had just come into the bedroom when she whirled around and hissed, "You had an affair with Carolina, didn't you?" He was a long time in answering, weighing the alternatives.

"Yes. It's all over now."

"Why?"

"That's my business. I don't have to answer that," he said, pleading the Fifth. "Just know I ended it."

"You ended it? Why? Why her? She's fat; she's slovenly!"

He interrupted, cutting her off vehemently, almost venomously. "I find her sexy—and raw."

"She's a pig, and totally immoral!"

"Oh, come on, Grace…" He tried to ignore that, waving it away with his right hand. But the flood gates of her pain were opened.

"No, you listen. I understood and wept with you when I learned of the affairs. I felt for your confusion and your sense of entrapment. I sympathized. I even read *Passages*! But now I find out you've been fucking my agent. While I'm out every night—first with my own show and then with 'First Day'—paying the price on the stage, she's taking 10% of my salary while she's screwing my husband!"

Sobbing and careening from one wall to another in their room, she laughed bitterly and choked out words between gulps of air. "You know, they always warn you that agents will screw you, but this is too much!"

He interrupted. "Now just a minute, Grace. It's over. She started it, and I ended it. It didn't last long, and it didn't mean anything."

"It meant that I haven't worked for four months. It meant that on the opening of my show—after six months of preparation and after a standing ovation—she comes backstage and can barely whisper, 'That was interesting material.' Now what is that? Is that loyalty? Is that honor?"

Keith the debater/lawyer surfaced. "I'm sure that this has nothing to do with you not working."

Grace screamed, "I don't care. It has to do with lying, with stealing, and with having absolutely no comprehension of what it means to be an agent. She is the worst of what's Hollywood."

Pausing for a moment, she muttered, "My life's become a soap opera. My life!" At that moment she heard her voice, really heard it, as if she were removed enough to hear a playback. She heard the shrill, raucous screams and the bleating pain. And she, who had always relied upon her intellect to supply compassion and understanding, felt true pain—raw, exposed nerves.

She saw her contorted face. She smelled the ugliness of shattered illusions, and, for the first time in her life, felt as if she were part of the human condition. Struggling against the role, she fell to her knees, rocking back and forth until, from the deepest center of her being, came the sobs. Only she was retching—something tearing inside with every fresh intake of air. She swallowed air, and retched faith in others, retched hope for something better, retched illusive honor. The final tearing unraveled the whole thread of her belief in how life operated.

Keith was on his knees, crying—terrified by the inhuman, gravelly sound—holding her as she unraveled. "Grace, I can't bear it. To see this happen to you, and know I did it. To *you!* I can't live with it. I have never seen such pain."

The next morning they called a marriage counselor. Keith went first. Several days later, Grace. Then together. Keith's first session was lengthy. The doctor who had listened to him describe his marriage, his wife, and his feelings for her and their life they shared, had laughed suddenly. She said, "You have just described the perfect marriage. Now, tell me why you are here?"

So much for all the writings on marriage and relationships. So much for the self-help books. Once again, the 99th percentile—only this time in failure. Her perfect marriage, her 100, might just as well have been a zero. It was the first ever for the All-American girl.

Several weeks later, she sat in her car outside her agent's office in Beverly Hills. She had requested a meeting, and Margaret, the owner whom Grace loved, trusted, and admired for her integrity, had suggested a spring Saturday morning. Hearing danger in Grace's voice, she arranged to meet her alone, with no possibility of interruptions.

The only problem was that Grace was paralyzed in her car. Knowing that she had to do it, she talked to herself as she stepped out into the Beverly Drive traffic. She saw only Gucci shoes moving past her and she told her legs, one at a time, to move. They were heavy—heavier than she was, it seemed—and her full concentration was required to move even one of them into the sidewalk traffic of wealth. She rang the bell and opened the door.

Margaret didn't notice her leaden legs. She saw only her face. Putting her arms out, Grace embraced her and tears spurted out. Grace left the office an hour later, calm. It was over.

Carolina was fired on Monday.

Several months later, the marriage counseling had shaped itself obviously into divorce counseling, and Grace and Keith were making peace with their pain. Grace had taken an apartment. She told everyone it was to overcome her fear. She could stay in her dream home, but she wanted to make certain she knew that she owned her things, and that they did not own her. Like a monk retreating from the trappings of a secular life, she started over with a new home, a few friends, and some new furniture. Her great fear of not being able to survive as an actress on her own was overcome rapidly. She worked more than she had ever worked, and earned more than she had ever earned. She was not wealthy, and not famous, but she was on the verge.

Her fear of being thrust into the dating scene at thirty-one was gradually being overcome. She had started to see her friend, Robert McGee. He was good company, understanding, and in love with a woman in New York. He was, therefore, safe.

She continued to see her therapist when the darkness was too much for her to handle. But, by and large, she was coming out of the tunnel into the light. She felt lighter, warmer, and richer as it became more and more apparent that she would not be surrounded forever by oppressive darkness. She rejoiced at the sky, the weather—any sensations. She felt that not only had she survived, but that she had actually been strengthened. She had endured a crisis and come through the pain more whole, and more compassionate.

Sitting in her psychiatrist's office, she read the plaque on the wall, which read, "There is no growth of consciousness, except through pain." She drank tea from a glass as the doctor said, "You are one of the strongest, healthiest people I have ever met. Your resilience, the fact that you have 'risked' it again so soon...no neurosis...I should come to you." She paused and added, "I don't feel you need to come anymore unless there is something in particular bothering you."

Looking back on it now, it seemed so long ago. She could barely remember the pain and concluded she must be healed. The sad thing was, she could barely remember the happy times either. They were just a few disjointed fragments that had disappeared into the shadows. The adhesive that had bound Keith and her for thirteen years was invisible to her now.

A light came on in the plane in front of her. She felt it and opened her eyes. *Christ, where am I?* she wondered. She checked her watch to see how long she had been daydreaming. *Two hours,* she thought. "God, that was a long one," she muttered.

It seemed oppressively hot to her in the plane. The woman in front had tilted her seat back and fallen asleep. Her pillow was squeezed between the window and her seat and had fallen backward, jammed now near Grace's left knee. The seat back itself was directly in front of her—no more than six inches from her face. *Perhaps if I tilt mine back to equalize the distance a bit,* she thought. It was stuck. She fidgeted with it until her row mate was awakened.

Eliciting his help, they both struggled with it until they realized she was in the first row in front of an entrance, and the seat would not tilt back. It was rigged to provide permanent clearance for the door. There she sat, strapped into her seat with a barrier in front, one behind, one at the window, and one to her right. She knew now how those monkeys must have felt when they were launched into space in constricted capsules. She vowed to send money to the ASPCA.

The heat was becoming unbearable now. She tried to uncross her legs to let some air up her skirt, but the area was so tight what with her purse on the floor, her book bag full of maps and Fodor's Guides, and the dreadful angle of the seat in front, that she achieved no relief whatsoever. She made one last attempt to finesse the right leg up and over. It popped out, her kneecap striking the latch on the table, causing sharp pain and springing the table loose. It promptly sprang to attention, ready to receive the latest goodies from the stewardess. Grace shouted, "Ow!"

She was beginning to hyperventilate, as she fumbled desperately with the table. If only she could restore it to its position and get out of there without waking the woman in front, she wagered she'd survive. She clawed at the table. *No luck!* Taking a deep breath, she admonished herself to relax—reciting "less is more," believing that if she just relaxed it would all work out. She did, and it did.

The next hurdle was to get into the aisle. If she stood, maybe she could breathe. Rudi, her companion for the flight, immediately rose and stood in the aisle. There she was, trying to maneuver her fortunately-svelte body between the tilted seats and the foot baggage. She took another breath, tilted 40 degrees to clear the seats, stretched her long legs, and dove for the aisle. Her left side careened into the seat in front. She bounced off, missing Rudi's briefcase, and stumbled into the aisle.

He reached down, taking both her arms above the elbow, pulling her gently to her feet. Seeing that her heel had caught the handle of his case, he leaned over and released her foot, acting all the while as if nothing out of the ordinary had transpired. Grace was seething and perspiring. She hated having been made to look clumsy. Rudi's quiet voice, however, said, "Are you all right? You don't look well."

Very gracefully executed, Rudi, she thought. In one turn he had saved her from falling awkwardly into the aisle, and, with his "it's terribly hot in here, something wrong with the air," he had gracefully excused the whole scene, sparing her any further embarrassment.

Straightening to her full height, Grace looked for the restroom sign. She saw none—at least none in German, French, or English—so she took a step to the front. Rudi's hand reached out, grasped her arm, and turned her easily toward the rear of the cabin.

"Thank you."

Grace would later describe the next few minutes as something completely out of character. As she entered the rear cabin, she pulled the red and gold curtain aside and was overcome by smoke fumes—or so it seemed. The cabin was full. It was the smoker's section and every person there was exercising his prerogative. The aisles seemed blue, the haze too dense to discern clearly the rear of the cabin. Like landing strip lights, the red glow of cigarettes guided her through the aisle.

Near the rear of the plane, several standing figures emerged in the smoke, waiting in line for the toilette. Grace was allergic to cigarette smoke. Actually, she was not allergic. The fumes made her nauseous and her eyes watered, but that probably did not qualify as a true allergy. It was near dawn—at least according to the plane's flying-into-the-future time, it was near dawn. By her clock, it was midnight.

Her breathing was no easier. She continued to feel flushed. Her breaths were getting shorter. There was nowhere to escape. She practiced breathing, mentally ordering herself to relax. Whether she relaxed or not was hard to say, but she became conscious of cigar smoke. *Unconscionable!* she thought, as she told herself that must surely be illegal. Then she remembered she was on a Swiss plane, and that they probably felt differently about cigars in Europe.

She searched to locate the offender. Instead of one there were three, seated in the center of the last row, right where she was standing. The three could all have been brothers. All were portly; all balding roundly on the top of the head; all with fleshy cheeks and thick, puffy lips; and all with stubby fingers and pudgy hands. Their suit vests were unbuttoned, their ties loosened, and they were totally involved in a poker game. The gentleman closest to her had set his cigar in the ashtray on the tray table in front of him while he skillfully dealt the hand. The gentleman in the middle was holding his as he picked up his cards, juggling the cards with the cigar. The third gentleman must have been losing. He clutched his cigar in his teeth, fiercely turning it with his tongue to the exact rhythm of his right forefinger, which was tapping the table in front of him.

A veil of smoke rose up to her nostrils. It was then that she lost it. Without thinking, and without remorse, she reached to the gentleman closest. As he finished dealing and set the cards down, she picked up his cigar. He froze for a moment, his right hand poised to pick up his own hand. Grace, however, intervened. Swiftly, she stubbed his cigar out on his cards, spilling them. Then she dropped the saliva-soaked shreds back into the ashtray. Whether the man was more distraught over the destroyed cigar or over the loss of his poker hand was hard to discern. After the frozen moment, his chubby mouth erupted into loud obscenities in German. He rose, shouting at her. The other two—whether wisely protecting their cigars and their poker hands or whether too stunned to react—did nothing.

Now, that woke everyone else up. Fortunately the view to the rear was obscured by clouds. The gentleman shouted and a stewardess ran down the aisle to join them. In the midst of the abusive German rhetoric, Grace babbled as best she could that she was claustrophobic, overheated, and otherwise not in control of herself. The cigar smoke had caused her to lose control, she explained. The stewardess, whose placid face looked as if it belonged in a Diplomatic Corps recruiting poster, did the best she could to assimilate the German expletives and the mad American's broken explanations.

Wisely she steered Grace to the other side of the cabin and motioned for her to go to the extreme forward cabin, explaining that there was one lavatory directly behind the cockpit. As Grace fled down the aisle, she could hear the low voice of the hostess trying to pacify the man with hasty explanations of the American's "illness." It seemed to quiet down behind her, and Grace began to breathe more easily. She didn't understand what had just happened, only that she felt a keen sense of exhilaration. She was always so gentile, so ladylike, so composed. Her behavior tonight did not fit the role.

Oh well, she thought, excusing herself. *It will make a good story for a* TV Guide *interview.* She entered the washroom, threw the latch, and waited for the "occupied" light to go on. As it did, she looked in the mirror and gave her smiling image a victory sign. She then washed her face and combed her hair, observing that it had maintained its blow-dry looseness despite the heat and moisture. Her eyes were slightly red from the smoke, but the redness accentuated their cool blue color, which seemed more pronounced against her teal-green silk shirt.

Grace especially liked this shirt because of the color it brought out in her eyes. Her eyes were like that—a shade of blue that becomes lighter or darker depending upon her clothing and her mood. Tonight they were blazing. She wore very little eye make-up. There was brown mascara, slightly caked on the lower lids, a thin soft line of brown eyeliner, and hues of subdued gold and bronze to highlight the lids.

Her eyes were perhaps her best asset. They were enormous, round, and open. She wore make-up, not to make them more pronounced but rather to frame them in order to keep them from looking too enormous. Even at that, they were so expressive that they dominated her full face. She had observed that, whenever anyone looked at her, their eyes went first and immediately to her eyes.

The only other feature which could even compete with her eyes was her smile. Her teeth were slightly crooked in the front, and her jaw was receding slightly, causing a bit of an overbite, but when she smiled, her face lit up. Tonight, however, she noticed tension around her mouth. Her otherwise relaxed face seemed tired, and her eyes looked narrower. She was glad she was wearing a vibrant color. To aid in her rehabilitation, she added a touch of rouge and a bit more of her mulberry-colored lip gloss, both of which made her feel presentable.

She had never had much patience with make-up. Even at the studios when make-up men would hover over her for an hour, creating a face they felt enhanced her best features, and overcame her worst, she paid little attention. She felt that all of their best techniques would not necessarily make her beautiful. And, conversely, that even a complete lack of make-up could not prevent her from appearing beautiful when she felt beautiful. She believed it all really came from inside—that our outer beauty is merely a projection of our inner selves. If the inner self were serene and joyous, then the outer self would be beautiful. Regrettably, the men in Hollywood either didn't agree with her, or

LEE KESSLER

there were very few people walking around with an inner peace and joy, because the emphasis was always on the outer accoutrements.

She had done what she could with the outer accoutrements tonight. As she looked at herself, she felt an odd sense of victory, a warming calm was returning. And she felt quite lovely. She bent over and brushed her thick hair forward twenty times. Her hair, by standards, was beautiful. It was long—just below shoulder length now and very thick, almost too dense to comb at times. It was very soft, fine like silk, very shiny, and moderately curly. A dark blonde highlighted throughout by natural streaks of sun. It was virgin hair.

As she stood up watching it fall back, full and tousled at the side, she was grateful she had steadfastly refused the studio's permission to change her hair. Twice, for mini-series, they had wanted to apply permanents and three times producers had wanted to change the color on a palette anywhere from bleached blonde to red. Never trusting them, daring to demand wigs instead, she had prevailed.

Yes, her hair was beautiful and natural, but always imperfect. No matter how it was styled, there would always be one section that would rebel, insisting on going its own way. Many an extra half hour she had sat in the make-up chair, the hair dresser and she battling a maverick curl—only to give up in the end.

She was reconciled to this by now. Grace had even come to think of it as a touch of "character"—a tell-tale contrast to the totally-together, stylish appearance she otherwise presented.

Tonight, perhaps because of the flush of victory over the cigar smoker, or perhaps because it reminded her of a nursery rhyme, she made no attempt to straighten the curl in the middle of her forehead. She smiled and thought, *Not bad for thirty-four.* Having passed muster, she opened the door to a crowd of people.

She felt a twinge of embarrassment for having kept everyone waiting while she primped. She was not normally vain, but her sense of disquiet had been so keen that those extra minutes of solitude had restored her calm.

She needn't have worried though. The line was not for her. The door to the cockpit opened and three people emerged. She caught a

- 32 -

quick glimpse of the pilot and co-pilot. Just then the head steward breezed up and selected the next three to go in. Because Grace was caught in the aisle, he presumed she was next and motioned her in with a middle-aged, sparrow-like woman and a young man, with a pimply forehead, who was eagerly loading his camera. She tried to protest but gave up and entered. As the steward closed the cabin door behind her, he lisped in German, "Nur drei Minuten, bitte."

"Ja, Ja," she answered, thinking, *Three minutes isn't very much time.* She turned, however, and looked out the front window. Grace was conscious of the woman eagerly talking to the pilot and co-pilot. The boy moved as best he could to take pictures from the pilot's point of view. Grace, however, was stunned.

Having never been in a cockpit before, the silence surprised her. The sensation of being stationary startled her. In her seat near the window, she had felt motion and forward movement, but in the cockpit—none. It was as if they were suspended, but absolutely becalmed. They were standing still at 570 miles per hour, completely disconnected from earth. The reality was so surreal that she felt as if she were on a movie set doing a "process shot," where they were getting ready to roll the sky but hadn't begun to move it yet in order to give the shot the sensation of moving.

Why are they staring at me? she asked herself. All three men were staring at her. Despite the fact that the woman was still talking and asking questions, with the young man joining in, the captain's face had brightened. He was looking only at Grace. He was a handsome, ruddy, Germanic man, who answered the questions of his co-pilot but who seemed distracted. He kept looking to Grace. Then the co-pilot turned. He was younger, darker, more intense, wore sunglasses, and stared at her through these.

He had been receiving directions from the Air Traffic Controller over Paris. Apparently they were confirming coordinates. He signed off without taking his eyes off her. Seeing that his mates were looking at her, the navigator, who was right beside her, looked up.

She wondered whether her blouse were unbuttoned but did not dare to look down. Perhaps she wasn't supposed to be there and was interrupting their work. *No,* she reminded herself, *the boy and woman would also be interlopers. Perhaps they've heard the story about the fracas at the back. Surely my fame could not have spread so fast.* She swallowed unobtrusively, licked her lips surreptitiously, and smiled, consummately maintaining her composure.

To assuage the awkwardness, she spoke to the navigator in German. He jumped eagerly at it and asked, "Guess what temperature it is outside?" He smiled as if he had a secret and couldn't wait for her to take the bait.

"Minus thirty degrees centigrade?" she guessed.

His face fell as his bubble burst.

"How did you know?"

Grace didn't know how to answer that. "Lucky guess" seemed too flippant. Besides, she swore she just saw the pilot check out her legs. The sparrow woman asked him another question, too quickly in German for Grace to understand. He responded by reaching between her and Grace, touching Grace's arm.

"Pardon, Mademoiselle," he said, apparently thinking she was French, "mais je…" and he went on to ask the navigator to punch some information up on his computer. And he never took his eyes off her. The pilot seemed to recognize her, looking as if he were going to speak, but didn't. The navigator realized he had a new toy to show and began to demonstrate the reams of information that could be acquired by punching in various codes. Presuming that she spoke German fluently, he got way ahead of her.

Grace stopped him. "Ich verstehe night. Spreche nur ein bischen Deutsch. Nur Englisch leider." She hoped confirming her minimal German would cause him to switch to English.

Before the navigator could respond, however, the pilot dropped the computer readout he'd been showing the boy. It fell between his legs and landed at Grace's feet. She retrieved it and handed it to the captain. In English, he responded softly, "Thank you."

My God, she thought, *the man is blushing!* At that moment, she realized that the three men were enamored of her. They were not staring, blushing, and otherwise falling over themselves to display their equipment because they'd heard she'd caused scenes over cigars. They were attracted to her and flushed with excitement over her presence in their territory. This surprised her. She smiled. It was returned.

Grace turned to leave, explaining that they had overstayed their three minutes. A flicker of disappointment crossed the captain's eyes.

"Danke."

A trio of "Bitte, auf wiedersehen" responded.

As she left the cockpit, she felt buoyant, almost girlish. Her step was light, and she tossed her head back, feeling the weight of her hair as she returned to her seat.

Rudi saw her coming, rose, stood back in the aisle, and said, "I wondered what happened to you. You look much better."

She nodded as he continued. "Did you hear about the disturbance back there?"

"No. What?" she lied. She thought she noticed Rudi suppress a smile, but she pretended to ignore it.

"I'm surprised you missed it. Some woman went crazy back there. There was all kinds of shouting, people running…"

"Really? I didn't hear a thing."

Rudi smiled now, and winked. She, however, showed no sign of comprehending his meaning.

CHAPTER FOUR

✿✿✿

As the plane taxied up to the gate at Zurich's Kloten International Airport, disappointment overcame her, for what had appeared to be cloud cover turned out to be a drizzling rain. The captain announced the temperature, in English this time—16 degrees Centigrade. *Hardly balmy, spring weather,* she thought. She had waited so long to return to Switzerland and had traveled so far, that it seemed to her an injustice that instead of mountains she saw shapeless mist; instead of green, she saw gray; instead of peace-restoring warmth, she felt penetrating chill. She felt sad and angry, as if a sadistic travel agent had played a trick on her. Grace had held this land in her recollections so delicately and reverently for so many years, and this is the way it was to present itself!

"It's supposed to be clear," she whined. "It just isn't how it was," she muttered to herself. She would have preferred to indulge herself a bit longer, to savor her disappointment, but she felt she should straighten around and behave like an adult. After all, she'd behaved like a mature adult since she was three years old. Everyone expected it of her. A little rain was surely no justification for a pout. So, she swallowed it.

Unlike her last trip to Zurich, the Customs officials were remarkably lax in either interest or pursuit. Grace was surprised that all her organization and preparation for a rigorous Customs questioning and search was for naught. Disappointed, she loaded her bags onto this marvelous new type of baggage cart. It resembled a huge shopping cart and was designed for its ability to ride on escalators.

The fact that there was no checkpoint for passports further surprised her. There seemed to be no prescribed path for incoming passengers, so she followed her instincts and tried to remember what to do based upon her last two trips to Zurich. After she had retrieved all her bags, she looked around for the Customs counter. She felt she had located it in the rear corner of the large baggage claim area but was surprised that the other passengers were merely exiting by elevators to taxis and other ground transportation. *Surely it isn't possible to just come into a foreign country and have nothing checked!*

Guessing that the others were all Swiss, and that this was the reason they were just leaving without having to open their bags, she told herself, *I just don't think I should risk it.* She went back to the Customs counter, carefully placed the bags in a row, and unlocked each. The only person at the counter was a sloth-like, middle-aged man whose back was curving from the excess weight he carried in front. He was sitting on a high stool near what appeared to be a computer terminal, reading a magazine.

"Entschuldigen Sie, bitte." She spoke in German to get his attention, asking if he wanted to check her bags. He seemed not to understand, and apparently had no desire to leave the magazine. Stubbornly, she pressed on. "I just don't understand. You're supposed to check to see that I'm not carrying contraband." Still there was no response from the sloth.

Grace stood fast. And then Rudi came up to her.

"Is there something wrong?" he asked.

Grace jumped in immediately. "Well, I don't know. I can't seem to get anybody to check me through Customs."

"It's not necessary," he answered.

Upon hearing that, she remained motionless for a moment, stunned, trying to put it all together. Seeing that Rudi was staring at her, she recovered, covering her confusion with, "Thank you, Rudi. God knows how long I'd have stood there. It's been a pleasure meeting you."

"My pleasure," he said, as he took her hand and squeezed gently. "Have a lovely trip." He was gone. He had slipped her his card, which, without really knowing why, she deftly secured in her wallet.

For some reason she couldn't understand, she did not find the ease of entering the country to be reassuring. It seemed important so she racked her memory. She needed to understand.

But when I was here with the band, they made me open my trombone case and they searched my horn, she remembered. *It was 1967...they even made me run the cleaning rod through the instrument. Probably looking for drugs then,* she argued with herself. "Now come on!" she said under her breath. But she couldn't let it go. *Even in 1970 they stopped Keith and me when we came here, looked through one or two bags, asked questions.*

Grace, for God's sake, that was during the time of all the international high jackings. She had to acknowledge that was likely the cause of the searches, but something still was unanswered.

"But we wouldn't do that in the U.S.!" She heard herself assaulting this issue as if her honor hung on it, but she was powerless to turn off the dialogue. *You can be sure we wouldn't be able to come into New York without a thorough check. We don't let anyone in without going through Customs. I mean, my God, I could be carrying dope, or goods to sell...* She felt two hot tears squirt out and run down her cheeks before she surrendered the debate. "I don't understand. It just seems like damned poor management to me!"

I guess times have changed, her other voice said, surrendering. She wasn't convinced though, but felt that in the interest of salvaging the day, she should drop the issue. Grace didn't like herself during these obsessive moments. It used to be that such obsessions were rare, but they had become more frequent in the last year. She had told herself that they resulted from the pressures she'd been under in New York, and she reassured herself now that they would disappear altogether once she got to Brunnen.

Pushing the cart with some trepidation about its effectiveness, she steered past the rows of cheese shops, confectioners, and camera shops, and gingerly pushed it onto the escalator. No disaster. As she pushed it off the top she discovered that, if she let go of the bar she was pushing down on, the cart, with its new design, came to a stop. There was no way it could get away from her. *This is a marvelous invention.* She smiled.

Two hours later, Robert's plane had arrived from Los Angeles, and he emerged red-eyed from his own Customs experience. Unlike Grace, he seemed satisfied with his whole entry into Switzerland and embraced her happily and enthusiastically.

She could see that although he was likely tired, he was happy to be with her, and looking forward to the adventure.

"All right, my dear, show me your soul place. I am all yours!"

The drive from Zurich to Lucerne was easy and pleasant. Although the dark, gray rain clouds obscured the view totally and dampened her spirits considerably, she occupied herself with navigating Robert through the streets of Zurich and onto the new highway, which led to Lucerne. The highway had changed considerably since she was last here, and most of her attention was required just to guide Robert.

He had always fussed badly in traffic—swearing profusely at the mistakes other drivers made, while making the same ones himself. Congestion made him uncertain, and uncertainty made him testy. Her directions were flawless, fortunately, and soon they were driving south to Lucerne.

Although Grace was keenly disappointed that they could not see the approach to the Alps surrounding Lucerne because of rain and fog, Robert seemed content to hear her describe in detail her recollections of the now-invisible terrain, responding politely when she pointed out an obscured river, a missing peak, or a change in altitude.

After about a half-hour, she had time to just relax and gaze out into the gray sheet, which was so effectively curtaining the beautiful landscape of her memory. She thought of the plane ride and her outrageous behavior over the cigar and was grateful she would not have to meet the gentleman again. She laughed.

"What?" Robert jerked as if he'd been daydreaming and missed a turn.

"Nothing." She did not want to tell him about the "mad American," although she guessed he would laugh roundly and enjoy it more than most. *I must have left quite an impression back there in Zurich—a madwoman who assaults cigar smokers and demands to have her luggage searched!* She wondered what Rudi thought of her. *Not that it matters,* she admonished herself, sneaking a peek at the card he had given her. It was just that she seemed so different now from the woman she had been a few years ago. And she felt so different from the image people had of her.

Whenever she looked in the mirror recently she knew she saw the same physical woman the outer world saw. They both saw the same tall, slim woman who perhaps had a bit too much of a tummy, or who was a bit too soft, but who was, overall, svelte and graceful. They would see the same long legs whose calves were firm, and whose stride was assured and strong. They would see the same small round breasts, and the slightly projecting sternum which broke up the chest profile, making her appear more angular and thinner than she actually was. They would see the same scattered crows-feet around the eyes, which were fairly unnoticeable unless she wrinkled up her face in laughter— the same dimples in both cheeks, giving her face a youthful, playful appearance.

If they were especially observant they would notice on bad days when she was nervous or insecure that she had a tendency to bite her cuticles. And that she had beautiful, smooth, white skin, which was translucent enough to reveal the blue veins and the occasional bruises that came so easily. If she spoke they would hear the same quiet, but crisp voice. Even when she spoke tenderly and reassuringly her voice was authoritative. Though she was an actress, those hearing her voice assumed she was a producer. She did not understand exactly what created that impression but was grateful for it, as it had afforded her access to many a casting director or director to whom she otherwise would never have spoken.

These were the externals that all could see and interpret as they would. All her life her parents, friends, teachers, and associates had always interpreted this data largely the same. To those she lived with, she was a polite, gracious young woman—reserved but not cold, quiet but not sullen. She appeared supremely confident, ambitious, and yet somehow humble, showing no outward signs of narcissistic self-preoccupation despite the profession she had chosen. She was intelligent and wise way beyond her years. Over the years, she had become almost a source to which friends and relatives came for advice and counsel, despite her young age. She had grown up wise, sympathetic, and intelligent. True, a few saw her as arrogant, but most just saw her as serenely self-confident.

Nothing could shake her. She could endure great personal pain and upheaval and still survive. She had been told she was an inspiration to others. Every man who had ever met and known her personally had found her to be inspirational—a woman whose discipline and determination guided them and strengthened them. This she did not imagine. Each had told her this. Robert had said, "You have liberated me. You're the only woman who ever allowed me to be myself."

She had always been strong. Her mother could count on her to defend her against her father when he would become violently angry. Her teachers could count on her to continue teaching despite protests and sit-ins over Vietnam.

Her friend, Mary, now in her late forties, could count on Grace to defend her against a beastly, abusive director. Her colleagues in the entertainment industry could count on her to defuse explosive situations between actors, or between directors and actors, or directors and Board of Directors. True, she was known to lose her temper occasionally, to snap or be impatient, but that was generally forgiven. She was for the most part caring, tender, and compassionate. She was strong and controlled. She was feminine. *And* she was mercilessly detached.

This was Grace's self-image—developed and sustained through thirty-four years. This woman would not have assaulted a cigar smoker on his way to Zurich, Switzerland. This woman would not even have thought of doing it. Were the others all wrong then? Had she changed so much? Or was there another Grace whom she didn't yet know?

How could she explain this to Robert—tell him of her fear that she might be trapped in a role—defined by all those around her to the point that she had lost the freedom to be herself, or even to identify what that meant. She felt that to even raise the question would be shocking to him. To dare to expose the uncertainty would reveal a chink in the armor that no one knew existed. She feared failure. She feared it would shatter his illusions, and possibly their relationship.

She had always felt, from her childhood on, that she had something important to accomplish. Robert knew and seemed to approve. He did not know, however, that she didn't know what that something was. Or that today she felt somehow as if she had perpetrated a fraud and betrayed a trust.

Her sudden desire to return to Brunnen was an attempt to gain answers. When she had first met Robert in Los Angeles, she had been driving a car with vanity plates BRUNNEN. He casually asked her what that referred to, and she had answered, "My soul place." Whether the mystery of that remark had intrigued him, or her coquettish delivery, she would never know.

In any case, he had persuaded her to explain her peculiar attachment for a remote village in Switzerland on Lake Lucerne. At the time, she had just completed the first presentation in Los Angeles of her one-woman show based upon the diaries of Anais Nin. This feminine, illusive woman had told a friend in her diaries, "Everyone, sooner or later, comes upon a city which is the image of one's inner cities." That line had so riveted Grace's attention that she felt an immediate kinship with Anais—a kinship which had led to months of research, writing, rehearsing, and the eventual performance of a show based upon Anais's bohemian life in Paris. The show was recognized as the finest piece of acting she had done, and it was the reason she had moved to New York.

Grace had her own inner cities, however. In 1967, she had spent the night in a town she felt was her soul place—totally matching her inner feelings and spirit. Three years later, she had taken her husband to see the town, as if to share a secret about herself with him. Ten years later, she was taking Robert, hoping he would understand something more about her once he had seen Brunnen.

As they drove into Lucerne, she came out of herself and eagerly looked to identify familiar landmarks. The town was the same—yet changed. First glance would not reveal how, however. The lake was barely visible because of the fog. The rain had slowed to a mist, and there was a stiffening wind. Through the windshield wipers she could see pedestrians struggling with their coats and sweaters. A girl crossed the street in front of them, dipping her chin to her chest, offering the top of her head to the cold. She folded her arms across her chest in a vain attempt to contain the warmth.

"This must have caught everyone by surprise," Robert observed. "Most are dressed in spring clothes."

"That's a good sign," she responded. "I'd hate to think it would be this chilly always in mid-May. I'm sorry we can't see Pilatus though."

"Who?" he asked.

"Mt. Pilatus. It's right over us. It's enormous, and totally obscured by this cloud on the lake," she explained.

"It must be obscured by that cloud." He spoke as if he'd just concluded an original thought. *Has he been listening at all?* she thought, trying to suppress a rising miff. Robert was slightly deaf in one ear, for which she was generally understanding. The fact that the degree of his deafness seemed to vary, as well as which ear was the affected ear, irritated her from time to time. He had an annoying habit of not listening and then excusing it by saying he had a slight hearing deficiency. He had an even more annoying habit of not listening, and then responding to what he thought she said, or wanted her to say. This almost always provoked arguments between them, with Grace insisting that he respect her enough to at least get angry at what she said, and not what he thought she said. She hoped he was not quite that distracted today, and she decided to let it go.

"Do you want to drive right on to Brunnen?" he offered.

"No. We might as well stay the rest of today in Lucerne. You'll like it, I think. We can rest today and drive on tomorrow. Hopefully it'll have cleared out so that you can see something of the beautiful sights I promised."

He placed his hand on her knee and squeezed gently. "I love you."

She thought of looking for the hotel she and Keith had stayed in, but thought better of it. Besides, she didn't think she could even remember the name.

"Let's find a hotel," she offered.

"Then we can climb under those famous Federbetten, listen to the rain, and I'll make love to you like you've never been made love to in Lucerne before."

Today, very uncharacteristically, that prospect numbed her.

A charming old world hotel was located just the other side of the covered bridge. The streets were cobbled—all the buildings were about 200 years old. The steep stairs that led to their third floor room sloped just enough to make climbing precarious. The large room was simply appointed with twin beds, a large wardrobe, a table, and two chairs near the window. Looking through the curtains, they could see the Reuss River, which cut the town in half, separating the old from the new.

Although the huge feather-stuffed quilts called Federbetten were indeed tempting, and afforded an opportunity to remove the damp chill, Grace confined the nap to two hours. She awoke restless, anxious to look for something. She didn't know what. By this time it was late afternoon, and Robert was interested in finding a place to sup.

She recollected the Fondue restaurant she had enjoyed the first time she was in Lucerne. She had been a member of a band comprised of students from all over the United States, and in 1967, they spent the summer touring Europe. In July of 1967, they played a concert at the Casino, and then were introduced to cheese fondue in a charming, local landmark. Today she couldn't remember the name but was quite sure she could locate it, as she had taken Keith there three years later, and they had located it quite easily in the vicinity of the Lion of Lucerne Monument.

Despite the cold wind and the intermittent showers, their sweaters and raincoats made the day tolerable, and they set out to explore.

Robert's first stop was to buy her a beautiful cut-crystal bird to add to her bird collection. It was a shimmering little creature shaped like a chickadee, which made Grace feel warm with affection. She suggested visiting the church, the Lion, and then returning to the restaurant for a relaxed, leisurely Swiss custom.

It was then that a disturbing sense of change occurred, making Grace uneasy. Upon first viewing, the town looked very much as she had remembered, but subtle changes had been made. The church was closed for renovation, and instead of the narrow street at the base of its steps leading to the Lion Monument, there was a broad direct thoroughfare that deposited visitors right at the base of the giant sleeping lion carved in stone.

For some reason she felt a sense of panic rising when she could not picture the restaurant's location. Grace didn't know why, but it seemed imperative that she locate this spot. Holding Robert's hand, they set out, roaming down one street and then another. Because this area of town was condensed, it took perhaps only a half-hour to cover them all, and each venture returned them to the base of the monument.

At first Robert was patient. As each street proved futile, however, and as Grace pressed more aggressively to locate the missing restaurant, he became testy. She could feel his irritation but was powerless to stop her search. For some reason she didn't understand, she needed to locate the spot.

They stopped and asked a young girl working in a boutique if there was a fondue restaurant in the area. The pretty, cherubic-faced girl knew everything there was to know about Swiss embroidery, but nothing of fondue, so they pressed on. By now it was raining, and water was seeping into her shoes. Robert, with a dangerous edge in his voice, approached a Swiss soldier. His uniform was a camouflage fatigue, the colors of which no doubt would be successful in the mountains in the autumn but made him stand out like a traffic light in Lucerne. Grace looked at his flaming cheeks, perfectly trimmed hair, and thought, *He's too young to be a soldier.* He also knew nothing of such a restaurant.

By this time, Grace had tears in her eyes. She began to cross a street toward the lake. Robert seized her arm and pulled her back. "Grace, you've got to stop this obsession. No one knows where the place is. Probably long gone—"

"But it can't be! It was a landmark. They wouldn't just—"

He interrupted her, shouting, "It's not here." In the rain, no one paid any heed to his voice. "Do you understand?"

She knew, of course, that it was gone. She knew further that this was not fun for Robert, that she was forcing him into a scenario in which he had no desire to participate. She knew she was being unfair. *You've flown all through the night to be with me,* she thought. Her mouth did not utter this, however. She merely dropped her head, nodding assent.

He cupped her chin in his hand and said, "We'll find a new place; start our own tradition."

Returning to the hotel, the desk clerk recommended a restaurant nearby. As they opened the door and entered the lower room of the restaurant, it felt and smelled like a room heated by a pine-burning fireplace. There was, in fact, no fire, but the red table lanterns offered a glow that warmed, befriended, and defused. The room was full of young boys in gray army uniforms. Although Grace knew they must be the regular army, she was stunned at their youth. They must have been more than eighteen, but they looked fourteen or fifteen to her.

Noticing a stairway to a second floor, she and Robert climbed to the second level of the restaurant. Their table had a single red rose in a vase in the center, the flickering candlelight striking the silver setting on the table. Relaxing into her chair, Grace sipped the house white wine and watched the rain tracing patterns on the lead glass windows. She felt welcome. Seeing that Robert was uncertain of her, she reached across the table, touching his right hand. He raised his eyes. She thought she saw sadness.

"I'm sorry. I don't know why it seemed so important to find that place," she said. "Something I wanted to give you, I guess. It's over now."

He smiled appreciatively, they drank the wine, ordered another bottle, and she felt close to him again.

"Tomorrow I'll see the only place that really matters, Grace. Ever since we met, you've spoken of your soul place. Tomorrow I'll see your Brunnen."

"And then you'll know all there is to know about me," she said, flirting, a twinge of nervous apprehension in the center of her stomach.

"Tell me how you found this place," he said.

"I've told you all that before," she demurred, sipping wine.

"Actually, you haven't. Only that you felt a kinship with it."

So she began. These memories were pleasant, and she shared them easily. She had first seen Brunnen with the band. They were scheduled to play a concert at the Casino in Lucerne but were billeted in a marvelous hotel in Brunnen called Le Grand Hotel Au Lac. The town was about 20 kilometers outside of Lucerne on the Vierwaldstättersee, the Swiss name for Lake Lucerne. Because this was about midway in their trip, and because the students had just completed a grueling series of concerts in Paris and Germany, a grand old-world luxury hotel had been selected. Two nights were allotted for their stay. At that time, it had seemed a luxury.

The hotel was indeed a magnificent specimen—set into the mountain base, facing the lake at the exact spot where it made a dramatic turn. Most of the spacious rooms had balconies with 14-foot-high French doors opening onto them. The entire front of the hotel was ringed by a strolling porch. The feeling was one of grace, elegance, peacefulness. The view to the lake was the finest in the town. The hotel's colors were gray and pink and, even as teenagers, all the band members were serviced as if they were very important and frequent guests of this pastel country estate. She remembered the enormous front doors made of etched glass. She remembered satin glass lamps, in the shapes of tulips and peonies, spreading soft pink light.

The view itself was overwhelming, with open vistas to the right and left on the lake—capturing the different personalities of the mountains across the lake, reflecting their height and detail in shimmering emerald waters. Each morning she awoke and found herself on her balcony, breathing the clear air, which was healing and strengthening. She had felt wholly at peace there. In fact, she had felt she was never meant to leave. The morning of the band's departure, she was frozen on the balcony, unable to continue the tour. She, who had never been flaky or irresponsible, or even outwardly emotional, who was a chaperone for some of the younger musicians, was unable to move. After the first bus call, she had explained calmly to her roommate that she wasn't leaving. The director of the band and his nervous wife appeared after the second call. She calmly told them the same. She did not tell them that, in standing there on the balcony, looking out, she was convinced she was looking into a mirror at herself.

"How did they get you to leave?" Robert asked, as he forked fresh bread chunks onto her plate.

"I don't remember." She paused, then joked, "Probably the Capricorn in me prevailed. But I knew I would return."

"Did you?"

"Yes, I took Keith there in 1970."

"Did he like it?"

"Yes." She reflected a moment and then added, "I think it frightened him." Her eyes were blazing now. She felt luminous, as if everyone could feel the energy, could see the light.

"You're very beautiful tonight, Grace."

"Thank you." The little girl in her dropped her eyes, lowered her chin, blushed slightly, and said, "I feel beautiful. And you, my friend, are very handsome." He looked very self-assured and relaxed at that moment. His voice, which became reedy under tension, was mellower and lower, and seemed to caress her. He looked into her eyes, and familiar palpitations stirred her. Their relationship had changed a great deal over the two-year period—mostly through struggle and compromise. Her feelings for him changed daily, like an electromagnetic current. Tonight she felt the strong pull of unlike poles.

She thought of the soldiers sitting below them, drinking half-liter mugs of beer, as they talked into the night.

"Robert?"

"Hum?'

"Did you notice how young they look?"

"Who?"

"The soldiers."

"I try not to."

She looked at him a moment, then smiled. "I love you."

"I love you, too." He poured the last of their second bottle into her glass, and touched the lip of her glass to the lip of his. The room twirled and danced for her.

As they left, all the young soldiers' eyes were on the American and his blushing companion as the two, hand-in-hand, exited into the street. They walked to the hotel, first hand-in-hand, then arms interlaced behind their backs.

Being the first one naked under the enormous feather quilt, Robert succumbed to the long flight, and the body-warming wine. He was asleep before Grace slipped into bed. She was relieved somehow.

CHAPTER FIVE

அひひஆ

arly the following morning, they loaded the car and, in a light gray fog, left Lucerne. It was market day and very difficult driving through the streets as the farmers streamed into town, parking their carts of rain-dampened fruits and flowers along the curbs. To Grace, the splotches of color were oddly reassuring.

Despite the fact that the day was cold, windy, and overcast, she felt strangely becalmed. The mountains were at least visible to about their tree lines. It was as if someone had drawn a gray line across the horizon, severing the mountains before one had a chance to view their true height and shape. Like the reverse side of icebergs, it felt like being under the waterline. She wondered whether somewhere up there, miles above, there were intelligent beings who could see the tip of the mountains, and who were conjecturing at that very moment about what lay beneath the sea of condensed moisture.

They had agreed to stay at Le Grand Hotel Au Lac in Brunnen, regardless of the cost. Grace wanted to make certain that if they were to return to Brunnen, she could treat Robert to a touch of the old world class. The last time she had been there, with her husband, they had been unable to afford such a luxurious hotel, and in fact had rented a room in a private home. It had been incredibly inexpensive, and offered the advantage of actually experiencing the lifestyle of a Swiss farm—as well as the pungent aromas of the family's cows as they breakfasted outside their room.

Today, however, would be different. She judged the retreating clouds to be a good omen of fairer weather to come, and genuinely looked forward to seeing the expression on Robert's face as he viewed the lake for the first time in the town of Brunnen. Robert was in terrific spirits—his natural ebullience heightened by anticipation. Each kilometer of driving elevated the excitement. Grace felt a sense of suspense—not exactly foreboding, but an unmistakable feeling that something was waiting for her in Brunnen. It was a similar feeling, which had caused her to suggest they change their plans from a cruise vacation through the Greek Isles to the visit here.

She lived in New York, working on the staging of her one-woman show, and Robert had stayed behind in Los Angeles, working as a writer and producer. The separation of 3,000 miles had put a considerable strain on their young relationship, and they coped as best they could with regular phone calls in the middle of the night, and cross-country flights whenever their work or finances permitted. Because the schedule of activity in New York theatres is on a different cycle from the schedule of television activity in Los Angeles, it was becoming more and more difficult to synchronize "safe" times—times when neither would miss important work.

Robert had called with the idea of a vacation together—a chance to be alone and to be away from the inexorable pressure and presence of the entertainment industry. The early part of May was agreeable to both, and they both had silently prayed that no major work opportunities would come up to interfere. Although both she and Robert worked fairly regularly, neither had gained major recognition yet, and neither had a regular, on-going job in television or on the stage. Like so many others, both were hustling the next job. This perpetual uncertainty about when, if ever, the next job would come, was the price of being in the industry. To Grace, it was one of the most debilitating parts of the business. To always be parceling precious energy out in looking for work, instead of preserving it for the actual work itself, seemed unjust. She did it, however—tirelessly. Or so it seemed to friends. This spring, however, she had especially needed a rest, so she had agreed to the vacation in Greece. Suddenly, one week before their departure, she asked to change it to Brunnen. And, he had agreed.

Soon they would be there. Coming around the north side of the mountain instead of along the lake, she wanted the first vista to be a surprise to him. The village of Seewen fascinated Robert. He marveled at the clustered houses, red roofs, the cemetery with pictures of the buried dead adorning each grave. *A startling Swiss custom,* she thought, *viewing the deceased as he looked at the time of his death.* And, of course, the trailings of a settlement up the side of the mountain were so unique.

"I hear bells," he said.

"Cow bells," she explained.

They came into Brunnen from the north through Schwyz and turned toward the lake. Grace needed no map at this point. She was on automatic pilot. As they came into the town, she noticed two rather large concrete buildings with double smoke stacks. Judging them to be factories of some sort, she frowned. They had not been there 10 years ago, and she fleetingly prayed that all would not have changed here, too. Just beyond them, however, were a series of farms, and she was able to pick out the house where she and Keith had stayed. She wondered whether the family were still there.

As they passed the house, a bedroom sash was thrown open on the second floor and a woman wearing a checkered scarf hung a giant Federbetten over the windowsill for air. She looked vaguely familiar.

Then, almost before she could prepare him, they were at the lake. Some things change: highways decay and new ones are built; old buildings are leveled and new factories erected; families move away and new ones move in. Some things don't change. The Alps do not; the lake had not. The shape and frequency of objects along its shore may have been changed by man, but the lake itself was unchanging. And Grace felt inexpressible relief.

Robert was already out of the car. Shedding his pale blue pullover, he stood alone along the boardwalk—transfixed by the panorama unfolding before him. Grace knew that most of the spectacular sights were suppressed by the still-present fog, and that the colors were thus drastically subdued. The effect was rather like looking at a charcoal drawing. She felt instantly calm. The nervousness subsided, and she felt sure that all she had needed was a vacation after all. Her recent dreams and recollections were just symptomatic of a need to get away. *Here I can rest!*

"Is that the hotel?" Robert was pointing to an imposing structure sitting on a ridge at the base of the mountain.

"Yes."

"Let's drive up there and get a room." And then, as if he'd almost forgotten, he added, "By the way, you were right," as he gestured toward the lake.

Surprisingly there were no cars in the steep drive as it circled around behind the hotel. The grounds were well taken care of she noted, and the lilies of the valley lined the porch entrance. It was disarmingly silent though. As they approached the double doors, the etched glass looked just as she had remembered. She excitedly turned the tarnished brass handle. It was locked. Peering through the window, she could see that the inner doors were boarded up, offering no glimpse into the lobby.

Trying to suppress the rising sense of panic, she quickly walked around the wrap-around porch to see whether they had built another entrance. The tall French doors, instead, were gated with winter louvres that lock and protect. A few scattered rocking chairs stacked in a corner were the only testimony that the hotel was still used. It was mid-May, and the hotel was closed.

She turned to Robert, grateful that he was hanging back, aloof, at the end of the porch. She hoped she was distant enough that he would not hear her voice as it faltered. Trying to make a joke, she choked out, "Well, that's that." She turned then and looked out over the lake. And she thought of July 1967. Whether he responded or not, she couldn't tell, for he turned and disappeared around the corner. Moments later, she heard the car start up and drive off. She was relieved.

How long she stood there, with the smell of lilacs causing her to reminisce, she didn't know. She knew only that Robert had returned.

"What are you thinking?" His voice was low—easing in.

"I was just wondering how much is enough?" Silence hung heavily.

He wrapped his arms around her, bit her ear playfully, and said, "I've got a surprise." Not to be discouraged, he didn't even wait for her response. "You see that yellow building directly below us, right on the lake?" She nodded. "That's a hotel—granted, it's new—but very nice. It has the same view as this, and is right on the water."

"What else?"

"It has a room right in the front on the third floor—with a balcony. I reserved it."

"Thank you."

"At least I think I rented it. I made a complete fool of myself trying to talk in German. But I think he understood what I meant."

Grace made the proverbial college try to bring herself out of her funk with, "Well, I guess I'll have to fix that up, won't I?"

Just then, a curly-haired terrier puppy skidded around the corner of the porch, yipping at them, before retreating to a safe distance, his toe nails clicking on the planks. Close behind was an older man, dressed in a black suit and tie, who was protected by a gray wool sweater under his coat, and who sported a dented Alpine cap on his head. Grace noticed that the peacock feather looked as if it had been chewed.

He asked what they wanted. They explained, and he informed them in limited, but perfect, English that the hotel was not open yet, that it wouldn't open until June 1. And even then, not to the general public. For ten years it had been operating as a sanitarium. The only difficulty in his explanation came as he fumbled for a word in English. They had quite a time translating his pantomime of what appeared to be someone rowing, into someone in a wheelchair, and from there into the word "cripple." Apparently, the hotel had been converted to a sanitarium for handicapped individuals and was used only as a summer spa.

She asked if he were the owner. He hesitated, as if mulling this over, and then rather inscrutably said no, that the owner lived like a hermit up in the hills. Then he changed the conversation as they were leaving. Grace turned to watch the old man. She didn't know whether he was the manager or the gardener. Meticulously dressed, he was snapping brown-tipped leaves from the tulips and lilies of the valley. Whatever, he worked as if the health of each blossom were his responsibility.

The dog would occasionally try to step into the tulips, and the old gent's gnarled hand would scoop it out while his aged voice lovingly admonished. It seemed a familiar argument.

At the foot of the hotel, across the road at the new hotel, it appeared that Robert had in fact successfully reserved the room. It was depressingly modern but had a gorgeous view of the lake and mountain ridges, and had a large patio with a small, white, wrought-iron table and chairs for relaxing. The wind on the lake had died down, leaving it looking like a silver mirror. The air was heavier and warmer, and the first snow-covered peaks were visible through the dissipating clouds. It was all lifting. *A good day after all,* she thought.

Later that afternoon, the air was genuinely moist and warm. It treated the skin like a moisturizer. Grace and Robert were sitting at a café table at their hotel, right on the promenade. Whether because it was early in the season, or because it had rained, there was no one promenading, however. Occasionally teenage voices would disturb the calm as they walked home from school. But there was general silence otherwise, the only sound being the lake gently lapping at their feet—and sometimes raucously a mother swan disciplining her five baby swans into a crooked line.

Probably their first swimming lesson, Grace guessed, as the formation was something less than perfect. Looking up at the hotel, she thought that the second "L" in Bellevue needed refurbishing.

About 50 yards down the stroll way were the dock areas. In the summer, there would be paddle boats, canoes, and small outboards—all for rent. Today, however, not a single boat interrupted the calm. Even the marina at the far end of town showed no signs of activity. They enjoyed a sweeping view of the entire lakefront curve of the town. At the other end of the curve was the Vierwaldstättersee Hotel—another grand hotel. This one was open. The town, however, was curiously empty—for which Grace was grateful.

Robert was turning left and right, trying to take in the changes in the scenery as the mountains framed the lake. The lake made a right turn where they sat, and they were at the vortex. The shape and power of the mountains changed at that point, too. The framing of the lake changed as well, and the colors of the water changed. To the left, it was jagged, clear, colder, higher, majestic. To the right it was soft, misty, supple, serene. And in the center—directly opposite them, high on a bluff—was a verdant green meadow. A few hundred years earlier, in that meadow, William Tell and his men had met and pledged themselves to the creation of an independent state. Brunnen had not been there then. As Tell looked out across the lake, he saw only the village of Schwyz, and it became the capital and eventual name-sake of a new country.

As Grace described this to Robert, their hostess, who was the wife of the hotel owner, stopped to chat. She was very pregnant, but carried it well. Robert responded immediately to the warmth and friendliness that characterize those who make their living in the Swiss tourist industry. He began to ask about the hotel and the town. As the woman spoke, Grace noticed her badly arthritic hands. The woman, perhaps in her mid-thirties, gestured with hands whose fingers were virtually frozen into cup shapes, the forefinger like the stem of the cup. Whether she felt pain or not was difficult to discern, and Grace felt sad that one so young would be so afflicted. The woman's voice was high and light, and she seemed to just skip from pronoun to pronoun—her lips pursed round, her jaw barely moving. Her dialect in English was charming, and Grace smiled.

Then she graciously excused herself and returned to the kitchen. Robert was silenced. After a few minutes, he recovered his desire to talk and began to describe a plan for the two of them in their middle age to buy a small hotel and run it. He said Grace could handle all the front desk and accounting activities, and he would hire and supervise the staff and the cook. "Maybe do the cooking myself—certainly the purchasing," he added.

She interrupted his fantasy with, "Are you talking about a business for us?"

"Sure."

"When?"

"Sometime in the future. Aren't we going to spend the rest of our lives together?"

Grace laughed and joined the fantasy. "What is that? A proposal?"

Robert looked straight into her eyes, lowered his momentarily like a blushing girl, lowered his chin, and then raised his eyes to check out her reaction. He shrugged and said, "Yes."

For a moment, she didn't move. Then she stuttered, "Is that a proposal? Did you just ask me to marry you?"

"Yes." He was more confident now—raising his chin.

"Oh my God."

The scene had apparently begun without his intending a proposal, but once it started he had regained his composure. Grace heard herself ask if he hadn't planned a more romantic scene. She heard him explain that he had planned to do it that night in their room—after dinner, wine, and lovemaking in the arms of these glorious mountains.

Grace was mute. She was falling away. She could see Robert's face. It looked serene and happy—certain. There were tears in his eyes, yet he was smiling. But she was falling backwards, away from him. She heard him continue that they could even have a baby—that he was willing to risk that—and that they could even make a little "Brunnen-baby" if she wanted. She felt even farther away. His voice grew more distant.

To try to stabilize herself, her eyes went to his stomach again. It seemed especially prominent, with each roll magnified. She felt herself still falling backwards. When they had first met, it was firm and flat. Now it was rolled, and he was seemingly reconciled to that. *Is this his middle-age self? Is this the beginning of what he will turn into with age and prosperity?*

She wished she could see into the future. When she was twenty-two and about to be married to Keith, it had not mattered—the unknown. She seemed to be on the same level as her life. Everything was in front of her—its magnitude unknown and, therefore, not threatening. For some time now, though, she had experienced the sensation of elevation and future sight. It was as if she were above her life—able to see patterns, crossroads, and forks in the road. She felt more frustrated by this than privileged, however. It gave her insight into people and their actions, but it failed to give her the view of the end of the road. She was high enough to see the forks and options, but not high enough to see the consequences of pursuing one path over another. And she was afraid. Because for the first time in her life, she felt a paralysis. She was blinded by the alternatives.

She was sure that Robert must see her fading from him at this moment, and she wondered what he was feeling. *If only the future were as clear as the past,* she thought. She remembered so clearly when they had first met. She was in a play at the Music Center, and he had come to see his friend's production. They were introduced at the after party.

Their friendship was at first cordial, one more of mutual respect for the other's abilities. She was suffering through the worst of the breakup with Keith at the time, and concealing it. Robert gave her massages, but she didn't know how much he knew of the turmoil in her life. She had abstained admirably from involving others—determined to brave it through. She knew also that, although he was in love—and had been for five years—with a wealthy New York art dealer, they were separated by 3,000 miles. She knew he was lonely, and she knew he was attracted to her. They both, however, maintained a distance.

Eventually she had opened up, revealing her pain at the disintegration of her marriage. Robert and she spent hours by his apartment pool, talking. He was a wise and temperate friend who genuinely and profoundly helped her deal with Keith. Although he was not in therapy, he lobbied so articulately for it that she had persuaded Keith to join her in counseling. Robert was supportive and frank. He challenged gently, and she valued his counsel and concern.

Once when they were barbequing at his place, for no particular reason, they had kissed. Grace had been so desperately in need of tenderness and appreciation that she had submitted to the impulse. The kiss had become passionate—too open. She pulled away.

Minutes later he had calmly said, "You know, I think we could be very good friends." He paused. "More than good friends." It had seemed like an observation, not an invitation. Both dropped it, and returned to the confidante role they had perfected—returning to their other loves they were struggling to maintain.

Several months later, however, when Grace was beginning to recover from the pain of separation, when she was buoyed by the tremendous shot of self-confidence that steady work engenders in an actor, she had invited Robert to dinner. That in and of itself was not unusual, since they met for lunch and platonic evenings out about once a month. Grace had decided, however, that she needed to overcome certain fears.

As a newly paroled thirty-one-year-old single, plunged into the world of discos, single bars, jiggling beauties, and partner shopping, she had rebelled. The presence of desperation in a room had always made her extremely uncomfortable, and she knew that romance, for her, could not be found answering "What's your sign?" questions in the haze of variegated smoke at the end of a bar. She did worry over her sexuality, fearing atrophy. But most of all she feared that she would never be able to have an orgasm with anyone other than Keith. She feared that, as difficult as life with him had become, perhaps he was the only man who could give her that pleasure. She'd always been one to face her fears, and she was determined to face that one. She had selected an unwitting Robert to be her guinea pig. *Surely, as a friend, he will be patient and understanding,* she had told herself.

She became more and more nervous as it grew closer to his arrival time, however. She began to breathe shallowly and felt great tremors in her stomach. *Suppose he reacts badly and is offended?* Then she would lose a friend, too. For Robert unknowingly was invited to a dinner. He had made the mistake of saying that nothing she could do would surprise him. Well, the gauntlet was laid. There was a surprise waiting for him that night—an Hawaiian fantasy to be exact. She had rearranged the furniture in her apartment, bringing in large potted palms, arranging them around a low, round table. Comfortable mats and pillows ringed the table, allowing one to sit or recline as desired. She had prepared an exotic Hawaiian dish, made enormous rum drinks, and had a florist make two large pink and white orchid leis. She was wearing a long, wraparound sarong. Naked above the waist, she wore only the flower lei—which accentuated her small, round, pink breasts. Her hair was thick and curly, swept back from her cheeks by a flowered comb.

For a fleeting moment, after the doorman announced Robert was on his way up, she frantically considered putting on a blouse before it was too late. But then, before she could act, he was there. She opened the door; draped the other flower lei around his neck; and, as his eyes registered her pink, erect breasts, she handed him the rum concoction and said, "Aloha."

Probably to give himself a moment to recover, he gave her a big hug and handed her a paper bag with chilled white wine. She wondered if he had even noticed. Doubts started to erode her determination.

"You look lovely," he said politely. That was all. *My God*, she thought, *I wish I could disappear. I started this charade, and now I've got to play it out.*

She served dinner, observing as she passed the mirror in the living room that she was totally pink all over. *Maybe he won't notice in the candlelight.*

She knelt opposite him. He was seated on the mat, turned to the side, his legs spread out in front, elevated at the knees. Resting one elbow on his knee, the other propping him up, he looked incredibly handsome in a pale blue shirt opened several buttons. She looked at the dense, slightly-grayed hair on his chest, and then into his inviting blue eyes.

"Aren't you going to put your blouse on?"

"Do you want me to?" she responded—more disappointed than embarrassed.

"If you want me to be able to eat this beautiful dinner, yes," he said, lighting the candles.

That had been the beginning of a rapidly escalating emotional and sexual relationship. Their sensual love had been full of understanding, passion, abandonment, and learning. He let go of his lady in New York, and they began the arduous work of developing a tenuous relationship.

Sitting now in Brunnen, Switzerland, Grace wondered whether he remembered. Although her reasoning during that period had not been the most sound, and her behavior a radical departure for this small-town, upstate-new York girl, she was glad she had abandoned some old guilt and ghosts. It had set her free, and reinforced both of them for the time when the relationship would be challenged by struggle.

She was struggling to stay close now. She called upon memories of an "Emerald Isle Fantasy"—that one had been great fun—and a "Sayonara Fantasy," which made her blush. These memories, however, were witnesses to pain. It was inevitable. As their intimacy peeled away layers of defenses, it exposed nerves. Robert, who was quiet and gentle on the surface, was filled with unresolved anger—primarily over his failure to be a successful producer and show runner after twenty years of work. He was angry over his inability to know his own worth, and over his laziness. He targeted his self-hatred often on those around him—particularly studios and networks who failed to provide the strokes or assurance he needed. He refused jobs often if someone offended his distorted sense of dignity, or when he merely thought they had.

And despite the fact that he had so effectively counseled Grace to seek therapy, he steadfastly refused therapy for himself. He offered the excuses that he couldn't afford it, didn't need it, or could solve it himself. His despair at time was so great that, in frustration, he took a baseball bat and beat his bed.

As shocking as that seemed to Grace, she had to admit that it was, in actuality, probably a healthy course of action for Robert. It released a physical tension and anger that otherwise might have been directed at her. Also, he enthusiastically played softball on Sundays with a team of writers, agents, and actors, and he spoke of it as "his salvation." He was twenty years older than the other players, but he hit the ball farther than any, and had the strongest and most accurate throwing arm. They called him the "old man," but all knew that his physical stamina was substantial.

Although Grace had never wanted a child in the years following that near-catastrophe in college, when she reached thirty, and as the awareness that time was running out hit her, she began to think about a baby. She found herself watching children in strollers, smiling at babies in the grocery line ahead of her, wanting to touch them.

Though her intellectual, independent spirit wanted to deny this, she felt an urge—an impulse sometimes when making love—to make a baby. And although she was meticulous in her use of her diaphragm, she caught herself occasionally wishing there'd be an error, and that she would get pregnant.

Robert found this a source of contention. He was adamant in his determination to avoid that responsibility. Intellectually she knew he was right when he had said, "I can't take on the responsibility, Grace. I haven't even started to live my own life. I'm forty-five years old, and have never had anything for myself."

The thing that distressed her the most, however, was what she called his "shutdown." Whenever Robert could not cope—either out of fear, anger, or guilt—he would shut down. On the surface it seemed a passive enough approach to an argument, but she soon came to view this as his most aggressive act. Instead of yelling, which God knows he could do; instead of hitting, which he had only done once; he would shut down. As if someone were systematically turning off light switches, he would turn off. His eyes went dark and blank, his jaw set, his face froze, his hearing turned off, and he withdrew. It was as if he were unplugging all connections to her right before her eyes. When he was finished, no matter how loudly she screamed, no matter how copiously she wept, no matter how desperately she pleaded and reasoned, he was unflappable. Totally unreachable. Within five minutes, he would generally be asleep. It was as if he denied—successfully—her very existence. She was a nonperson—totally non-existent, incapable of reaching him when he shut down. Impotent in her rage, she hated him then.

What's more, he hated himself when he detached himself like that. He knew he was hiding, refusing to accept responsibility for his actions. They had had many battles over this, over his yelling and impatience, and over his interrupting her before she could finish her sentences. Grace felt that revealed a callous disregard for her as an individual—an arrogant assumption that she had nothing new or worthwhile to contribute.

She had told him she would not tolerate such behavior. He had believed her, and he had learned to stay with an argument. For the first time, he had begun to let go of his rage. His work went well, he worked steadily and was earning more money than ever, and, as with most men in the industry, that fact reinforced his sense of worth. She knew that the terrible, inevitable trap for all of them was the eventual succumbing to those who were in control of their financial welfare. It was all too easy to lose a sense of your worth or accomplishments, and to measure them only against the fame or fortune. Wealth and recognition seemed to validate those in Hollywood. Without it, they so easily floundered, doubting their ability and their stamina—tragically sometimes even their very significance as human beings.

But all that was in the past for Robert—at least for now.

Now, sitting in Brunnen, she feared it might return again, dragging her down with it. *Still,* she told herself, *I have learned and grown tremendously through the struggles with him.* She had been forced to work on her impatience and bossiness. More importantly she had learned that love—real love—is sustained through conflict. She learned to trust that love can endure, despite disagreement and tension. With Keith, she had had a relationship devoid of conflict. They had seldom argued. Keith feared argument, and believed that fighting and disagreement were signs of a dead love. Any time they fought, he viewed it as further testimony of the demise of the relationship. He had held a grudge sheet. Instead of growing, he had kept score. She had bought this, and it had nearly destroyed her. With Robert, she had grown very secure in the knowledge that, insomuch as growth comes out of pain, conflict was not necessarily the harbinger of a dead love. Far from it. Their love seemed to grow as *they* worked. She had come to trust this. He *had* given her that.

"I'm grateful to you," she shouted across the great gulf between them. She was no longer falling backward, but he sat now, seemingly very far away. She hoped he could hear her. He had.

"I love you like I've never loved anyone in my life," he confided.

She wondered why he couldn't see that gulf between them.

That night she was unable to make love. He was unable to understand. They faced away from each other in their bed in this room in paradise. They did not touch. She believed he wept, but said nothing.

Whether she had slept or not, she did not know, but she was aroused by a presence in the room. She felt as if something infinitely strong and forceful had entered the room. What was the communication? She was almost afraid to turn over. As she did, she glanced at her watch. It was light enough in the room to see 4AM on the dial. The curtains were open—the door to the balcony ajar—and she realized that the silence, the light, and the mountains had awakened her. She sat up, drawing the white feather comforter around her. Looking across Robert, she saw that he was asleep. Then she saw the mountains. It was the middle of night, but the moonlight reflecting off the snowcapped mountains illuminated the sky, throwing light into their room. The clouds had disappeared, leaving a flawless midnight blue sky that seemed to dissolve into a teal blue near the jagged peaks. Each was starkly outlined against the hue, and each appeared like giant sentinels—monolithic presences guarding the night. She had seen Brunnen several times in the past but had never witnessed this particular phenomenon of stark white in the blue night. She felt they were watching her, and had awakened her with their silence for a reason. Was it only to let her know that they had returned, shedding their gray shrouds? Or was it to say they were happy she had returned? Whatever, she felt welcome—totally—and she slept.

When she woke, Robert was standing in the door to the patio. He was totally naked and seemed oblivious to the early morning chill. It was just predawn, and he had been looking out the window for some time. Occasionally he would turn his head to the left as if he were following some movement, then to the right, as if studying something.

Curiosity got the better of her, and she said, "What'cha doing, my friend?"

He jumped, startled out of his vigil.

"Watching the sun come up."

"Are you personally escorting it?" She hoped he might laugh, giving her some sign of how he felt about her this morning. Instead, he continued to gaze out the window. He turned to the dresser and pulled out his powerful military-grade binoculars from their brown leather case. He looked boyish, so vulnerable, standing at the window studying something. After several long moments, he turned, tears brimming, and then spilling. "This is the most beautiful place I have ever seen." Almost as if he could not collect his thoughts, his lips moved to form them, and then stopped. She said nothing. After a while he said, without lowering the binoculars, "I thought nothing could surpass the Grand Canyon. That was so awesome."

"Hmmm," she agreed.

"But this goes beyond that. It's enduring." His voice broke.

"I understand."

She got out of bed, dragging the Federbetten with her. Standing beside him, she wrapped it around his right shoulder. He grabbed the other end after she'd wrapped herself in it, and they stood there in a feather cocoon, silently watching the sun play its overture to the day on the mountain peaks.

Still looking out to the sunrise, Robert said, "I meant to say more yesterday. I meant to tell you why I want to marry you."

"Tell me now."

"I've had a lot of time to think since you left Los Angeles for New York. I know at first I was punishing you for abandoning me. I was hurt. I couldn't understand how you could leave, just walk away from us just as we were becoming so close."

"It was something I had to do," she answered simply, quietly.

"I know. I know. I see that. I've had time now," he continued. "Believe me, I admire your courage to leave your friends, your home, to go to a strange city. It's brought me to a great appreciation of your spirit."

Grace was uncomfortable now. Her desire for approval seemed to be shadowed now. But by what? Could it be shame? Rather than explore the feeling, however, she suppressed it and tried instead to dampen his praise by cutting in.

"Please. You don't need—"

But he in turn cut her off.

"Yes I do," he said, waving off her objection with his one free hand. "You're a lady who has always had strong principles, things you believed were right or wrong, and you've always acted on those principles. You felt our work was only concerned with deals and Nielson ratings, and not quality. So you left to find an environment that would nourish you. I love your spirit. I want the best for you."

"I know, Robert. I don't doubt that."

"But I have to tell you, Grace, I need the deals—the money now. I've spent twenty years with nothing. I need to have something for once in my life." He looked directly into her eyes now. "But that doesn't mean—and this is very important for you to understand—that I don't feel the same as you. I do."

She nodded.

"But I realize I'm not getting younger, that I won't have anything if I don't take it now. I love you. I want a life together. You've told me you want marriage and a baby. Well, I'm willing to do it." He must have felt her stiffen, for he qualified it quickly. "If you want. I love you, and don't want to lose you. I want something finally in my life that I chose."

Softly she said, "I understand, and I'm touched." Wishing to end this, she said, "Robert, I want to climb that mountain just outside of town today." He hesitated for a moment, and then on quick rebound, agreed.

"Fine. We'll go after breakfast." He started to unwrap the cocoon. She stopped him, placing her hand on his chest.

"I mean, I want to go alone."

"You don't want me with you?"

She knew there was a limit to how much rejection he could take, so she tried to be gentle. "Of course I do. But not today. I need some time to be alone." And then, as if to reassure him, she added, "To think about this."

"Yes?" He looked defeated.

"Yes. I thought maybe we could use a little time apart, okay?"

He waited, looked out to the sunrise, and then back to her.

"Sure. I understand," he said, stuffing the binoculars back into their case. "We've been together a whole 24 hours now. I could use a little solitude myself." The sentences tumbled out too quickly. She thought she saw fear in his eyes as he disappeared into the bathroom.

He walked her to the outskirts of town, pointing to a low peak that seemed walkable. As she was dressed only in jeans, shirt, and a heavy cardigan, with her blue and yellow running shoes serving as her only traction, he recommended a gentle hike.

She left him at the beach. It was too early in the spring for anyone to be swimming, so he settled in to do a little reading, and was once again using his binoculars to do some swan watching. His blue eyes reflected the elegant blue of the lake, and the gray-blue of the nubby sweater she had given him for Christmas. He was wearing his old red-striped shirt, dark brown corduroy jeans, and looked quite handsome. His hair had curled beautifully today—shaped to his head, with the intermittent gray catching the sun. Only his blue and iridescent-orange Nikes seemed incongruous. They kissed lightly.

"Have fun," he said, kicking off his shoes and adding, "be careful."

"I will."

"See you later."

And for no reason that she understood, she said, "Goodbye."

As she walked along the north shore, she wished that she had told him she loved him. To have proposed and then to have heard only, "I want to be alone," must have startled him—probably hurt him. She reproached herself for not being more tactful, told herself he deserved better, and promised to make it up to him when she returned that afternoon. With that admonition the guilt instantly dissolved. *I suspect*, she thought, reassuring herself, *he will enjoy being alone, too.*

The real truth, however, whether Grace would admit it or not, was that she could not wait to do a little exploring by herself. For years she had been waiting to return—had even thought of buying a chalet in the hills around Brunnen. Lately she had felt strong, insistent urges to return. She even had dreams regularly—all but one telling her to return. The one maverick dream confused and frightened her more than the others, but she chose not to think about it now. For now that she had returned, she found this day more beautiful than any of her previous days, and eagerly looked forward to an afternoon of contemplation.

Having returned to Brunnen, she could no longer avoid facing the reality that she had been very anxious lately about her work, or lack of it. She seemed to lack the single-mindedness and determination that were characteristic of her. She felt less joyous and more confused than she could ever remember. And now there was a marriage proposal—a whole new twist to the future—to consider. But she felt confident that here, alone, she could work it out. Looking up at the mountains, one ridge in particular seemed to beckon her. She had the odd feeling that something was waiting for her there. She dismissed it, however.

Grace decided to climb to the top of that ridge. It marked the beginning of a circular mountain range that ringed the lake. Although there was snow on the top, she thought that was due more to the previous day's rain than to a formidable elevation. She could see a few houses near the top, and judged the area to be fairly gradual in its gradation. She had to ask a passing bicyclist how she could walk to the top, as she saw no roadway. He looked at her in disbelief and said, "Sie wollen spazieren?"

"Ja, ja."

"Nein," he protested. "Nehmen Sie den Luftseilbahn. 500 meter weiter." The man was quite old, and she assumed that's why he appeared so shocked at the prospect of someone walking to the top. Nonetheless, if a cable car were the only way to get up there, it would make the ascent easier.

About 500 meters down the road was a large sign pointing to the base of the mountain. A little farther on, there was a small white shack with a sign LUFTSEILBAHN. It looked more like a machine shop than a spot for a cable car, but she suppressed her doubts and entered. There were tools hanging on hooks on two of the walls, and cables were spooled and stacked in a dusty corner. On the other walls were detailed maps of the entire area around Brunnen. She was just glancing at these when a man jumped off a platform near the center of the shop and came toward her. His hands had grease on them, and he wore a moth-eaten wool cap on his head. She judged that there was about two days' growth on his tanned face. Grace explained that she wanted to go to the top, and he asked her if she wanted a one-way or round-trip fare.

"Round trip," she answered immediately. *Surely he doesn't think I would want to stay up there,* she thought.

"Fünf Minuten," he said, just before he hawked and spat into a container near the steps. She assumed he meant she was to wait five minutes. She paid her fare and glanced superficially at the maps. Then, shortly thereafter, he said he was ready. He helped her into an old, red cable car. It tipped slightly as she entered. Before he closed the door, however, he loaded in two large steel milk cans. They must have been full, because he was straining and groaning just rolling them in, and the car sank a few inches on its cable. So, Grace and two full milk cans made the ascent.

The only thing reassuring about the trip was that there would be someone at the top to greet her—if for no other reason than to pick up their milk. Although the view was breathtaking as she rose up the hillside, the wind caused the car to swing vigorously, and every time it passed one of its support towers, it swayed sharply—pendulum-like. It was rather like riding the top of a very tall Ferris wheel. She found it harder and harder to look at the view, and turned instead to see when the next tower would jolt her again—as if advance knowledge would assuage her trepidation. She wished Robert were there, and envied him his safe, stationary spot on the rocky beach. She told herself repeatedly that there was nothing to be afraid of, that the car was obviously safe, and that accidents surely were rare. Logic doesn't alter fear, however.

The car passed the snow line, and all around there was a white blanket. It was strangely incongruous since the temperature, although cooler than down below, was still reasonable. Moments later the car slowed and entered a large wooden structure. As predicted, a man was there to pick up the cans. He seemed more interested in them than in her, and she felt rather like a stowaway. She knew logically that this car must be used regularly for passengers, but that did not dispel her feeling of being an intruder.

The Swiss are gracious, friendly as a whole—particularly to tourists. This man was no different on the surface. Except for one moment, as she turned to pull her bag out of the car, she caught him looking at her—scrutinizing her actually—as if he were sizing her up. She thought she saw him frown as he quickly looked away. And her intuition told her that, for some reason, he disapproved—either of her, or of her presence on this mountain—and that it was an effort for him to conceal that. Yet, he was polite. *Perhaps I'm too sensitive today,* she admonished herself.

He extended his rough and tanned hand, helping her out. His eyes, which were barely visible beneath dark, scruffy brows, quickly and more openly now passed from her head to her foot, passing judgment. Before she could discern what the verdict was, however, he turned away, rolling the milk cans to the edge of the station. She noticed his clothing. He wore somber, sturdy pants and an eminently warm shirt. Though he was a youngish man, whom she guessed to be in his late 30s, he seemed older. His sunburned neck and wind-chafed cheeks gave him the appearance of being either hard-drinking or hard-living, or both. She suspected life was tough for him here.

She thought of asking his name, but thought better of it. Besides, he had started to do the most amazing thing. He was loading the cans onto a flat wooden cart, which resembled the shape and size of a child's large wagon. It had sides perhaps only 12" tall, and no top. It was, however, suspended by a pulley from an overhead cable. The cable was attached to the end of the platform they were standing on, and extended outward. Curious to see where this crude shipping apparatus would end up, she moved close to him. He released a hand brake on the pulley, and the wagon with its load of milk skidded easily through the air, picking up speed as it descended slightly, heading toward a wooded area below.

Grace leaned over the edge to catch a glimpse of its destination but was thwarted by the disappearance of the wagon, cable and all, into a grove of pines. She could see a chimney smoking in that clump, and guessed that the milk cans were arriving there at about that moment. There was no road leading to that area—at least not one that either car or cart could reach. A footpath wound up the side of the slope, entering the grove just at the edge of her vision. *Fascinating,* she thought, *to think of someone living this isolated.*

She turned to the man to ask a question about the system, saw that he was biting the end off of a cigar, and decided not to press her luck. Telling him she was going to walk up the hill a ways and that she would return later in the afternoon, she made a hasty escape.

The top of the ridge was perhaps 100 meters above her, and there was a path into the woods just behind the structure that held the cable car. She noticed that the zig-zagging path had split-rail railings to hold onto, and that leveled steps had been cut into the slope. Once she was in the woods, where she could look down at the man's house and cable car station, she noticed that part of the house had a large patio with a restaurant, and she realized it must be some kind of way station.

It was raining on her, despite the sun. Looking up, she spotted that it was just the sun melting the snow, which had blanketed the trees, creating an isolated shower. So she pressed on.

At first the climb was easy, although slippery, as the rain was making the ground snow very slick. Soon the steps disappeared, and then the railing, and she was left to climb the rest of the distance without support. It was difficult, since she had on only sneakers. Not only were they soaking wet, but there was no traction whatsoever. She found that turning her feet sideways into the path helped to keep her from backsliding too badly. About 10 minutes later, she reached the top. A sign-post greeted her pointing in several directions, giving the names and distances of nearby towns. It was then that she realized the top of the ridge was an apparently much-used hiking path. Hikers could walk the ridge and completely circle the lake. In order to get their bearings, signs would tell them which towns they were standing over, and the distances between the next town and other cable cars.

That explains the restaurant, she thought. No doubt it was a stopping place for those on the long hike in need of refreshment. It also explained why she had been asked if she wanted a one-way ticket. It would be possible to ride to the top, climb to the ridge, then hike to the town of Küssnacht, descending there.

By now her feet were quite cold from the snow, and starting to feel numb. She realized why the two men had looked at her as if she didn't belong. The slope was gradual. Hiking the ridge was not like mountain climbing, but it did require certain equipment. A walking stick would help, and hiking shoes would be essential. She wished she had either, and settled instead for a bench at the very peak of the ridge. She had to leave the path to reach it, treading through virgin snow. The ground seemed solid underneath, and she sank onto the bench to relieve her legs.

At that moment, she allowed herself to take in the view for the first time. It was astonishing. Not only could she view the mountains and the lake, but the considerable elevation afforded a complete overview of the area. She felt as if she could see the patterns—how the mountains were carved, how the lake filled the crevices, how the snow and trees parted company at the timberline. It was a hostile break, revealing irreconcilable differences. From below she had always been transfixed by the height and majesty of the mountains, and by their power and serenity. From above she felt exultant—as if she were at one with something eternal. She felt as if she had left her life behind her, and existed now only in symbiosis with an ongoing, all-knowing Nature.

Gone were thoughts of New York: of her initial expectations related to her new adventure, of the subsequent disillusionment as her enthusiasm and commitment were once again met with indifference, of the exhaustion of picking herself up and starting over one more time, and of nightmares about prison mortgages and shadowy stalkers.

She felt truly at peace with herself, as if in harmony in a pure environment. Then there was the earth, and the smell of the grass as its vibrant, green blades cut through the snow, triumphing once again. The snow yielded, retreating in the face of spring's earth. She smelled the spring grass. Although it was raining here on top of the mountain, it seemed to evaporate before it could strike her. Her sweater felt untouched. She made a snowball and ate it eagerly—as if she were devouring clarity. She wanted to internalize the purity of this place. It all had structure and purpose—a past, a present, and a future. If she could just take it in, she could perhaps possess a like serenity.

How long have I been here? By the shadows she knew it must be late afternoon. She remembered that the last cable car down was at 6PM, and she rose to leave. Although Grace had solved nothing, she felt very relaxed and encouraged. Tossing the snow ball away, it struck a snow patch. The patch moved, slipped, then slid intact down the slope and out of sight. Seeing this, she told herself to be careful walking through that area, lest she slip and end up with a soaking bottom as well.

She started down the path, but found the going difficult. Her feet kept slipping out from under her, and she had to keep from falling by dropping her hand to the ground, digging into the snow with her bare hand. Her bag was filling up with snow each time she took one of these dips, but she managed to hold her balance fairly well in a crouched position. Inching down the slope, she wished that she had thought to buy a walking stick, and vowed to do so tomorrow.

The path curved slightly outward now. As she rounded the curve, she slipped again. Actually, the snow patch slipped, dropping her to her bottom unceremoniously. She reached to stop herself, but the momentum of the slipping snow patch carried her down.

Damn! she thought, as she slid around the curve. *I'm going to be soaking wet.*

By then she was sliding down the slope, picking up speed. Were it not for the fact that she was getting wet by rolling in the snow, she thought she would have enjoyed the slide. It made her recall sensations of coasting on those "saucers" when she was a kid, and she felt the same spinning movement. Grace giggled, thinking how she would look to

Robert if he could see her. Looking ahead and below, she saw a sharp turn with a bank of snow, and knew that would stop her. She rather hoped no one was around to witness her ungraceful descent. After all, she'd slipped about 20 meters. Moving rapidly now, she hit the snow bank, dropping her bag, which had been dragging along behind her. She started to stand up, but she didn't stop!

Instead, her momentum carried her through the bank of snow, jolting *it* loose. The packing texture of the snow in the light rain made it all adhere, and the whole bank now moved forward with her weight. Grace couldn't see that not only had she gained momentum, but she had also left the winding path and was sliding south now down an open meadow near the edge of the ridge. There were no obstructions—no trees, few bushes—and she was rolling now with considerable speed.

She wasn't laughing now. That vague impression of something waiting for her returned. She felt something stuck in her throat. A scream? She couldn't seem to stop herself. Then, her sweater was torn open, and she felt pain in her right hip as she struck something under the snow. She saw only what seemed like a flying sky above her. She tasted unwanted snow, and felt it burn. Sliding over the top of a round slope, she saw suddenly that the ridge appeared to end.

Just as suddenly she knew she was sliding very rapidly and uncontrollably towards the brink of the ridge.

There couldn't be a drop off, could there? She didn't remember seeing one on her way up, and that reassured her just enough that the fear subsided momentarily.

Grace had no way of knowing that she was about 50 meters east of her original starting point now, and that there was in fact a steep drop off of about 20 meters to a narrow path, and then below that, another 30–40 meters vertical drop before the slope tapered once again, and descended reasonably to Brunnen below.

In the last instant before the snowpack she was riding on hit the edge, she thought, *It can't be this innocent!* And then she went over.

Grasping desperately for anything to stop her fall, she grabbed at the base of a small bush along the edge. For a moment it held, causing her to slow, but she couldn't hold it, and her right palm burned with pain as the cold-stiffened branches tore her flesh. She screamed, flailing helplessly, as she let go.

Suddenly, her left arm ripped, as if torn from its socket, and she jerked to a halt, suspended just over the edge. Through water-filled eyes—gasping and choking on her screams—she struggled to see what had caught her.

A strong, tanned hand held her wrist firmly and, in German, a voice said, "Be still. Be still. I will lift you up."

He had lifted her up, careful to avoid her bleeding hand while precariously holding his own balance on the edge of the ridge. All Grace could think of as she regained her footing was that it didn't even look dangerous. It was just a field. She favored her right hand, wincing.

The man extended the arm she was favoring, tentatively moving the elbow, then the wrist, then the fingers, and finally he reassured her that she was all right. He wrapped the hand in a handkerchief. She could not see his face well. She didn't know why, and ascribed it to probably the shock and the tears. He was taller than she, and his low voice was reassuring. There was a peculiar accent to his German.

She stood shaking, trying to pull the muscles, which were in spasm, under control. That effort held her silent. He retrieved her purse and slid it over her shoulder, as she wearily thanked him.

"Be more foresighted next time." He started to move her gently along the ridge toward the path.

"Foresighted?"

"The next time you hike, use a walking stick and proper shoes." His voice was firm, perhaps impatient. Her vision was not yet clear, but she was able to see blue, penetrating eyes and a tanned, smooth face. He was a young man.

"How did you…" Her voice trailed off, leaving her unable to complete her question.

"I saw you fall," he answered, saying nothing more for a moment as he used his walking stick to probe the ground. It seemed to click as he stepped. Finally he added, "I was lucky. I reached you in time."

"You mean I was lucky," she said, correcting him, venturing a skeletal laugh.

"I wouldn't have wanted to see you fall again."

Grace had no idea what he meant by that. Fearing to ask, she decided he probably meant seeing her fall off the second ledge down below, so she let it drop. When they neared the cable car station, he shouted ahead, "She's had a rough tumble here, Fritz. See that she gets down right away."

Fritz came out the back, ran to them, and Grace was handed over to him. She observed he was sans cigar, for which she was *very* grateful. Both men helped her into the car. There was no conversation. She was beginning to feel the chill from the wetness, and her shoulder and hip ached badly. She squeezed out a thank you, and the car left the station. Grace was already out of the dock and headed down the mountain before her head cleared enough for her to realize she had never even learned his name.

As the car plunged routinely, she kept her eyes focused totally on the rapidly approaching lake below.

Robert was not at the beach—something for which she was glad. When she slipped into the hotel room, he was sitting on the balcony, facing out over the lake. Although he must have heard the door, he did not turn. Relieved that he was not disgruntled over her late return, she slipped into the bathroom to clean up her scrapes, soak the aching joints, and to change into dry clothes.

Later, toweling her hair dry, she came up behind him and kissed him on the nape of his neck in an attempt to make their first contact. He responded by holding up *The Return of the Native*. She had just begun to read it and was surprised when he said, "You've read the last page, haven't you?" She had no idea how he knew, but she was caught and forced to admit it. It was a habit she'd had all her life—or at least all of her recollected life—reading the last page first. Knowing that it was a source of consternation to Robert, however, she did it surreptitiously. Now, somehow, he had divined that.

She played with the curls around his ears and calmly said, "Yes."

He said nothing. Grace came around beside him, combing the snarls out of her wet hair, and observed his steely silence. He noticed her hand but said nothing this time.

"What's wrong?" she asked, bracing herself. He made the effort to shake off whatever was bothering him—like a wrestler trying to rid himself of the awful weight—then slumped backwards into the chair as if he'd lost the round.

Again she probed. "What's wrong?"

"I was just thinking about Ruth." Before she could ask why he was thinking about his agent, he added, "And about what you said."

"I don't understand."

"You warned me about her." As he spoke, Grace felt the emotion of fear welling up, and a sense of foreboding overtook her.

"I didn't tell you because I didn't want to spoil the trip, but just before I left Los Angeles, the office called and told me they no longer wished to represent me."

Nearly speechless, she stuttered, "Why? But you've been working all the time recently."

"I know. But they said they only wanted to represent major show runners. They're going to concentrate on packaging and only wanted major deals." He stopped for a moment, closed her book, and said apologetically, "I guess I should have told you before. It's been on my mind."

"Why didn't you?"

"I was afraid to upset you. And I remembered you warned me about her and the whole agency. You told me all she cared about was the 'deal.'"

Grace had warned him about that agent, but so much time had passed, and he had been doing so well, she assumed she had been wrong. Now, however, she could feel her temperature rising. All the old buttons were being pressed. She had left Hollywood to escape those buttons, but here they were again. And, without being able to stop, she heard herself begin her pre-recorded message.

"Goddamn it, it's just not fair! There is no such thing as honor in our business. No one with a sense of loyalty and very few with a sense of integrity. We're not human beings to them, let alone artists. We're just dollar signs. And if someone comes along who's more suited to the big-money fad that TV creates and advertisers promote, then out the window goes loyalty!"

She noticed he looked pained as he tried to interrupt her. "Grace, I know all this. You've said it before."

"But when will you learn not to let your ego be stroked by these dilettantes and find someone who cares about you, about working in partnership with you to develop a whole career?" By this time she was "Chautauquaing" around the room, Robert following, almost pleading.

"Grace, please, I can't take any more."

"But don't you see how little honor there is? Principles and responsibility have bowed to the almighty buck." Her eyes were flashing now, her voice strident. She would have continued the diatribe had he not shouted, "Stop it, Grace! I know all this. I've heard it before. All I wanted was some sympathy."

"But I am giving you sympathy," she said, as she sat next to him on the bed.

"No. You're haranguing. I wouldn't have told you. But it was bothering me. Let's just drop it."

"Great. You want to drop it? You drop a bombshell on me with 'Grace, I lost my agent this week,' and that's all you want to say about it?"

"Yes it is. The rest doesn't affect you."

This really irritated her, and she threw her towel across the room as she spat out, "Doesn't affect me? If that isn't just like you. You think you live in a vacuum—that what impacts you does not impact me. Well, it's not true. You just asked me to marry you!"

"Yes. So?" He was defensive now. She could see he was struggling valiantly to stay in the room, and not to disappear.

"Well, if you don't think your professional success has some bearing on that, you're naïve," she explained forcefully.

"Only because *you're* not working," he retorted. "You can't get a job and are having a difficult time of it. That's why you're upset about me. Otherwise you wouldn't care."

Grace saw no validity whatsoever in that argument and chose not to even acknowledge it, continuing instead with, "How can I commit to marriage without considering the ramifications?"

At that he shook his head and had that look which said it's hopeless to deal with her, so she overrode him with, "When I was young, it didn't matter. But I don't have that same freedom now. And you want to have a baby. Well, how do I know we'd be able to support a baby? How do I know you could take care of me while I was too pregnant to work?"

"You don't. You can't know. You can only know I will try."

"Well, that's not good enough. I can't take a chance like that when so much depends upon the choice. Robert, I see that the future is determined by each choice—one affecting the other until the future takes shape. And I want to *know!*"

He looked stunned. "Are you saying that you can't make any decisions because you don't know what the future holds?"

"Yes." She responded quickly, and then dropped her face into her waiting hands. "No. I don't know."

"Well, that's crazy. You're the one who told me that I was not in *training* for my life. I remember you saying it was not some event to take place in the future—that it was happening now. You're the one who made me stop postponing my life and start living in the present. Now, how can you sit here and say this?"

"I don't…it's just different somehow. I don't know." She was weakening, unable to grasp the subtleties, and unwilling to try. She seemed to possess no strength these days.

As if to capitalize on this, he made the peace offering. "Love, let's just forget about it. There's plenty of time to worry about that when I get home. Let's just go on to Vienna and enjoy the trip. We need it. It'll all work out." He touched her cheek. "You wait and see."

It was suddenly very clear to her what she had to do. She felt no doubts. Instead, she felt a wave of calm that dissolved tension. Her voice changed, and from deep within, a stranger's voice said, "I can't go to Vienna. I must stay here."

"But you said just a few days here, and then to Vienna for our trip." He apparently had difficulty dealing with this new voice, and he dropped his hand from hers.

"I know. But I can't leave. I shouldn't have left thirteen years ago. Now I have a second chance."

"I don't understand," he said. But he did, in fact, understand.

As he rose, to separate himself from her, he turned and spoke forcefully, as if he knew the stakes. "Grace, I've indulged you all I can. I gave no argument when you suddenly changed our plans from Greece to Vienna by way of Brunnen. I told myself it would do you good and that, as I'd seen none of Europe, it didn't really matter to me. I have sympathized with your compulsion to get to Brunnen. I listened to your exaggerated claims about your purpose in life, your disrupted search for a meaning, and about Brunnen and your 'soul place.' I've listened to all of this. I've loved you through all this, for God's sake, even asked you to marry me!"

She was conscious of his dressing and packing—separating her things from his. She made no effort to either interrupt or stop him as he continued talking. "Well, I'm not going to indulge you anymore. I've said what I have to say. I've told you I love you. I want to marry you. I even want to have a baby. And that's enough. I can't force you to love me. I'm not going to beat you into marrying me. It'll either work out for us, or it won't. We either go forward from here or we recognize we've reached the end, and accept what that means. The rest is up to you, Grace."

Again, the inner stranger's voice answered, "I know." Then it merged with her known-self's voice. "Robert, my love, I never meant to hurt you. I know you're proud. You've offered a great deal, and I know you won't beg. Please know, from my heart, that something's missing. I don't know whether it's in you, or me. I suspect me. But I must find out." She sat silently for a while, giving him time to nod in agreement. Then she added, "I promise I will work it out."

He snapped the right latch on his suitcase, then the left; grabbed his jacket; retrieved his passport from her bag; and turned to face her. "I'll be in Vienna. I'm leaving the binoculars. I have the feeling you'll need them more than I."

She laughed and nodded. *An ironist to the last,* she thought. Her eyes teared up.

He stopped at the door, as if thinking, and without turning said in a steady voice, "Take care of yourself, Grace." Then he was gone.

CHAPTER SIX

T his time she did not cry. Momentary sadness yielded quickly to relief. Anxiety yielded to calm. She was no longer breathless. Grace knew that, although she risked losing it all with Robert, there was no other way to go forward. The time with him had made her progressively more exhausted, and the time of solitude seemed a gift.

Unable to afford to remain at the Bellevue, however, she checked out and walked to the edge of town, stopping across the street from the farmhouse she remembered. Nothing seemed to have changed there. The geraniums in window boxes were blossoming spring red, and patches of color clung to the base of the house. She did not hesitate when ringing the bell. The only one who seemed to notice was a family cow. He was lazily mowing the front lawn and raised his head, turning sad, brown eyes on this visitor.

When the door opened, Grace recognized the woman. She looked as before—only spread more. The face, the breasts, the hips, and thighs occupied more space in the door this time. She showed no sign of recognizing Grace, but she was polite.

"Haben Sie ein Zimmer zu vermieten?" Grace inquired in passable college German.

"Ja. Ja."

Grace rented the room—nodding silently as Sophie showed her the location of the bath and demonstrated the closets and the location of extra comforters. *She's a pretty woman,* Grace thought, *a hard-working woman whose gray bangs are betraying acquired age before justifiable age.* She decided not to mention that she had been here before.

So, she spent the next few days restfully exploring the tiny town, sitting on the water's edge watching the boats being delivered for summer sports, and sleeping alone on the beach, comforted by glacial waters. A peculiar sense of exhaustion still controlled her. She had always been so full of energy and zest, awakening each morning with a jolt as if someone had pulled a switch, turning all her circuits on at once.

This had been a source of consternation to Keith who rose and awakened slowly, and it was a bother to Robert as well. For Grace had seemed to bound out of bed, determined to hit the floor running. It had always been so. Recently, however, no amount of sleep seemed to satisfy her. And now, in addition to exhaustion, if she tried to think of Robert as she had promised herself she would, her thoughts fragmented, leaving her incapable of focusing upon her present life. A kaleidoscope of characters from the past intruded instead, with ever-changing pictures. And she gave up the effort of trying to hold them still, let alone dispelling them.

Instead, she slept, letting warm air soften the insistent knot in her stomach. Today she had fallen asleep on the rocky beach, watching her swan teaching its youngsters to fish, when she saw very clearly a wall-sized map of North Vietnam, then South Vietnam, then the separation by the Demilitarized Zone. There were blue lines for rivers, green shadings for forests, black crosspatches for military access roads, brown lines for major highways, and hundreds of orange dots scattered throughout—along the routes and in the jungles—each a Howard Johnson Restaurant!

Then she heard a helicopter overhead, felt the throbbing of its propeller, saw the camouflage coloring. Looking up, she saw the pilot in helmet and elaborate headsets. He spoke into a microphone, squinted down at her. She recognized George Hazeltine, from her college, remembering him as a haughty waiter in her freshman dorm when he was a junior. He seemed to recognize her, for he smiled—and then froze. The helicopter stopped throbbing and plunged before her, his face frozen in surprise as it plunged into an orange dot of a Howard Johnson restaurant. The orange dot flared, swollen momentarily as it consumed the fallen bird, and then the conflagration swept the map entirely.

She woke, shaking, knowing she had never said what she wanted to George. And she thought of the time, two years ago, when she had played the wife of a helicopter pilot missing in action in Vietnam. In the special, her first starring role in television, she had played a woman who had become an alcoholic after her husband disappeared. Her hard road back to reality had provided Grace with her finest TV role to date, and she knew she had performed to the test. Her performance had been weighted in truth, courageous in its approach, hopeful in its resolution, and everyone around her had expected an Emmy.

She did not receive one, however. Her co-star did. And George, long dead, never knew that he—and her regret—were the source of that performance.

To put these thoughts out of mind and to dispel the nightmare, she rose and decided to hike up into the mountains to a nearby town called Morschach. The estimated climbing time should be 90 minutes, which would give her ample time to explore and return by dinner. The day was sunny, but cool. She tied her sweater around her shoulders as she began the climb. By this time, she had a walking stick and sturdy shoes with cleats. They disturbed her, however, because of their weight and their decidedly "square" appearance. She did feel somehow crippled though, and thought they were an appropriate addition. And above all, they were safe.

Passing two older men who were exercising in the mid-May afternoon, she chatted with them briefly, in the best German she could muster. The communication, however limited by her marginal German, nonetheless warmed her, and made her feel close, tied in again. Other than Sophie, she had spoken to no one in several days. She enjoyed their company until they all arrived at a signpost. The Morschach route narrowed and steepened considerably as it made its way up through dense, pungent pines. The two old gentlemen stopped to catch their breath, remarking that the path was for youngsters, not the faint of heart. They mumbled their approval as they seemed to assess her legs, and then returned the easy route to Brunnen.

She was alone now, lightly treading on ferns and winter-worn pine cones, occasionally catching moss-covered rock with her cleats. Overhead a jay chattered at her. Alongside a squirrel followed her, darting from tree to tree as if part of a surveillance team. She stopped to stare at him. Apparently satisfied she meant no harm, he blinked and departed. She was alone.

Filtered light illuminated the path. Her legs stiffened and her calf muscles ached as she pushed on with her stick to the next sign. Given three choices of villages, the signs to Morschach and Sisikon both pointed to the right, so she continued. About 50 meters along, the path forked, one angling sharply left up the hill, and the other a gradual right, and then on up. But there was no sign, and Grace had no idea which path led to Morschach, and which to Sisikon. Both were well-traveled though, and clearly progressing to some destination far uphill.

This annoyed her—to be following such carefully marked paths, and then at a critical fork, to find they had omitted a marker. She needed total details—always had. She felt lost now, but, since she had been climbing an hour already, she had no intention of getting lost at this point. With an angry determination, she cursed under her breath and proceeded to climb hard left, breathing deeply as the path narrowed further. She saw no more signs, and could barely see to the next bend, given the density of the uncut maples that grew beneath larger pines. She was afraid she had taken the wrong fork, and was considering turning back, when she heard movement on the path ahead. Something was coming down the path toward her.

"Please God, let it be someone, not something," she muttered under her breath, not really expecting Him to hear. Using her walking stick, she stepped to the far edge of the path and looked up, just as a man stepped down off an exposed-root directly in front of her on the path.

"Guten Tag," she offered hesitantly, before she realized she was staring into familiar eyes. *Very intense blue eyes,* she thought, as she recognized him. His eyes registered surprise at seeing her, then something else. She couldn't grasp what. It passed, and he smiled politely.

"Guten Tag. Wie geht es Ihnen?"

"Sehr gut, danke," she responded politely, unable to take her eyes off his. There was silence for a moment. He broke it with, "Ich sehe, daB Sie ein Wanderstecher gekauft haben." Snapping out of her daze, she held up her stick, proudly demonstrating it, thanking him for his advice. She saw him look to her feet. Knowing he was checking to see if she had followed all of his advice, she nonetheless wished she could hide those clod-hopper feet. Too late. She awkwardly modeled them, turning her right ankle from right to left to display the cleats.

The conversation had ended, and he made a move to leave. Very self-consciously, looking at the ground, tucking her right foot behind her left leg as if to hide it, she said, "I'm afraid this time I'm lost."

"Oh?" He spoke in English now, with what sounded like some kind of British accent.

"Yes. I want to go to Morschach."

Tapping his stick against his shoes to dislodge some dirt, he pronounced simply, "Then you are not lost."

"I don't understand."

With a perfectly placid face and an edge of assertiveness, he almost lectured, "You know where Brunnen is, right?"

"Yes, of course, it's down there." She pointed down the slope.

"And you know where Schwyz is, right?"

Again pointing down the hill in another direction, she said yes.

"Well, there you are. You know where you are, just not where you want to go."

She looked puzzled, so he continued.

"Morschach is where you want to be. Here is where you are. You can never know where you are in relationship to the future, only where you are in relationship to the present. That you know. You are above Brunnen between Schwyz and Brunnen, and you can go down easily to either town. Therefore, you are not lost." Reverting to German, he tipped his suede hat, "Auf wiedersehen." And he was gone quickly into the afternoon shadows.

Grace was too exasperated by his arrogance to figure out the meaning of his statement. She was more preoccupied with his attitude than his content, and felt that he had spoken condescendingly. Very few people had ever spoken to her as if they stooped to reach her, and she resented this smugness.

She remembered his energetic eyes, then dismissed him, reminding herself, *His ashen hair is very thin on the top.* Nonetheless, she pressed on stubbornly to Morschach.

She took walks regularly now. Her legs were strengthened and her breath control much heightened. She enjoyed immensely the ever-changing view of the lake afforded by walks along the ridge.

Then one day, a week or so after meeting her stranger-friend in the woods, she decided to hike along the ridge where she had nearly fallen. All snow was gone now, surrendering to the day's sun and the mild spring nights. That part of the ridge was the highest, with vistas in three directions, and Grace felt she was ready now to return. Only this time, she would walk across the ridge to that point, rather than take the cable car. It frightened her, and she now had more confidence in her climbing than in her riding. Also, she had an adventurous desire to meet that mountain on her own terms.

Today she felt a need to get up high—to escape. Depressingly, she felt surrounded down below, unable to breathe. The feeling of being pursued, and that twisting knot in her stomach, returned regularly, making it almost impossible to collect her thoughts. She would ask herself what Robert was doing, wondering how he fared alone in Vienna, wondering if he had taken a lover and was sampling Austrian "dumplings." But the vision would be interrupted by pictures of Keith's graduation from law school, of their first furniture, purchased second hand from an estate in the Rossmore District of Los Angeles, and then, blackness. She could remember nothing much from the '70s—no low lights, no high lights—just a blank. *How could I lose a decade?* Maybe if she went to the top where the air was clearer, this mental constipation would disappear.

On top, the air was, in fact, wonderful—but her mind was still blank. She felt uneasy, as if she'd lost something of value. But because she couldn't remember what she had lost, she couldn't search, and she was overcome by nagging feelings that she must find what was lost before she could go forward. So Grace traipsed along the top of the mountain in present vivid color, searching through past blackness.

Then, too, there was the vague future. That morning Sophie had come to her room. She had her ubiquitous scarf tied around her head, this time tied in a double knot. She handed Grace a postcard forwarded from the Hotel Bellevue. It was from Vienna and, in Robert's boxed, engineer-style handwriting, said only, "Leave tomorrow for Los Angeles. I love you. Robert." The picture on the front showed the incredible Baroque interior of the Opera House, and she envisioned Robert there listening to his beloved Mozart.

Because Grace had always been a practical lady who could rationally analyze a problem, she had sat down to draw up a credit and debit sheet on Robert's proposal. But today the "what ifs?" stopped her. What if it were wrong and didn't last—if they separated after a few years? She would be forty and starting over again. What if they had a baby and neither she nor Robert could support it? She would be trapped in financial horror with less than she had now. What if she didn't like the baby, and had forsaken her vital privacy and independence forever? What if she couldn't be faithful to Robert, finding new places and new men stimulating and reinforcing? What if Robert grew old, taking her youth with him? What if she gave him all her strength, leaving none for her own battles? What if she could no longer dream, and ended up settling instead for security?

These thoughts so overshadowed the credit column that she gave in to misgivings and seriously doubted whether she could commit to anyone again. *Surely not with the same blind faith I did before,* she thought. Pain and setback had jaundiced her view. What others considered to be her indomitable spirit had been dampened. She was but a "shadow of her former self." She knew that, and was powerless to stop the onslaught of fear and indecision. Grace was acutely conscious that a wrong choice now would drastically affect her entire future path. Fortunately she was astute enough to recognize that the ubiquitous character Depression had made his entrance, sneaking onstage when her back was turned—upstaging her clear, purposeful performance, veiling it instead in darkness. She had angrily resisted his return by ceasing the internal debate and going for a walk instead. Once again, she was on the ridge.

The sensation of elevation always seemed to clear away the darkness, to restore good, warm feelings. She shed her sweater and strolled easily, letting the sun stroke the exposed parts of her arms and breasts under the chemise she was wearing. Her skin tingled in response, and she began to relax.

She was directly over the spot where she had fallen now. As she looked down the slope, she reminded herself how innocuous it appeared, and yet how near she had come. *A simple choice, a potentially devastating result,* she thought. That idea disturbed her—stirring troublesome analogies—and she decided to wash it out with a cold beer. Remembering the overlook café at the way station, she made her way there. On the way, she spotted an Edelweiss and knew it was a good omen.

The sun had brought out many hikers. Every table was occupied, although there were individual seats remaining at most. She approached a vacant seat, stopping suddenly. There he sat. Like an apparition with his back to her, she recognized his thinning hair immediately. He was alone at his table and was talking in a subdued manner to a black man opposite at the next table. The vigorous German language was loud and pervasively masculine throughout the rest of the patio restaurant. This made her uneasy, and she considered leaving, hoping he would not find her impolite. Besides, she had not forgotten his curt remarks of a week ago. Before she could act, her decision was made for her. The man he was talking to noticed her, averting his eyes to her, stopping midsentence. Almost as if on cue, all other voices stopped, heads craning to see the feminine interloper. Her stranger-friend with thinning hair, however, did not turn. He simply set down his beer.

Grace had never really been one to make the first approach to a man. She was far too insecure and had always waited for the man to show his colors. But she had no intentions of being left standing awkwardly in the middle of a Swiss way station, surrounded by hard-drinking, hard-laughing local boys. She had always had a knack for appearing to know exactly what she was doing—whether she did or not. She never floundered or looked embarrassed.

That poise was challenged today. Determined not to lose it, she walked up to his table and, as if they had a prearranged meeting, she said assuredly, "I believe I owe you a drink."

There was silence throughout—all eyes shifting focus from her to him and back again. For a moment she thought he looked disturbed at being interrupted. He recovered, however, looked to his friend opposite, and then to her.

"For what?"

"For catching me." Curious eyes now observed them both. Hesitant eyes checked his reaction carefully. He nodded and said, "I was afraid you were going to say for redirecting you."

She broke into a huge smile, laughed appreciatively, and answered, "That would take a bit more doing than even you might imagine."

Smiling, too, as if she'd gotten the best of him on that, he said, "I see. In that case, ein halb Liter Dunkles, bitte," he requested, as he ordered a dark beer and motioned for her to join him.

There was a noticeable relaxation of tension in the room as Grace set down her things and slid onto the bench opposite him. Other men returned to their drinks, their voices at first tentatively conversing and then crescendoing to a normal din. Her friend glanced at the man opposite and seemed to wink as Grace ordered two half liters of a dark beer. Her companion tried to discourage her from ordering that for herself. Explaining that it was a very heady, dark beer, he encouraged her to try the local Helles.

"I'm not as faint of heart as I may appear," she said.

He demurred, and she ordered. They waited in silence. Grace observed him a little more closely. Although his hair was thinning on top, he was a young man, perhaps her age. His face was tanned and weathered, but youthful, intelligent, and alive. And his crystalline, flashing eyes again penetrated. He was wearing a plaid flannel shirt—partially opened, with sleeves rolled up—revealing slender, muscular arms and a firm chest. *An athletic build,* she thought, *showing not even a single fold of flesh. He's rather like a runner.* Curiously, she felt warmth now from his silence, instead of coolness. And she felt depth—or perhaps mystery. That was all, before their beers were placed in front of them.

She raised her mug to toast, "For catching me."

"For catching you." He waited as she took a swig. She nearly choked. It was like warm, diluted molasses and was sickeningly sweet. Determined not to give him a victory on this, she smiled and persevered, thanking God her acting talents hadn't abandoned her. He had topped her before, and she would be damned if he would best her on this.

Watching her valiantly swig the near-molasses, he rather cryptically said, "Hartnächig," as he raised his mug. She made a mental note to look that up in her dictionary when she could.

They fell into silence. Although this confrontation had occurred in silence, they had spoken with their eyes for a moment. She felt a nebulous sense of connection before she broke it. Looking out over the lake and village below, she remembered the day she had stood in Keith's Century City office looking out over the Pacific to the gleaming Catalina Island and the always hazy Pt. Dume. That day, looking at the splendid panorama of blue water from the office they had dreamed of having for so long, she had the distinct feeling—a certainty actually—that her life was changing irrevocably. She and he had just decided to separate and at that instant, looking out, she knew that regardless of whether they got together again, their life was changing and would never be the same. Something was leaving.

Now, in Switzerland, she had a similar feeling—the sensation that her life was changing irrevocably. And she who had always resisted the word *irrevocably* on principle—who was terrorized by it actually—resisted that feeling now.

Instead she drew a new book from her bag, *Jude the Obscure*, and opened it. She noticed he was watching her, but made no attempt beyond a smile to communicate further. She read the first page quickly, but before she turned the page, she skipped to the last page and read it through. Her mind's eye saw his mouth drop open, saw his lips move as if to speak, saw him change his mind, and return to the tranquility of his beer. She then returned to the second page and read a while.

After a few minutes, she returned the book to her bag, paid for the beers, rose, and looked into his eyes. They seemed to want to speak—questions mostly. Uneasily now, she said, "Thank you."

Without removing his eyes from her, he responded, "Thank you." She walked to the door. He did not turn. But as she reached the steps, he gave the exit line, "Miss Archer?" As she turned, he added, "You forgot your walking stick."

How does he know my name?

She was sitting now on a bench along the path. Unable to shake questions from her mind, she waited for answers. Unable to shake either the feeling of a force—something waiting for her here—or the fears of returning to the stifling world below, she sat paralyzed.

His voice intruded, gently. "What's wrong?"

And for the first time in months, she verbalized her fear with a blindingly truthful answer. "I'm stuck." There was silence as a hand touched hers, and she added calmly, "I can't seem to leave the mountain."

"Then don't." That was all he said.

It was late night now. She had been on the mountain, stuck to that bench, for six hours. He sat beside her in the dark. They had not moved. He still held her hand.

He asked finally, "Are you still stuck?" She tugged his hand and nodded. Then she swallowed and asked, "How did you know my name?"

He took a very deep breath and held it interminably—as if exhaling the wrong answer would be fatal. Slowly he released, and in exhaling turned to her. "I've been waiting for you."

A thunderstorm was beginning at the far end of the lake near the town of Altdorf. From where she was sitting, she could see jagged lightning revealing flashes of purple and red around the peaks. There was darkness in the distance where the rain must be falling. But here, at her seat high on the mountain, it was clear and fresh. There was ozone in the air, and she felt somewhat high. For a moment she thought she could see into the future, and that Altdorf, and its early summer storm, were that future. The darkness was waiting there for her. By the time she reached Altdorf, if she were to go there, perhaps it would have moved on, leaving a bright, clear evening. But here, in Brunnen, with a stranger holding her hand, it was already clear and open.

Below, the lights of the town were on for the evening. Rising out of the darkness was laughter from one of the cruise ships that regularly journeyed from Lucerne to Altdorf. It stopped at each town along the lake and had just left a few revelers in Brunnen. Now, from the diagonal path it cut into the lake, Grace heard voices tinkling. And she heard an alpine horn in the distance. A dog barked, and a child answered—all probably 10 kilometers away. The night air carried the sound without static or interference. She felt suddenly joyous at the effortlessness of penetrating the night in Brunnen. And she thought of New York City—the sounds of the trash hitting the street, ground in by 1 million joggers; the thunder of trains dripping spray paint and blood; the millions of strained voices as each man, woman, and child strove for recognition. And yet here, from 10 kilometers away, she heard a boy and his dog, now laughing together. The balmy spring air was exhilarating, too. In the spring, the body joins the surrounding air—as if fusing with it—being nourished by it.

The joy she felt made her face shine. Her eyes were teary but she felt relaxed. Letting go of her stranger-friend's hand, she asked softly, "What is your name?"

"Klaus," he answered succinctly.

"Klaus…?" She protracted the sound to draw him out.

"Klaus Urhaber."

She repeated it—less to memorize it than to try to recollect the name from her past. *Although, I've always had difficulty remembering peoples' names,* she reminded herself.

"Do I know you, Klaus Urhaber?" She had no such recollection, and assumed his mysterious remark implied only that he had wanted to see her again after her near-fatal fall. She sensed nothing sinister about this man—quite the contrary. He exuded great gentleness, a centeredness, and a complete lack of tension. She had no fear of being alone with him here in the dark on an isolated mountain, surrounded by none but sentinels. And for that reason, she was not prepared for his answer.

"Yes." He laughed diffidently as he leaned over to pick an Edelweiss whose white petals shimmered in the moonlight, which was now punctuated by lightning. She noticed his broad, perfect smile as his surprisingly delicate hand gently stroked the white flower. "But apparently you have no recollection of it."

"I'm afraid not." She felt uneasy now, albeit unspecifically, until he reassured her.

"It's all right. It was a long time ago. July 7, 1967."

That was the day she had left Brunnen on the band tour. She felt a rush of adrenalin now, and knew it was not from fear. From what then? Grace felt a keen sense of anticipation and turned to him, her eyes widening, pupils dilating to see him clearly in the half light.

His voice was low and husky. It filled his frame. "You were on your balcony at the Grand Hotel Au Lac. Do you remember?" He spoke gently now, like one who is trying to coax an amnesiac back to awareness. "It was early morning."

"I remember the day. I *was* there then. But I don't remember you." Even as she answered him, something stirred. From deep inside her mind an image long-repressed was surfacing like a developing photograph.

"I had the room next to you and your roommate. I was on my balcony enjoying the morning," he explained. "I remember it was an especially beautiful day in Brunnen. And you came out on your balcony."

"I'm sorry, I don't remember." Her mind was struggling to expand, to reach back, to recall the image.

"You stood there for a long time before a short, dark-haired girl—"

"Yes, Pam," Grace interrupted, supplying her roommate's name.

"Before Pam," he said, gracefully incorporating the supplied detail, "came out and told you it was time to leave and could you help her with her saxophone. You said, 'I'm not going.'"

Grace smiled. She remembered that well enough, but little else.

He continued, this time poking the Edelweiss into the curls above her right ear.

"Pam disappeared, and after about five minutes, a man and woman returned."

Eagerly now Grace spoke. "Yes, Dr. Nugent and his wife." But the returning memory failed her. "What did they say?" she pressed.

"The man spoke first and told you they were all waiting in the buses and that it was time for you to leave. You said you couldn't leave. I'll never forget this, Grace. You said, 'This is my soul place. I cannot leave.'"

She said nothing now, but rather sat looking out over the lake. He was putting her in touch with her lost self, and she reached backwards in time to assist him, even though she still had no recollection of having seen him there.

"Then you stood looking out across the lake until the woman spoke to you," he continued.

"What did she say?" There was urgency in her voice now. "Please tell me what was said to me."

"That the band needed you, that you were a responsible adult, that you couldn't let them down. The man added that the younger musicians looked up to you, counted on you. He said, 'You're an adult now, Miss Archer. You must stop this childish talk, and come with us.'"

Grace was numb now, for she remembered those words—having successfully buried the actual words for years.

"What did I do?" she asked eagerly.

"You doubled up as if you had a pain in your stomach, and froze there for a moment. Then you stood, turned, and—as you turned—you looked right at me and said, 'I'll be back.' Then you left." That was all.

Now Grace had always had a penchant for romance and mystery, but this was too much. *It isn't possible,* she told herself. She heard his voice, but it was muted now, as if her mind were erecting barriers.

"You meant it," he continued, sounding certain. "I could see that. And you included me. I knew in that instant what I had to do. So, I waited." He was staring at her now, smiling at some private victory.

"So you waited?" she repeated, as if the sound of the words being repeated would provide a sense of reality. She dug her fingernails into her palm to wake herself in case she was dreaming. She was not.

He smiled and nodded. "I waited."

She thought he looked completely open and felt that those seer's eyes were looking deep into her soul. This time they were not questioning eyes, however. They were confident, resolved. They were reassuring.

High on a mountain, above Brunnen, Switzerland, on a summer night in May, the sound of feminine laughter joined with a rich, throaty male voice, and the duet wafted out over the lake. Perhaps the boy and his dog 10 kilometers away could hear.

No one could see them, however, as the man in a plaid shirt lifted the lady with his arms, whispered something about "still being stuck," and supported her with sure steps to his cabin in a clump of tall pines—whose only access to the outside world was a peculiar wagon-like assembly that delivered his supplies from the station of a Luftseilbahn.

She was having the dream about the Dark Stranger who followed her everywhere. Unlike the character Depression, the Dark Stranger was a mystery to her and therefore, more terrifying. In her dream, she drove from unnamed city to unnamed city, but he was always there. He frightened her because she could never see him, and this day he kidnapped her. He stepped out of the shadows, but before she could see the face of her shadowed stalker, she woke.

It was always the same. She always awoke before she could learn who followed her. She had dreamt many times about her jobs, her home, her lovers, the cities and towns of her past. And always there was a stalker, and always he remained a mystery.

Sometimes she cried; she begged; she threatened. But he was impervious and remained in the shadows. This dream was no different. She felt no fear upon waking—only frustration. *Rather like coitus interruptus.* She tried joking with herself, as if a sense of humor could lift her spirits. That rarely worked though, since the dream always seemed a precursor to Depression.

Grace turned her thoughts instead to the room she was in. It was enormous and seemed to be the entire top floor of a cabin or a mountain chalet, for the ceiling sloped to a point in the center giving the feeling of an enormous loft, three sides of which were pine-paned and one of which was glass. Heat from an enormous 8' tall, rough, stone fireplace made reassuring crackling sounds. *Surely no heat is necessary in these spring nights.* She wondered whether the fireplace had been designed for another purpose.

Apparently so, since she noticed the irons within the fireplace made it possible to cook and bake. Hanging from the ceiling were large iron pots and bowls, and along the wall was a tall stack of wood. The furniture pieces were massive and wooden. Most seemed to be hand-carved. None were rough, however. The wood was smooth, treated, and cushioned by strategic pillows.

The bed she was lying in was large and had no frame. The mattress rested on the floor and was quite firm. Then she realized that the floor was covered—not by rugs or, God forbid, animal skins—but by mats. Stepping out onto them, she recognized the tatami mats of Japan and thought that was curious. Although there were some few glass and porcelain chess sets on wooden tables or shelves, there was an austerity in the room—not a coldness, just an efficiency, or perhaps a self-sufficiency. It was, in fact, a warm living area. The only decidedly masculine thing in the room was a large hat rack on the wall near the bed. There were at least 20 hats hanging there, from ski caps to suspiciously Texas-style, suede cowboy hats.

In the center of the room, about two feet of ladder projected into the room, and she guessed the loft area was connected to the lower floor only by ladder.

A man's steps preceded his climbing entrance through the hole in the floor. Grace, caught naked as she stood on the tatami, sputtered a protest and leaped under the enormous, cocoa-brown feather down quilt.

He apologized as he entered. "I'm sorry. I didn't think you were awake."

"It's all right," she said, as she tucked the quilt securely around her, leaving only embarrassingly messy curls showing. She felt very awkward—almost compromised. She regretted that she was intruded upon at her decidedly least attractive moment of the day, and wished that she could at least brush her teeth. To do so would mean getting up, and she was not going to do that in his presence. So here she was, wondering why, or if, she even wanted to appear attractive for this man. And she chalked it off to conditioning, force of habit.

"Did you sleep well?" he asked, as he crossed to the fireplace, opened a wall cabinet, which revealed a sink unit, filled a coffee pot, and hung it over the fire to heat. She noticed he was in stocking feet.

"Not too well." She stopped for a moment, thought, and then added so as not to appear rude, "The bed was lovely, but I had a bad dream."

"I know," he said, without turning toward her. He placed a colorful woven basket full of fresh-baked rolls on the table and set out a marmalade jar.

"Did I talk in my sleep?" she asked, hoping she hadn't snored.

"No, I didn't hear anything. Of course, I was down below and probably wouldn't have heard you even if you had."

Grace wondered how he could possibly know then that she'd had a bad dream, but decided not to even get into it. The whole situation was a little too bizarre for her. In fact, she remembered only having fallen asleep before she could get her mind to fit together the significance of their conversation on the ridge.

"I have a few questions," she said, sitting up somewhat, careful to keep her breasts covered.

He laughed. "I expect you do."

Amazing how he's always ahead of me, she thought. "You say I spoke to you that day?"

"You seemed to," he answered calmly, almost disinterestedly, as he pulled up the chairs, pouring a mug of cream.

"And as a result, you decided to wait for me?"

"That's right."

Overwhelmed with curiosity, she fired rapid questions at him. He responded equally rapidly.

"Well, are you from Brunnen?"

"No." He volunteered nothing else.

"Where then?"

A slight beat of hesitation was all he showed before he responded. "I don't think it would have any meaning if I were from Brunnen."

Again, she felt as if she were running to catch up. "What were you doing at the hotel?"

"The same as you. I was on holiday at a grand old hotel some friends had recommended."

"What did you do after I left?"

- 99 -

"I bought the hotel."

Grace was so stunned by this she almost dropped the quilt from its shielding position. "You bought the hotel?"

"Aber natürlich," he said casually. "I guessed that when you returned you would come back there, so I bought the hotel to make sure I didn't miss you."

"Were you in the hotel business?" She spoke calmly, but her mind was racing, trying to grasp the implications of a man her age taking those actions.

"No." Again, he offered nothing else.

She decided to press on. In the meantime, he had crossed to the fireplace, pouring coffee for them. "Do you live at the hotel then?" she asked.

"No. I moved up here to the mountain in 1970 and converted the hotel to a spa for invalids shortly thereafter. I have a gardener look after it now."

"I know. He spoke of you."

This time Klaus seemed surprised. She was ahead of *him*. He crossed quickly to what appeared to be another built-in closet.

"May I ask you why you gave up running the hotel?"

She thought she saw his jaw close tightly, exposing a double twitch of the jaw muscles. He ran his right hand through his already-disheveled hair. This was something she had seen him do before. He said nothing, however, in response as he pulled out a soft, pale yellow cashmere robe and handed it to her. Taking a seat with his back to her, he served himself a roll.

Putting on the robe, she crossed and sat opposite him. His eyes looked lighter today—almost less friendly. Deciding not to tell him that she never drank coffee, she poured the warm cream into it and asked casually, "Why did you make it a place for invalids?"

"It seemed appropriate." He looked right at her. His eyes were more of a challenge than a barrier this time. They were certainly not welcoming. "Constructive." He modified his answer, softening a bit. She said she understood and asked what time it was.

He told her 10AM, then added as an afterthought, Monday morning. This caused her to choke on the roll she was munching. It had been Friday night when they sat on the mountain. Now it was Monday. *What happened?*

He answered her unspoken question. "You slept for quite some time."

She was too stunned to even respond. But she could see that he found this amusing.

"I took the liberty of having your clothes sent up here. Sophie, is it? She sent them up Saturday."

Feelings of resentment started to rush quickly now. Whatever numbness had suppressed her emotions was dissipated instantly, and she shouted fiercely, "How dare you? You had no right!" She felt her face flush red with anger at his presumptuousness. Feeling surges of energy racing through her properly restrained body, she watched him set down his cup without making a sound. He, too, was properly calm. *Too calm,* she thought.

In a steady voice—a disarmingly steady voice—his now-blazing eyes burning into her, he said, "I waited thirteen years, Grace. You've been a long time in returning. But now that you're here, you're not leaving until it's resolved between us."

CHAPTER SEVEN

꧁꧂

Grace normally would not have been held against her will by anyone. Male domination, as most of her peers had described it, had never been applicable to her. She was the one who usually made the decision about relationships, particularly since Keith and the realization that she had surrendered control of her self-esteem to him somehow. Even if fear were a motivating force in her life, she would not yield to bullying. But in this circumstance, she felt no danger physically. The thought crossed her mind that perhaps Klaus was fulfilling a romantic fantasy in her life. That was contradicted by the fact that there seemed to be nothing romantic passing between them.

Her curiosity was further augmented by the fact that for months she had experienced compelling forces. Some were merely vague feelings of anxiety or confusion. Others were dreams of heightened uncertainty, of being chased by the mysterious stalker, and being unable to stop running. Still others were feelings of mere pressure and thought, which kept leading her to return to Brunnen.

It had therefore not surprised her that Klaus said they must resolve it. Instinctively, before meeting him, she had known that whatever was here for her in Brunnen had to be satisfied. Before she could decide about a future with Robert—or even face him—and, she suspected, even before she could work again as an actress, she would have to discover what she was running from. Her instincts told her that her recent doubts and paralysis, her almost contradictory desire to escape a suffocating labyrinth-like world and climb instead to a free mountain top, were all part of this.

She therefore had no fear of Klaus. She had entered the crucible voluntarily. She had chosen to come to this mountain, and on three occasions now, to return. And it certainly wasn't Klaus's fault that a stranger had entered his life those many years ago with the words, "I'll be back," thereby disrupting his path and altering his life with seemingly equal compulsions. She hoped they would turn out not to be combatants, but rather partners who needed each other to be free.

This at least was understood between them that morning, and in the ensuing truce she grew to love the mountain. She went regularly into town to be with other people, to sit by the lake, to chat with Sophie, or to pick up mail. Once Grace had asked Sophie if she knew Klaus, and Sophie had said she did not—only that there were a number of people on that ridge who were completely self-sufficient and who never came into town. That was all, and the conversation ended. To date though, Grace had met none of these other people, or didn't think she had. Meanwhile, very practically, she had notified her parents, her agents, and her banker that she was staying on in Switzerland and not to worry about her. She heard from everyone except her parents.

This afternoon in June, as Fritz helped her off the cable car, she thought she heard music floating over from the woods to the east. She asked him where it came from, and he merely shrugged as if he didn't know. *I don't think he likes me,* she thought.

Fritz, more than anyone, seemed to resent her presence. He was married to a quiet girl, with fawn eyes and enormous glasses, who rarely spoke. She looked tired—like one who, although young, has lost life's energies, as if age were draining her strength. She was probably around thirty-five but seemed old. She said very little, and Fritz was quick to discourage even the exchange of amenities with her, hovering close by as if he were running interference for her. Grace didn't know whether that was because Ursula was ill—she certainly looked pale—or whether she just didn't have the inner strength to resist his domination. She couldn't help but think of her own mother, imprisoned in marriage for fifty years, and wondered whether this relationship were an example of burgeoning repression, of the slow process by which many women surrender their identity to a stronger force.

She said nothing of this to them, nor to Klaus. There was no doubt in her mind, however, that Fritz was piqued at her arrival and, most especially, when she was with Klaus. Every attempt at conversation only yielded a perfunctory acknowledgment. He was never rude exactly—just a master at making her feel like an odd man out.

And, reasonably, she couldn't blame him. She had not met Klaus's other friends, but he spoke of them and most seemed to have spent their lives—or most of their adult lives anyway—on the mountain. Once, when she asked Klaus about what brought them there, he said she would eventually discover that, and changed the subject. He was equally reticent about himself. Despite his assertions of needing to settle it between them, she had learned nothing about him in the two weeks since that morning in the cabin—except his age. He was her age.

She was thinking now about how two weeks had disappeared as she walked along the path. A two-week period in her life in New York would have been marked by numerous auditions, meetings about her one-woman show, lunches with friends, evenings out at the theatre, and phone calls to Robert in Los Angeles.

Today, here, she could remember nothing but long walks, quiet hours of meditation on ridge overlooks, deep restful sleep, steaming Swiss meals, and a sharp increase in the quantity of beer imbibed. It amazed Grace how much beer the Swiss consumed. She remembered having been astonished as a college student from a dry town in western Pennsylvania at how much wine Frenchmen consumed—both children and adults—and now she realized that the Swiss had their own version of thirst-quenching anesthesia. Nonetheless, she was definitely more rested and at times almost invigorated by the rare mountain air.

The sound of a single flute was still floating on the air. It soared up over the trees soulfully, and seemed to improvise its response to the changing clouds and temperate wind. It was truly beautiful and seemed to speak just to her. Until she had met Robert, she had never enjoyed flute music. Having been a trombone player, her proclivity was for brass—powerful, solid, ripping brass. The beauty of a single light voice had been beyond her grasp until recently. Robert loved Mozart, and he loved Rimpal. As Grace had grown to trust her femininity more, to appreciate her vulnerability, and to feel confident with the two, she had come to identify with the lonely, lilting voice of a flute.

Today it tranquilized and mesmerized her, and she followed the sound through the trees behind the chalet. Klaus was sitting on a flat rock, which projected over the edge of the ridge. Facing north, he and his flute seemed to be conversing with the clouds and intermittent sprays of sun. She hesitated to interrupt. Klaus must have felt her presence, however, because he stopped. And as the last notes were carried out over the valley below, he said, "What brings you here?"

"Your music. It's beautiful. I followed it."

"No, I mean, what brings you to Brunnen?"

Something within her stirred, and she knew that the time of bucolic recuperation was ending, that the time of their coming to terms with one another was at hand.

She stepped gingerly onto the rock, hoping their combined weights would not topple it, at the same time trying to overcome the vertigo she was experiencing. Dropping to her knees, she crawled out to the point where he was sitting and sat beside him. It was an extraordinary sensation because she could not see the ridge behind her, and therefore felt suspended out there in space, 1,000 meters above the valley. Below, it was very quiet now, and she hoped she wouldn't get the urge to fly that she'd heard described by people who had perched along the Grand Canyon.

"I'm a refugee from Norman Layton," she answered abruptly. He didn't understand, for which she was grateful. It afforded a little grace period as she decided whether or not to talk for the first time to anyone about this time of her life. "Actually, I'm a refugee from Hollywood."

"I'm listening," he said, sounding reassuring.

At first it was difficult to put her thoughts into words. But each sentence shared made the next easier, and she spoke very directly about the High Roll/Low Roll Syndrome, and about Norman Layton. Klaus was patient and coaxed answers where she was unclear.

"Grace, I don't understand a high/low syndrome. Is that a psychiatric term?"

She laughed. "No, it's my term for a phenomenon of the acting business. Because of the way the people in the business think, success is not success unless it's success." He looked confused—apparently not catching the subtleties or subtext inherent in the repetition. *Probably the language difference,* she reminded herself, so she explained it. "What I mean by that jumble is that only fame and fortune are acknowledged criteria for success. In Hollywood, your professional worth as an actor is most often—not always, but most often—defined by your box office potential, or the actual dollars you bring in to your agent, or the cars you drive, homes you live in, restaurants you eat at.

"Success as an actor is equated with money, with fame, or the size of the roles, or the billing you receive. It's the number of fan letters you receive, the number of people who recognize your name on the dreaded TVQ lists—which almost no one in America is aware of, but which fill actors with fear. Almost no one measures an actor by his growth or his spirit…by his quality. That's pretty much the given in the business."

Taking one of the oranges he offered her, she continued. "Now an actor is supposed to know this. His job is to seek and maintain the quality while all around him seek the tangible results. Gradually, unless he's very strong, though, he succumbs to the value system of those around him. He begins to identify with their criteria. In other words, he measures his own worth by the tangible results: jobs, billing money, party invitations. If those elements are all there, he is reinforced by agents, managers, friends, fans, and he is on a high roll. He may, if he's lucky, even be able to sustain the quality of his work through this. He's high, and bolstered by the reactions of those around him. He's confident and invincible. I personally experience it as a sensation of being unstoppable. I feel I can do anything."

"And?"

"And, the eventuality is that for every high roll, there's a low roll."

"I see. Like the…" he struggled for the term in English, "what's the word for that ride in amusement parks that goes up and down?" he asked, using his right hand to pantomime the peaks and valleys.

"A roller coaster," she supplied, smiling, and then continued. "Yes, very much like that. And it's inevitable. Do you understand?"

There had been a distant look in his eyes during her explanation, as he sucked on the orange. As she questioned him, then however, he eagerly met her eyes and said, "Yes, I understand." And as if that weren't sufficient, he added, "Completely."

"Well, when the low roll hits and there are no jobs, no money, no fans, no letters—whatever—all the criteria that identified the actor as successful, and therefore good, have disappeared. And those around him begin to doubt and to disperse. Just as a high roll breeds confidence, daring, and more success, a low roll breeds doubt, cowardice, and more failure. In a low roll, an actor may lose agents, managers, the attention of fans. Some of these disillusioned people may even be hostile to him. And unless the actor's sense of worth is hinged on something other than dollar signs, he's in trouble."

"Is that what you felt?" he asked gently.

"I don't know. Honestly, I don't. I didn't think so. I mean, an actor doesn't lose his skill just because he's unemployed. His task is to sustain himself, and his sense of worth, through the low roll, until he has a high roll again. I think I knew that." She corrected herself. "I mean, I think I know that."

"Then what's the problem?"

"Oh God, this is hard." She exhaled self-consciously but decided to keep going.

"The double D's." She laughed nervously as he watched her, and then added, "Discouragement and Disillusionment." Grace paused for a moment, listening to the wind in the spruce trees behind them, brushing the hair from her eyes. "I got very tired of inventing a catechism of encouragement for myself. But mostly I think people disappointed me."

Resting her chin on her knees, she said, "People in my life dripped the words 'brilliant,' 'staggering talent,' 'gifted'—and then disappeared. Or became distant. And then I had an experience with Norman Layton."

Klaus touched her hair, removing a tiny dried leaf that had lighted there, and looked into her eyes. She smiled a thank you.

"I was in a high roll. Actually, I see now in retrospect I was coming off a high roll. Anyway…" She told him the story, which was the beginning of her problems.

She had been working very steadily since her separation. As if to cushion the blow of being alone and totally financially on her own for the first time since graduate school, she had been regularly working. Each film project was interesting, worthwhile, and each role was getting larger. She had never felt she particularly belonged in the world of episodic TV and was content to work in certain miniseries that prided themselves in being "quality" television. But she had told herself that if the perfect series role came along to tap her special abilities, she would probably take the series.

Enter Norman Layton. While directing a gentle turn-of-the-century piece, she had received a call from her agent to report to Layton's office for an audition for one of the starring roles in a miniseries about the Depression South, which hopefully would convert to a series if the first eight hours were successful. She picked up the script, and, after studying it, made some very distinct choices about the character. She was a simple woman, a mother who was again pregnant and having difficulties. Grace had gone to great lengths for the initial meeting. Having decided to go into the meeting in character, she searched antique dress shops until she found a dress from the '30s that suited her own color needs and the earthiness of the character. She also bought comfortable but worn "clodhopper" shoes, as she called them. Last, she created a simple hair style with a bun, and wore absolutely no make-up.

At home in her apartment, after working out the relationships and character actions that seemed appropriate, she developed a physicality of a pregnant woman in an advanced stage. She practiced, using pillows to make herself conscious of the sitting and walking exigencies of advanced pregnancy. Then, discarding the pillows, she practiced the scenes to see if she could create the illusion of a nine-month pregnancy on a 5'7" frame at her 120-pound self.

Satisfied that she had done that, she analyzed the kind of sharp pain the character was to experience in one of the scenes, isolated it in herself, verified it with an obstetrician over the phone, and then made it part of her character. She knew they would believe the pain. After all, she had once created an imaginary bowling alley in a producer's office, and when she released the imaginary bowling ball, two of the network executives had raised their feet! She was confidant, and totally prepared. She arrived in Layton's office and waited with a group of actors. All were dressed in normal street attire and several were recognizable actors who had previously starred in TV series.

She—by then totally in character in the '30s—sat alone, quite relaxed with the gamble she was about to take. For Grace had felt that this part had "her name on it," so to speak. It was a series with humanity and had values. It expressed an earnest earthiness—her strong suit—and it was written just weakly enough to require first-rate actors and not just "talking heads."

When her name was called, she was as relaxed as she had ever been. She waddled into the conference room in complete pregnant character. There were perhaps ten people in the room: Layton, the writer, a studio executive, a previously-cast cast member, and some casting people.

She observed that some eyes opened wide, but nothing was said of her character choices, even as she struggled with a chair until she was finally able to drop back into it—her imaginary belly creating an obstacle. During the scene, her imaginary belly made rising difficult enough that her acting partner instinctively helped her up. Layton, who always wore that white, inverted sailor's cap, asked her to remain, and an actress was brought in to read the scene between the character and her black midwife. The awkward relationship between black and white was important and seemed to be working well. Then, on cue in the scene, Grace suffered the pain she had rehearsed. The audience of ten gasped. Her partner dropped her script and rushed to help before she realized what Grace was actually doing. When she did realize, the two proceeded with the scene—totally improvising and, apparently, totally believably—for Layton rose, came to her, embraced her with tears in his eyes and said, "I can't tell you how much it means to me to have met you." The casting person winked and only then did she drop out of character, virtually bounding out of the room.

Over the next week, she was called back to read with a black actress flown in from New York, and both worked beautifully together. She, the other actress, the writer, and Layton began to flesh out the relationship between the two women, based upon a connection he had seen in the scene the two actresses had read.

Then she was called back on sudden notice to Layton's office to read with a man. She was told that he and she were the number one choices and that Layton needed to see their chemistry together. Both were responsive to each other, tended to work similarly, and enjoyed improvisation. They felt comfortable enough to extend the scene into improvisation, allowing Layton ample time to see their listening and adapting abilities, and their emotional range.

Layton kissed her upon greeting her, introduced her to the president of his organization, and toured her around saying, "This is Grace Archer, a marvelous actress." Then suddenly, the whole thing collapsed. Within 24 hours, Layton had decided not to use the man and, in pushing him out of his thinking, had turned thumbs down on Grace as well. Feedback through her agents revealed that several people were still fighting for her, but Layton was searching the country for someone other than Grace.

Over the next three weeks, an inside source later told her, the role came to her three times. And each time, just before authorizing the deal, Layton would back off. He ended up in an "eleventh hour" casting of a girl from Chicago who looked just like Grace, but who had never been on camera before. He further hired and fired both the girl from New York with whom Grace had read, and another actor who would have been perfect as the husband. The series failed.

"So, it was a great opportunity that you missed out on," Klaus said.

"Yes, exactly. The fact that it was the closest I'd come to the largest, most challenging project I'd come in contact with made it hard." Showing regret, she added, "And the money. But what really disillusioned me was what followed."

"What?"

"Several months later Robert—"

"Who's Robert?" he asked, interrupting her.

She paused for a moment, deliberating how to answer this, and said finally, "The man I've been seeing." After a longer pause—for she knew she was not being totally honest—she admitted, "My lover."

"I see." He ran his hand through his hair quickly.

"Anyway, Robert took me to the Writers Guild Awards months later. He had had several scripts produced and wanted to go. Layton was giving one of the speeches. And in the lobby during the intermission he was within five feet of me. He looked right at me, *and didn't recognize me!*"

Klaus whistled. Or was it the wind? She reached for a pine cone as it rolled by, propelled by the warm air.

"What did you do?" he asked.

"I tried to think he must not have known me without my pregnant character." She laughed, too quickly, and knew that she had failed to cover her certain knowledge that it was not the character Layton had forgotten.

"And what did you learn from that?"

"That if you're going to play, you'd better win."

They sat silent for a while, sharing another orange. Grace traced a design in the loose dirt with a stick and did not look up. A few moments later, she continued. "And that was the beginning of a low roll—a deep, long one."

"When did it end?"

"It hasn't."

This didn't seem to assuage his curiosity. Surprisingly diplomatically, he asked, "How long has it gone on?"

"Two years." This time she was sure the whistle was not the wind. *There is nothing to add to that*, she thought, hoping he wouldn't press it further. But that was not to be.

"Was that your first?"

She attempted to make a joke by saying, "Christ, you sound like you're asking me if that were the first time I'd been laid."

"Was it?"

He had her on that one, and she laughed. "In a manner of speaking, yes, actually."

They both laughed, and then he added perfunctorily, "It'll end."

His casualness made Grace angry. As mercurial as she knew she was being, she resented that. It was the easy answer everyone gave—those who listened without hearing, who answered without feeling. *But then again, how could he, or anyone for that matter, know how it felt? That rejection?*

Still, she had expected more of him somehow, had sensed a greater kinship between them. Perhaps she was wrong in her assessment of him. Perhaps she was romanticizing. She concluded, "Anyway, I became disgusted and left."

"Okay. That explains why you're a refugee from Los Angeles. Now, why are you a refugee from New York?"

This was not the appropriate amount of sympathy she had expected. She had anticipated commiseration but had received instead another challenge. She was decidedly annoyed—and too much of a lady to show it.

Klaus lay back just then, opening his shirt in deference to the sun. Looking at him now she thought his slender frame looked slight against the rock—almost vulnerable. Yet, he was the one who pointedly interrogated with an almost infallible ability to penetrate to the core of a discussion. She had never met anyone who could so artfully cut through the, as Robert would say, "bullshit." Klaus had a precision mind. Sitting on the rock, as if suspended in space, she felt somehow that it was appropriate to be served up so—without any camouflage. He could just lie there, and as acutely as if he were a surgeon, cut away layers. Her pride made her want to resist—to argue even—but she felt somehow that it was useless.

Instead she looked out for a while, enjoying the sensation of the wind and sun against her face. Then, as a cloud passing between them and the next mountain obscured the view and a bit of the sun as well, she began her answer.

"That's a bit more complicated."

"I'm listening." He lay still and did not look at her. In a tall pine along the ridge, she thought she saw what looked like two mountain bluebirds frolicking. It was the time of year for nest building, and, given the frequent chatter of the pair from this indigenous species, she smiled, deciding that they were mating. Her voice joined theirs.

"Robert and I had been fighting over the general state of television. I was preoccupied—nearly obsessed—with a degenerating quality of projects, with a total lack of responsibility on the part of networks and producers, with a firm belief the American public was being sorely misjudged and underestimated by those who controlled programming."

"Did he *disagree* with this?" Klaus seemed surprised. He turned his head as he spoke in order to observe her reaction.

"No. No, of course not. It was my jealousy that hurt him."

"I don't understand."

"Well..." She had difficulty continuing with this. She began to gesticulate with her long, slender hands, as if the gesture could generate the words. She noticed he was watching her hands as if their uncontrolled activity were speaking directly to him. "I had run into sex discrimination...for the first time in my life. Robert produced a pilot and cast me in it. I found myself with an actor who made more money for saying two lines than I made for a starring role." Before Klaus could speak, she cut him off. "And if that doesn't seem possible, it is. I had to risk losing the role to get only two-thirds of what that man would walk into the project and be offered, and not even have to negotiate. And then the guy was disappointed that his agent hadn't gotten him more!"

"You didn't feel he was entitled?"

Her voice choked now for she had been this route before. "Yes, of course, he was entitled to get the most he could. It just was a constant reminder of a part of the business I was encountering all too frequently. Robert was paid more too for his writing and producing than women were." She stopped for a moment, frowning. "This is not easy for me to say, but I was jealous. I wanted it to be as easy for me as it was for them."

Klaus laughed briefly. Grace merely looked at him. Her throat was dry now, and she wished she had water. "Anyway, I came to believe that people worked for profit only—without any other purpose, and with no integrity."

"And why does that disturb you, Grace?"

"Are you serious?!" she asked incredulously. Apparently he was, so she explained feverishly. "Because I believe that you first decide or feel what you enjoy, what you want to create or give, and you then find a means of expressing that, of earning money, and of re-creating with that money. I have never felt that the objective in life is to make money, by whatever means available. That leads to manipulation and dehumanization."

She shimmered now with zeal, her very spirit committed to this point of view. Her voice quivered slightly, her hands delicately but frenetically still cutting the air. Her eyes were misty. "And you see, I have always believed that the purpose of art is to guide those who may be lost, to entertain those who may be despondent, to enlighten those who may be in darkness. Basically to open up the world—for all to better understand mankind and themselves."

"I agree," he responded noncommittally, "but that's merely the recent discovery of the rest of our generation. You're just discovering it now, too. That's good. But you must know that you're not in an art; you're in a business."

"I know. I know that—now. I realized that when I fought with Robert, and I knew that I would either have to change the business, or leave it. That's when we quarreled over "Gang Chronicles." And she told him of her outrage at an upcoming series to be based upon the lives of notorious American gangsters, chronicling their careers and lives. She spoke about her rage at being asked to look at these people as human beings—however slickly the show was produced—and to overlook their criminal legacy. "Kennedy died and left a legacy. King died and left a legacy. Vietnam left a legacy. The women's movement, space exploration—even the Beatles. And TV is reduced to the senseless justification of criminal behavior and shows like 'Apartment 66'—a jiggling, lascivious lapse in taste about a swinging singles' apartment complex. Was that what so many died for?" she cried. "To give the American public the luxury of being fed salacious garbage?"

There was silence now after this regurgitation. Even the bluebirds were muzzled. Not even a dragonfly or beetle dared approach the raging rock. Then she whispered, "I felt trapped with no control over my life or the future. I was not—am not—strong enough to change it."

"You may never be." Their eyes met, and she swallowed hard. He always challenged, however gently.

"Perhaps. So I went to New York."

"The Mecca of the artistically committed, right?"

This made her smile and she blushed, gracefully sidestepping the easy jab of her listener.

"I was exhilarated about the move—optimistic that my one-woman show would meet with the response there that had eluded me in Los Angeles—confident that I would be exposed to artists who would appreciate my talent, who would give me the roles I deserved. I anticipated the energy, the colors, and vivid vitality of the city. Have you ever been there?"

"No, but I have a close friend there."

"Well, I knew quality would not only be recognized there but revered. And that purity of purpose would be rewarded."

"And?"

"I was robbed the first day I arrived."

Klaus barked, "Hah!" She laughed now, too, continuing the rest of her story through her brave mask. It was a role she knew well. It was an effective role. She stretched out beside him as if to appear to be as casual about this as he seemed to be.

"Yep. Before Robert—he came with me to help me—before we could even unload the rental truck, it was broken into."

"What was stolen?"

"All my jewelry, mostly family heirlooms. And an antique Oriental table from my ex-husband's family. I used it in my show, and he had agreed to let me have it for my show when we divorced, rather than keep it in the family."

"Was he angry?"

"No. I was. New York was not what I thought it would be. I was alone and lonely. My show was received with encouragement, but not with an actual production. I had auditions for plays, did well, got very close, and then failed to be cast in any. I think you could say I succumbed to the second 'D.'" Then, as if to remind him, she explained, "Disillusionment. I just ran out of strength."

At that moment, a raucous crow flew by, his harsh and incessant voice pursued by the swift, menacing silence of a large hawk. Then the crow disappeared into the trees. The hawk veered off, rising once again to scout another meal.

"I read the *Riverworld* series to occupy myself—maybe to escape."

"Grace, did you read the last pages first?"

"Yes," she answered assertively, hoping to ward off any intimidation. Then he responded.

'Well, at least the final book hasn't been written there yet."

"Oh yes it has, it just came out, and I read it before I came to Brunnen."

He shook his head in disbelief, squinting his eyes as if he could see her more clearly that way, or perhaps, just to see her differently. Apparently he was unsuccessful because he spoke, rather emotionally now. "You amaze me! You do know that you rob yourself of the pleasure of discovery that way?"

"I know. I've been told this before. And I don't care," she said, as she waved the thought away.

"But don't you see what it means?" He was sitting up now, and she sat up to meet him. "The fact that mystery is part of the quest is what makes life worth living."

"We're not talking about life. We're talking about reading books! I enjoy and appreciate the writing more as I read if I know the ending. I see so much more of the subtleties and connections, and I comprehend not only the author's intent but also his methods and techniques. I get the whole picture, Klaus. Things I otherwise would have missed or overlooked stand out if I know the end. And I feel richer for it."

"Ohhhh, you're quick," he pursued. "No doubt you find that the signposts of life would also be clearer if we knew the end."

"I wish you'd stop talking as if this were a metaphor for my life," she retorted angrily now.

At this point, he threw up his arms, turned his face to the sky, and said, "Beautiful visionary's eyes, and she's totally blind!" And then he lay back, actively silent.

She decided, as she glanced at him, that his thinning hair must be caused by his habit of running his fingers through his hair.

Many minutes passed. There were no sounds except the occasional crunch of dried grass and leaves as a small, invisible animal skirted the ridge close to them. The clouds were coagulating now, forming a blanket—as yet too high to bring precipitation, but pervasive enough to chill the air slightly. Their brief argument had been like a summer storm—arising quickly, carried on balmy winds; briefly skirmishing with the earth beneath; and then dissipating, leaving exuberant moisture, gentle sun, and tranquil air in its wake.

Grace bridged the gap finally. "I don't want to argue. But I resent your presumption that you know me as well as you think."

He said he understood. And then, in an effort to get away from the topic of controversy, she added, "I was telling you why I left New York. Well…" She searched for the words. "I feel that each of us has moments when we have the handle, so to speak, on who we are and where we are. Those moments are turning points, and I reached mine in New York at a Puritan Oil audition."

"Is that like Mobil?" he asked.

She had forgotten that he might not understand Americans' predilection for market research and advertising—let alone know a particular cooking oil sold only in the United States. So she explained what she could about TV commercials, and he said he was well aware of America's advertising obsessions.

"All my life I've wanted to make it count. I don't know whether my parents told me this, or I arrived at it alone, but I feel I have been given certain gifts and I have an obligation—no, a responsibility to use them well, to make them count. I have always been attracted to theatrical pieces about the triumph of the human spirit against all odds. I want to continue to play roles of people locked in a battle of some sort and who triumph somehow—who make peace with themselves. To me, that's what acting is about, and I want to enlighten those who see me work. I want to widen their experience and hopefully stimulate their compassion and resolution."

Then, almost self-consciously, she laughed self-deprecatingly and asked, "Do you understand?"

He said that he did. Her voice, though strong, was liquid now, flowing to new thoughts and embracing them. She told him of a notation she had made in her Diary, which upon rereading, had provoked her to escape from New York.

She had been on an interview for a Puritan Oil commercial. Needing money, and having gone without work for so long, she was especially vulnerable. She had received a callback and a first refusal, meaning that they were seriously interested and clearing dates with her agent. Just the fact that she'd received a callback restored her confidence. She experienced feelings of belonging once again, and of being wanted. So much so that she had even made a bold phone call to an Off-Broadway producer regarding her own show.

She had also composed and mailed several confident business letters to possible producers. And then it had happened. She realized she was responding this way to a mere commercial callback. Never mind her dreams of film stardom, of recognition for inspired performances, of money enough to validate her acting, even of being cast in small roles in worthy projects. She was restored—by the mere prospect of a cooking oil commercial. She had sunk a long way, and the realization of this had brought her face to face with the common man—the average, unacknowledged, unrewarded man who tries to find a job and is rejected; who tries in the process to hold his self-esteem together and, with each rejection, finds it takes more and more courage to try again. Face to face also with the man who is perhaps unable to work, even if he wished to, or who lives in Harlem where few do work. Who faces the futility every day and must summon the strength from his imagination and dreams to even try. And who may eventually sap his dreams of so much strength that they lie bankrupt at the back of his mind. If dreams, and dreams alone, sustain and motivate, the ongoing dips into them for the resources to struggle on may dry them up. Outside reinforcement is necessary—for everyone—to keep the dreams vital and fertile.

Some make it, and some don't. And for the first time Grace had come face to face with her own arrogance. She was confident that she was one of the special ones with stamina and determination enough to make it, regardless. But even she grew tired and wanted to quit. She was still struggling, trying to regain her footing, but she realized for the first time that she might not make it. It was possible that, despite her brains, energy, and determination, events could combine themselves in such a way as to overwhelm her, causing her to give up. It was a shocking acknowledgment from the Golden Girl who survived the '60s upholding the American Dream.

"You'll survive this," he said, responding to her calm resignation. His voice, too, did not falter. For the moment he seemed supportive, not combative.

"I *know* I can *survive*," she said, elongating the sounds. "But is that all there is? To survive? Isn't there something more?"

"I think not." Klaus seemed to be looking into the distance telescoping and scrutinizing—his voice as distant as his eyes. Then he returned, affixing placid eyes on her again. "I think not."

Grace laughed nervously, secretly wishing she could escape this planet. "Well, that's unfortunate, because you see I'm plagued with the dream, but do not know if I have the courage to go the distance."

Looking at her now as if to give to her, and not to observe her, his young, lineless face relaxed, and she thought she saw self-recognition in his eyes. Then he asked, "Did you discuss this with anyone?"

"Yes, but they saw only what they wanted to see."

"Or what you wanted them to see," he admonished.

She stiffened over this, too proud to acknowledge any accuracy in that.

"They saw my so-called resilience, what I now feel may be a masochistic tendency to subject myself to repeats of situations that a wiser person would walk away from. But they all called it 'courage' and told me I was 'inspirational' to them. One actress friend told me that she looked to me to provide guidance. She watched me struggle and knew that if I could survive it, so could she. If I could do it, so could she. As if I held the answers!"

She paused for a second, found this amusing, and then added, as if reading from a prepared list, "My friend, Mary, called me before I left for New York and said, 'I have never known anyone like you. I've never known anyone who's gone through what you've gone through. I have a sustaining love, which keeps me from capsizing, but you've been robbed of even that. I just don't know how you have functioned.'

"Then, Klaus, my friend Laurel told me her fiancé, Howard, who's a former TV star said, upon hearing me cry on the phone one day, 'My God, if Grace is crying it must really be serious. You'd better go to her. Grace crying? I can't believe it. Even her?'"

She then added, "Laurel said, 'Whether you know it or not, you're a role model for even the men!' And Robert says I'm either 'the most vulnerable strong person he's ever met, or the strongest vulnerable person he's ever met.'"

"And what do you think you are?"

"Me? I think I'm a fraud. I'm not what I appear to be. I don't feel strong, not lately anyway. Actually I feel like I have some kind of terminally debilitating disease. I'm dying inside, and I marvel the others can't see. If it were cancer at least my skin would yellow, or my hair would fall out, or I might smell." Her bitter laugh could not mask her sadness, however, and she tried not to look at Klaus.

"Vulnerability and weakness are not synonymous, you know." He spoke softly, and was watching now to see if she understood.

"Oh?" she snorted sarcastically.

Ignoring that, he continued. "A truly vulnerable person may be the strongest of life's creatures."

Although the juxtaposition of these apparent contradictions interested her, she was too fatigued by now to engage in any more mental jousting. She said nothing. Moreover, she didn't understand his apparent alignment with Robert on this.

Realizing that the distance was increasing between them, Klaus rolled a pebble to her, as if to arrest her attention and erase any separation he had caused. "So, what did you do?"

"I decided to write my memoirs." There was a moment of silence, followed by a simultaneous burst of laugher from the two of them.

"Marvelous," he purred, with infectious laughter, "just marvelous."

"You see, if I do guide others—just *if* mind you—and if they do draw strength from me, whether it's drawn from an empty vessel or not doesn't matter. So I decided to actively do something."

As she spoke, her hands again energetically stirred up the air. He was completely silent now, watching her. The clouds were so dense as to blanket them, and without squinting, she was able to look directly at him. For a moment she considered crawling off this promontory to safer ground. But for some reason she did not understand, she stayed. There was no question that he had some power over her, however illusive it was in her mind. Instead of leaving, she told him something she had never confided in anyone, including Robert.

"I titled it *Keep On Keepin' On.*"

He smiled and nodded.

"And I remember the opening paragraph very clearly. I wrote, 'They say a writer's life is a lonely one. And they asked how I could have the audacity to write my memoirs when I'm not even famous. I do not know if a human being needs to be famous in order to have lived a life worthy of memoirs and, not being a writer, I have no way of knowing about the isolation. I suspect the latter is true. I hope the former is not.'"

"Nice sentiment."

Grace did not know him well enough to know what he meant by that, but because of that mysterious sense of competition she felt between them, she feared he was making fun of her. He sounded somewhat critical, and yet he was smiling, nodding his head and looking at her as if he was seeing something for the first time. She asked him what he was thinking. He said, "Nothing."

And then he changed the subject. "What about the book? Is it finished?"

A sad wind chilled her heart as she, having opened the issue, was forced to confess, "I didn't write anymore."

"Why not?"

"A lot of reasons." As she looked up, she laughed and joked, "All of which I'm probably now going to have to share with you, right?"

He, too, laughed. "Exactly."

"Well, very simply, I grew afraid. I had never hoped to be prolific, only to be profound. But I was overcome by fear that my innermost thoughts would be shallow, that all of my principles would be but vanities, and that the body of my self-esteem would be but a skeleton. And worse—once revealed—would shatter my self-image." The wind was coming up, prompting the trees to stiffen now against its assault. *Soon, they, too, will bend,* she thought.

"Every writer takes that risk," he said simply.

Klaus's perfunctory attitude once again annoyed her somehow and she snapped, "How would you know that?" But he took only a deep breath, silently buttoned his shirt against the cooler air, disassembling his flute as if preparing to leave.

Apologizing, she said softly, "I know nothing about you, Klaus, except that you say you are a friend. I'm sorry."

He said it didn't matter, and she told him why she wasn't writing.

"I fear I will not possess the wherewithal to write what I feel. I admire the command of language and imagery that writers have—their ability to use sound and images to evoke an emotional or intellectual response. I admire those who follow a florid poetical impulse, or those who laconically juxtapose images, which would otherwise be contradictory—all to stimulate and guide the reader."

She paused, then added, "Let alone the command of the grammar and structure required to achieve the desired result. And I doubted my ability to put even my paltry thoughts to paper. Then again, I thought maybe it's all self-indulgence."

"Is that why you came to Brunnen?"

"I can't say for sure. I have felt a compulsion to come here, as if some force were pushing me."

He was wiping the end of his flute with a cloth and, as she spoke, she noticed he hesitated for a moment—just a moment—and then asked, "In what respect?"

She wondered now if she should have told him this, but decided that once embarked there would be no harm in continuing. "It's difficult to explain. Los Angeles was not what I had dreamed it would be. New York had definitely failed to live up to my expectations. All the exuberance I had felt upon arriving there—in a new city with a better chance to perform as an actress, to begin a new life and make new friends—all seemed to be sputtering in a harsh environment."

Large, soft rain droplets were dotting their rock and the light was dimming now as a summer storm signaled its entrance. She did not move, however.

"So I came back to Brunnen. It was the only place where I had felt whole. And totally safe. It is high and serene, away from the 'No' world I live in. Here surely I can be happy. Even if it is just an escape… even if I am running."

"Are you?" he asked.

"Running?"

"Happy here?"

She knew the truth and knew he would know it. She dreaded to acknowledge it, for to do so meant she must first admit it to herself. "No."

There was silence. She wished that he would hold her but knew he would not. "Happier," she qualified, "but not happy. I thought it would be different somehow."

"You know, Grace, the trouble with moving to a new place to make a new beginning is that you come along."

Instinctively she exhaled, as if struck in the stomach, the wind knocked out of her. She laughed nervously to cover the blow.

Quite suddenly, he rose and extended a hand to help her up. She took it as he continued. "It's not the place you're in, but who you are in the place. You came to Brunnen, but you brought yourself along—and your baggage."

He hoisted her up as the rain assertively joined the scene. She felt rather dizzy and presumed that this must be what vertigo felt like. Seeing this, he took her hand, at the same time handing her his flute to protect in the front of her shirt, and placed his arm around her waist to support her as he guided her off the rock.

They, like the squirrels and rabbits who had been reconnoitering nearby, scurried into a grove of pines to wait out the flurry. The sound of an angry jay was the sole counterpoint to the gentle but persistent rain.

Grace looked up at Klaus, realizing for the first time that he was not really much taller than she. But he seemed so unencumbered. As he lifted his head in silent conversation with the jay, she observed his pronounced Adam's apple. He shook his head to dry his hair, running his fingers through it once again to keep it clear of his face. She thought that, although thinning on top and a bit mad from the tousling, it had a nice wave when wet and fluffed. His face was relaxed; his full soft lips parted as if to receive.

"Do you ever feel old?" she asked, her question startling even her.

He grinned broadly and responded spontaneously, "Hardly." Then, noticing her frown, he asked, "Do you?"

Confidingly she answered, "I first knew I was getting old when I looked at the policeman who took my theft report in New York, and he looked like a kid."

Klaus laughed, and she added, "They'd always been 'authority,' and now all the cops on my beat look like kids!"

"Now that you put it that way, I see what you mean."

"And I *really* knew I was old," she continued, "when I went to a King Karol record store in New York, asked for the Peter, Paul and Mary *A Song Will Rise* album, and the clerk said, 'who?'"

"You're kidding?"

"I wish. Then this kid says, 'Oh yeah, them. Well, lady, I think you'll have to try one of those antique record shops. They handle all of the out of print stuff.'"

Klaus's smile had changed to a look of disbelief. "Out of print? It can't be."

Grace nodded a conspiratorial yes, and then put the cherry on top of the charlotte russe with, "And on top of that, he called me 'lady.' That really did it. He was just a kid…he probably only knows John Kennedy as a man in his history book!"

Unexpectedly, Klaus reached out, pulling her close, his arm around her shoulder consolingly. "What did you do?"

"I had an affair with a twenty-five-year-old stud from San Antonio." She said this so matter-of-factly that she knew he didn't know whether to believe it or not. In any case, he found it amusing. To her surprise, she hoped that he found it provocative.

"And then?" he persevered.

"Then I came to Brunnen." She looked up at him. He was squinting at her again. "You don't believe it?"

"No, no, I believe it. I just don't believe you know why you're here." His tone of voice was so different now from his seriousness a few minutes ago when he had spoken about her and her baggage. She sensed his playfulness, and hoped he *was* teasing. However, she looked at him blankly, scarcely knowing which cue to pick up on.

Rather self-consciously, he dropped his arm in order to lean against a tree, scrutinizing her now-puzzled face. When he spoke there was disbelief. "Surely you know that you are far more beautiful now than when you were twenty?"

"So they say." She shrugged, uncomfortably shifting her eyes to the ground.

"No. I say," he said, reassuring her. "You forget, Grace, that I knew you then, and I tell you, you are more beautiful today than I remembered. And far more sensual. Anyone who looks into your eyes can spot that subtlety."

She hardly dared look up, afraid he might be kidding her. "Anyone?" she fished.

"Anyone who does not have, uh…" He struggled for the word, searching the air overhead for it. "How do I say it?" He found it, as if plucking it out of the air, "Glaucoma."

This made her laugh, and she dropped her head, hoping he wouldn't notice she was blushing. Taking a moment to let the tension dispel, she finally looked at him, complimenting his command of the English language. He thanked her, smiled, and said he regretted only that he had no sense of humor in English. "Now, in German, I'm quite a witty fellow."

Something told her he spoke the truth. This released a playfulness in her. "So you find me sexy, huh?" she fished outrageously now.

"I do."

"I didn't know."

"Language barrier," he explained, mock-apologetically. He looked at her for a long moment, raised his hand as if to say something, but instead gestured to the patches of blue emerging overhead. The connection was broken. The summer storm had dissipated as quickly as it had arrived, and he walked out of the grove—his eyes on the ground.

Those are the first personal words he's spoken to me, she thought, as she followed him onto the path.

CHAPTER EIGHT

N either one of them spoke again about that day of the summer storm. For a while, Klaus had behaved as if he had overstepped his bounds. That mystified Grace, and she wondered what internal editors he listened to. She decided that perhaps he did not want to be involved with her and, momentarily finding himself attracted to her, had thereafter withdrawn. But, she argued with herself, that was so inconsistent with a man who had been waiting for her for thirteen years. Or had she misunderstood him? After all, she had been here six weeks now and knew almost nothing about her host—neither about the life within his head, nor the external life.

Whenever they talked, he mostly listened—serenely—as if there were no exigencies of time. But he remained always distant. He was attentive, but uninvolved. That made her feel simultaneously precious and insignificant, and there were no adequate barometers measuring her odd new life with her stranger-friend. Some quiet voice within her urged her to accept this mystery though. And for no reason that she could understand, she listened to that voice.

It was the height of summer now. Although she could hear and watch the boats on the lake below, she had less and less desire to go downhill. She rarely went below to mingle with the tourists or townspeople—all of whom were savoring the nominal warming of the lake. Their laughter filled the town and echoed up the hillsides. She could almost see the rainbows of ice cream consumed daily by visitors to this once-tranquil resort. She herself longed for the solitude of the lake, for the serenity she'd discovered when she and Robert had arrived eight weeks ago.

Suspecting that a return to that state of grace would not be possible until autumn, she confined her activities to her ridge—walking, reading, and gardening. For that was one thing Klaus agreed to some help with. Where he lived while she was occupying his house was a mystery to her, but he checked on her regularly and came to work his garden. The sunny patch was yielding the fruits of cucumber and tomatoes now. They enjoyed carrots, peppers, onions, and lettuce daily. She watched eagerly as his herbs—sprinkled throughout the garden—were growing. The cool nights were fragrant with the wafting of thyme and rosemary.

Klaus's self-sufficiency fascinated her, for she didn't believe it had actually been tried since the mid-1900s. In addition to the chalet, which was a marvel of efficiency and economy, there was an ice house dug into a hill some few yards away. Ice blocks carved in winter were wrapped in dried long grass, cooling the earthen chamber and preserving the meat of small game and all kinds of vegetables—fresh, as well as dried and preserved. Klaus was proud of his design and his ability to preserve and store fruits and vegetables. His pride revealed itself, however, in a calm assuredness that this was the only way to live. He was so confidant of his self-sufficiency—not so much as an escape from society but more as a duty. He told her that it was his "duty to live life as he met it." He believed he was a keeper of the earth and he therefore would painstakingly lecture her about the earth, seeds, growing periods, and independence. But something about this made her suspicious. Or, was it jealous? She didn't know. Certainly, she experienced the feeling of being behind, of running to catch up.

Before too long she began to look for chinks in his armor—for flaws in his reasoning. Pouncing on two areas where he was decidedly in contact with, and dependent upon, outside sources, she harbored them—waiting for the proper time to trip him up.

The opportunity came one morning as he was demonstrating his woodworking, using a resin found in nearby pitch pines to soften the wood. He was wearing only cut-off jeans—a product of the outside world she catalogued to herself. The jeans revealed his long, muscular legs and trim, firm torso.

He is beautiful to look at, she thought, and that thought disturbed her.

She herself was wearing short shorts and a pink t-shirt—only the t-shirt had a lace applique around neck and sleeves. She had always dressed this way, sporting a conscious feminine touch. Even if she wore a sweatshirt, hers would probably have embroidery or appliques to soften its effect. Even her t-shirts were embroidered, ribboned, or appliqued so that—no matter what she wore—she was adorned somehow with satin or silk, flowered if possible.

Klaus was gently rubbing the top of a small end table he was building. He had simply softened the edges of a natural slice of wood from a fallen oak, its near-circular shape supplying the beauty. And he spoke of the simplicity of the piece whose "unadorned and unencumbered shape was in harmony with its environs." As he spoke, he looked up, his eyes falling on the lace rosettes adorning her loose bodice. Whether he intended to draw a negative analogy or not was immaterial. Her sensitivity over her appearance and over his apparent criticism of her made her prickly. Or was it the heat? In any case, she decided the time had come to remind him of certain inconsistencies in his own life.

"Then why do you bring milk up from below? And flour for your bread?"

What is in his eyes? she asked herself. *Disappointment? Withdrawal?*

He returned to rubbing, more vigorously. She pressed her advantage. "There are ample cows on the hill and certainly grains or grain substitutes."

"Exactly," he almost barked.

She knew she had him now. "Then why do you allow yourself to be at all dependent upon a commercial product?"

"I have a friend down below. She's been unwilling—so far—to move up onto the hill. Buying flour and milk from her is our only regular communication," he answered, not even interrupting his rubbing.

That was all he said. His face told her that he had said more than he would have liked. Was he angry at her impertinent questions or pained at speaking of his friend? She could not tell. But she knew for certain that she wished she had not attempted this one-upmanship. For there was distance enough between her and this curious, mysterious man, and she knew for certain she had driven the dividing wedge in farther. *When will I ever learn not to ask questions—the answers to which I am unprepared to hear?*

And, moreover, the scalding familiar sensation of jealousy swept her, cramping her brain like a record caught in a groove, repeating a refrain until she could free herself from the rut. *The idiocy of it all,* she thought, scolding herself. *The man, after all, is not even my lover. Just an acquaintance—an unknown really.*

From that moment on, she was obsessed with wanting to know more. Fearing he would hibernate further, she knew she would have to be cautious. She considered his private room, connected to his unified living area only by a ladder. Despite the fact that he did not stay there, she had never been down below. All the accouterments of his daily life seemed to be in the giant room she was using—a room for cooking, dining, sleeping, reading, and working. Below was an unknown, undefined territory. She knew only that he kept musical instruments, as she had heard him play. Sometimes his flute—but more often guitar and an occasional mandolin. His strong hands were nonetheless sensitive—slender and facile like those of a keyboard player. And there was certainly precision in his grasp, tenacity as well.

He was gone now. *Perhaps I should go below. Surely he will not discover me,* she thought, *because he is on a separate walk along the ridge to the east.* He would often go off in that direction and be gone for several days. She wondered now where he went. Why, responding seemingly to his own time clock, he would disappear to the east? In an effort to escape the groove of jealousy she was caught in, she tried to rationally describe their relationship. But it eluded even circumscription. Illusive it was; amorphous it was; problematic it was. Her mind grappled for an anchor, but the truth in fact was, it was non-existent.

After all, she told herself, *he has rarely touched me, even casually.*

Whether because it had been eight weeks since she and Robert had made love, leaving her body now sensitive and demanding—restless for attention and comfort—or whether because she was in fact attracted to Klaus, she would catch her mind trying to decipher not so much who he was or what he stood for, but rather whether he was sexually attracted to her, and what his role was in this romantic fantasy. She also felt that the healing effect of time and the mountain air were creating a separation between her former and present self. And Klaus was leading her present self. To the extent that she trusted him, she also desired him. Yet she could not speak of this to him, for there was an unspoken agreement between them—or so she believed.

Then, too, she wondered also where his money came from. In addition to apparently having had the capital at age twenty to buy a hotel, he had had the money to support himself on the mountain for thirteen years without having left it, as far as she could discern, for even so much as a single day. *True,* she told herself, *he is remarkably self-sufficient.* But she guessed that there was something else, some other source of support. Yet, he spent almost all of his days in his garden, either tending or planning the various fruits and vegetables that delighted them, and which would sustain them through the winter. His cherry trees, clustered near the foot of a summit, were fragrant and sharp, prolifically yielding fruit. But they were nothing compared to the burgeoning fruits of the nut trees found amongst the heavily wooded area. Acorns, chestnuts, walnuts were all budding, ostentatiously enticing the resident squirrels to circle, inspect, and anticipate the autumn harvest.

His forestry techniques seemed to subscribe to a policy of non-intervention. There was a natural course—a natural death of trees—resulting in air and space for younger, needier fledglings; a natural use of dead and decaying wood for fire; a seasonal replenishing of fruits and nuts left wild.

Only his garden showed structure. But even that was tended without artificial assistance, certainly without chemicals and fertilizers. Klaus fertilized his crops with manure—not imported manure but rather from the deposits of the cows down below on the hillside.

Although she passed the solid brown bovines regularly in the lower areas of the hill, none resided up on the ridge. At least none that she knew of. The familiar tinkling of their bells was a reassuring and daily medley—but never proximate. Therefore, in order to procure a supply sufficient to regularly replenish the land, Klaus received a cart load of cow dung weekly. Of course it was conveyed on the cart with the milk cans. Miraculously, on that first trip Grace had made by herself in the Luftseilbahn, however many weeks ago, the shipment had been only one or two milk cans. Recalling her terror over the steep ascent, she was more than modestly grateful that the swaying ascent had not been accompanied by 100 pounds of "meadow muffins," as her father used to call them.

The aromatic residue was sufficiently difficult to deal with as it was, and she was eternally grateful that Klaus made effective use of his strong, home-made oatmeal soap, scented with natural pine.

Klaus had a pet raccoon. Fairly small in size—more like a cat actually—he had a face either smashed flat or mutilated naturally so that it appeared almost like the face of a Persian cat. The raccoon had been injured, probably by a bobcat or a dive-bombing hawk, and had been restored to relative health by Klaus. In that, she'd found yet another inconsistency. For all this contradicted his statement to Grace about his aversion to interference with the forces of Nature. He had talked reverently one day about his appreciation of Nature, and of the power, beauty, and ultimate justice of Her forces, and had told Grace that he never interfered—a fact borne out on one of their excursions in the woods on an afternoon when a bobcat stalked, attacked, and captured a lackadaisical hare. Klaus observed this with seeming indifference—not a coldness, but more of a resignation—as if accepting things as they were. None of which had made it easier for Grace to view the death of the hare that afternoon as she stood helplessly watching from the path the animals had crossed, one in pursuit of the other.

But then there was flat-faced Deliverance. It was therefore surprising to her that Klaus had made any effort to save the raccoon who had appeared in the garden, bleeding from the left hind quarter.

Whether it was due to the raccoon's endearingly squashed face or its pathetically puny size, Klaus had exercised interference. He had washed and treated the animal, assuming it would leave when healed. That was eleven months ago, according to Klaus, and the raccoon, now named Deliverance, was long-healed and well-heeled as a member of the household. His residence was established in the brush near the ice house, and under the chalet in winter.

Deliverance didn't think much of Grace. No doubt she was an interloper in an otherwise unchallenged domain. Whenever Klaus was around, Deliverance would waddle close to his legs, always positioning himself between him and Grace, but never close to Grace. In fact, whenever Grace, instead of Klaus, would bring out food, Deliverance would very disdainfully stand at a distance and observe her, as if to demonstrate his disapproval of this disruption to his normal life.

Grace was dumping corn cobs into a trough for Deliverance when she turned in time to see the two men conversing, apparently in discord over a package held precipitously between them. Fritz was tapping the package with one hand, and motioning toward her with the other. He looked tense and angry. Klaus was silent. He was listening, but appeared to be absorbed in the package itself. She could hear nothing, as they were too far west along the path at the edge of the woods, but she knew somehow that Klaus distrusted the object he held.

Shortly, the two broke up and Klaus slowly returned along the path. He did not know she had been watching. Spotting her as she put the empty basket in its place beside the garden fence, he approached and said, "This is for you." He handed her a thin box the size of a record cover, and then walked into the house.

The box, forwarded from the Hotel Bellevue, was postmarked from Los Angeles and, she noticed as she turned it over to open the sealing tape, had printed on it in large familiar letters, "Fan Letter"— and nothing else. She laughed. *So typical,* she thought as she hastily opened it.

Inside was a collage unicorn, mounted on a heavy mat board and created from pieces of fabric. His body was white satin with a gold, watered-silk horn. He was lying in a bed of magenta and violet nettings against a blue chiffon sky and silver lame moon. Robert was a producer, not an artist. The artistry was rather crude, but the vibrant colors and textures created a mesmerizing fantasy, like an incipient dreamer materializing out of the mist—his golden horn penetrating the moon. It was Robert's way of reaching out to her and her world— an acknowledgment of the dreamer self she identified with, and the misty pastels that softened her life.

She thought of his indecisiveness and his inability to keep promises. She remembered countless scenes of self-recrimination as he, teary-eyed, talked of what he wanted, had intended to do, and had failed to act upon before the opportunity had slipped his grasp. The sad irony being that now, late in his life, he had decided what he needed and had taken action to get it—only to find her slipping from his grasp into her own cloud of indecision. This fan letter, as he called it, reached out to her. It was the perfect attempt to reach her in her own atmosphere. On the back he had written a love poem.

Grace read it, fingering the mat board as she absorbed his tender thoughts. He was no poet either, but nonetheless his desire for her was obvious. It was signed, "Robert."

A small footnote was added below the signature—barely legible. It said, "I'm going into EST to get my life in order. I thought you'd like to know." Was this an afterthought, or a thought written with regret, thereby printed so unobtrusively in the lower right corner?

Of all the effects the card might have had on her, the immediate one was shocking to Grace. In the past, the smile induced by his attempting such a communication would have led to a lessening of fear and a softening of anger, to a closeness between them. But today, standing alone at the top of the world, she remembered only when— rising in the early morning hours in Los Angeles as a hot summer morning was gathering strength, looking at her love in bed with half his face buried in the pillow he held pressed tight against him like a lover—she had made a diary entry.

That entry, upon rereading, had catalyzed her decision to leave for New York. She had written, "I awoke at 6:00AM and for the first time in my life thought, 'I have no confidence that things will ever go right for me again.'" Two years ago she had dreamed of love and a marriage proposal, and her man wanting to create a child with her. Today, however, as the brass ring was within her grasp, she was numb.

Dreams die hard. More often they wither, usually after a long and painful discoloring. Could this unicorn bring her back, or was it merely the last flicker of a dying flame, all the more colorful for its desperate errand?

Klaus had come back outside and was unconsciously watching her. She took it inside and placed it against the mirror on the sideboard— there to stand as a reminder. Coming back outside, she noticed that Klaus was completely silent, and his hair was unruly again. His angular face was calm, but he looked sad somehow, as if his cheekbones— normally camouflaged by flesh—were rising up, throwing his eyes into shadow. *He has aged,* she thought.

He asked who the package was from. She told him. He asked if she loved Robert. She said she thought she did. But she added that she didn't think that was enough, and he exhaled a bitter laugh.

His eyes fleetingly registered something. She thought it might be fear, but she did not understand why. Her thoughts were interrupted as he responded, "What more is there, Grace?"

Now it was her turn to laugh. "If I knew the answer to that I would not be stuck on a mountain in Switzerland."

"What is it you fear?"

"Missing opportunities." The answer was formed more easily than she expected. In fact, it startled her that she had an answer at all. Her voice was angry now as she continued. "I don't want to cut off my options." But rupturing upward inside was the horrible suspicion that perhaps she loved him only because she was alone and didn't want to be. Always the unanswered question reoccurred. *Do I love him REALLY, or am I merely allowing him to satisfy a need to be loved? Would I leave him for someone else if an intriguing opportunity presented itself?*

She felt strongly now the tension in her body as she thought of the opportunity between Klaus and herself. Was this perhaps the one situation she feared? Was it the unknown she would feel compelled to explore—even at the cost of another man's great, and growing, love?

Klaus was sitting on a rock, elbows resting on his knees, leaning forward and watching her, as if waiting for her to make the next move. He was in a neutral position both in body and in face. Fleetingly she pictured his arms around her, fantasizing his strong legs easily parting hers, his as-of-yet undetermined maleness entering and filling her. She struggled to dismiss this, and to focus on the reality of Klaus, but instead saw only supple limbs—tanned and golden from working in the elevated sun—and his lips, certainly fuller than she had noticed before. She felt contractions deep within her, a subtle lift of her inner thighs, a feeling of wet warmth within, and she surrendered her mind to the momentary speculation of lovemaking, wondering if he did the same with her.

She guessed it would be total, as all else he did. Klaus, more than anyone she had known, and despite the mysteries about him, expressed emotions honestly when he did so. When he laughed, it came from deep within, erupting into an almost melodious roll. It flowed smoothly, with no hesitation or editing. Likewise his anger was always real and intense—never violent—merely a true and seemingly exact expression of his feeling. She never felt it was misplaced or impotent. That seeming perfection had irritated her in the past few weeks, but as she looked at him now, she felt certain his lovemaking would follow the same abandoned, centered path—a total focusing of his thoughts and feelings into one bursting moment.

Almost as suddenly as those thoughts swept into her mind, Klaus rose, entered the house, and returned with a moderately worn, but unmarked, volume of Thomas Hardy's *Justine*. Without looking at her, he handed it to her and said, "Read this." Returning to the reality of lost options, she heard him add, "Then we can settle this."

Settle what? she thought. *My love for Robert, or my fear of missing one of life's jewels by virtue of a wrong choice?*

"Whether you're staying or leaving." He seemed to have read her mind, for he answered her unspoken question.

Grace took the book, decidedly resentful now that he had once again assumed his role of teacher. His tendency to speak to her as if she were virtually blind, as if she scarcely knew her own thoughts or feelings, was unspeakable presumption to her mind. To his credit, she had to admit he never spoke as if he were above her, but rather ahead of her. To her consternation, she felt humiliated by this, because she seemed unable to surprise him.

Keith had once said, "You amaze me. Just when I think I know your limits, you push beyond." Robert, certainly after the Caribbean Fantasy, had never made the mistake of thinking he could anticipate her actions. Her gift for surprise was one of her most appealing traits, she thought.

So now, what was wrong with this man that he couldn't or wouldn't acknowledge the uniqueness of this mind he was encountering? Who was this man with whom, for the first time in her life, she was playing catch-up?

She capitulated, however, and took the book, gingerly opening and reading the first two pages. Then, routinely, having at least found them intriguing, she turned to the last page.

It was then that Klaus changed. Swiftly he attempted to retrieve the book he had given her, like a disappointed gift-giver recovering an unappreciated gift. She resisted and said, "I'll understand the purpose better this way."

"The mystery is the purpose!" With a cold, separating look in his eyes, he seized the book, turned, and went below. Moments later, the lone voice of an English horn playing a haunting Spanish folk song stroked the air. Klaus played from within the chalet. Grace sat motionless. Each was in their shared isolation—one at peace, one on a mission of survival.

By dusk, as the evening breezes cooled the upper room, Klaus finished playing and returned. Offering an apology for an argument that hadn't really materialized, he told her he was sorry, not for *what* he had said but for *how* he had said it.

"I misplaced my frustration, Grace. You were not the appropriate target."

"Who was? Fritz?"

He nodded.

"Why were you arguing this afternoon?" she asked.

"The package. Fritz was angry about the package."

"I don't understand."

"He does not like intrusions from below."

"He wishes I would leave, doesn't he?" she ventured with certainty.

"Yes. We argued over that. I told him you would not." He stopped then, breathing softly, careful not to look at her.

"Do you want me to?" She braced herself again to receive the answer she did not want to hear.

"No." He did not look at her as he breathed the addendum. Then mercurially, before either could react to his answer, he ran his fingers through his hair and jokingly added, "Fritz had some crazy idea I would leave, too." He crossed quickly to the door, stopping en route to grab his alpine cap, apparently to constrain the unruly waves.

"Anyway, I was really angry at him, and directed it toward you by mistake. It won't happen again."

"You promise?" she teased in her little girl voice, hoping he would respond to the playfulness, hoping she was not too blatantly manipulative.

"I promise," he responded far too seriously, ignoring the playfulness. "It's time you *all* met. Then it won't happen again." With that, he left.

What Klaus had in mind was a party. Actually, he and his friends met regularly down below in the "inner sanctum," as Grace privately referred to it. But this evening he asked her to join them. Those evenings could best be described as times of camaraderie. Whether beer drinking was part of it all was fairly immaterial, given the joviality and vitality of the music making. Everyone either played an instrument or sang, and the evening materializing down below sounded like a guitar-studded, Jews' harp jam session from another era. The only addition was a set of drums. She had never heard Klaus play drums and didn't know whether they were his own, or belonged to one of his cronies. In any case, they were played by someone with an adept and enthusiastic hand whose vigor caused the floor to vibrate with sound. Her bare feet tingled on the tatami mat as she dressed, and her curiosity was aroused.

Since Klaus never left the hill, or if he did, never in her presence, and since the lift closed down at 6:00PM, she presumed all his friends lived on the ridge. They entered his room from below and had never intruded upon her. When they spoke, they spoke in German—the speed of which was impossible for her to translate if ever she were tempted to eavesdrop—which she had been. Tonight a nervous twinge irritated her stomach as she realized she might be spending an evening with a group of people, none of whom spoke English, and that she further would be unable to either communicate with them, or comprehend. She told herself that Klaus would surely help her out since he had specifically invited her to join them tonight, and that moreover, if there was one thing she did well as an actress, it was listen. Surely just quietly listening and observing would enable her to comprehend the essence of the conversations. She relaxed a little.

But will Klaus help? Doubts sprang up. *Yes,* she finally told herself.

Grace selected her cream, satin blouse with its fine, diaphanous shoulder lace and high collar, voluminous sleeves flowing to tight, lace-trimmed cuffs, and twenty compact satin-covered pearl buttons. She assessed herself in the mirror and approved of the soft framing the neckline afforded her face, the warmth and healthy color the creamy hue supplied. Her eyes were large, peeking curiously from under curls—for she had taken the trouble of curling her hair in order to look the way she enjoyed looking.

To be honest with herself, she knew she wanted to make a good impression, and to feel feminine and confident. Her cheeks were flushed with trepidation, and she prayed silently to no one in particular that all would go well. She wrapped the wine-colored dance skirt around her waist, stepped back into the rosy shadows of sunset, and then crossed to the ladder. She knew she looked radiant, beautifully attired in a costume that was totally symbolic of her sense of self, and she was prepared to make an entrance that would allow them to accept her for what she was—graceful and unpretentious. Such an entrance should ideally be made through ornate double doors, allowing the entrant to sweep in and alight somewhere.

Such an entrance, however, could not help but be undermined by a crude ladder through the ceiling of a room, which would force the entrant to descend backwards through the ceiling into the room below. Grace, for whatever reason, had not foreseen the obstacle. If she had, she might have chosen to go outside, maneuver down a sloping path, and slip in through the door used by Klaus and his friends to come and go from the basement. She had not, however.

If she felt anxiety about feeling out of place, she had good reason, for as she slowly navigated her heels down the ladder rungs into the group below, they stopped singing and watched, as if she were climbing down into their den. She arrived, rump first—never her most flattering angle—and promptly caught her lace and satin sleeve on a nick in the wooden ladder. Not wanting to snag or rip her favorite blouse, she did not dare to move. Grace stood there awkwardly, her snagged arm bent behind her, as Klaus introduced her to Fritz, Ursula, and a black man whose name she did not catch at first. Each said, "Guten Abend," and to each she responded, hoping they weren't expecting her to move from her spot, praying they would return to playing so that she could turn her attention to the offending sleeve unobtrusively. But, they did not. Rather, they merely looked at her—tension mounting.

At last, she broke the tension by laughing shyly, boldly calling attention to her embarrassment with a girlish, "I seem to be caught." But this, too, was greeted with silence.

Hardly remarkable, she thought, as she observed they all wore jeans and t-shirts, various styles of sandals, and nothing more. *I must certainly look absurd to them,* she thought, *impaled upon a rustic ladder in my Upper Westside satin.* "God, get me through this," she whispered to her mind's ear.

Then Klaus graciously rescued her from the clutches of the ladder, and from the clutches of mortification, with his typical grace. "I should have warned you about that ladder." She noticed that Fritz seemed to be chewing the inside of his right cheek. His eyes shared some secret communication with Ursula.

An hour later, however, she was adapting. Actually, the others had merely returned to their music-making, leaving her alone, but at least no longer the center of attention. She judged that Klaus and his black friend must be professional musicians—or rather must have been. The black man, whose name she still couldn't capture in the conversation, played drums with considerable skill and versatility. Klaus, tonight, was alternating on keyboard and guitar, mixed up with a variety of other instruments including flute and recorder. Fritz, on the other hand, played less well—mostly guitar and some rhythm percussion instruments.

His voice though is very pleasant, she thought. *Clear, with a twist of an almost ironic humor in it.* The music was familiar somehow. Not the songs, for those she didn't know, but the sound was familiar, as if she'd heard that unique sound before. She wasn't sure, and there was no time for her to really try to recall.

Seeing Klaus play with others, singing ballads, folk melodies, some rock numbers, Grace sensed for the first time that she was finally learning something about him. In the many weeks she'd been his guest, she knew nothing about him except that he lived alone in a place where Nature governed his actions. He never spoke about himself. But tonight was different—as if, for some unknown reason, he had decided to let her discover what she might. She didn't really like his voice though, as she listened to him sing. It was husky, impure, as if he sang through smoke. And it quivered painfully when he would reach beyond his abilities. But he was sincere. Near-laryngitis or not, she concluded, he could communicate a lyric. She had to give him that.

The combination of wine, the second-hand high from a little bit of grass that Ursula was smoking, and the music was very intoxicating, and Grace let go of tension. She believed, whether it was true or not, that her companions, too, were relaxing somewhat.

Ursula did not play, but she occasionally sang—her small, breathy voice reminiscent of the sounds of the '60s in Wisconsin. For she sang mostly ballads. Most were in German, some in English—some about love, some about peace. The rest of the time, she lay back on a cushion in a window seat and stared dreamily out the window to the village below. Grace wondered, *Where is her mind? Why does she seem so removed even in the midst of friends?* Then she noticed that Fritz was watching her if she spoke to Ursula, even as he was playing, much as a bodyguard sees everything. She didn't know why that image would come up, however, and dismissed it, concentrating instead on Ursula and Fritz.

What an odd couple, she thought, as she tried to imagine what had caused this frail, blonde, wispy woman to marry the tall, weathered man, whose bushy brows provided a ferocity to his demeanor. His jaw was tight, forcing him to talk between clenched teeth, with or without a cigar. There were several cigars in the breast pocket of his t-shirt and, thanking God that he was not smoking or chewing on one, she turned her attention to the black drummer whom, she now understood, the others called "the African."

He was very small, very black, with hands and feet that virtually flew over the drums and pedals. His very spirit poured out into the rhythm. His face was soft and innocent-looking, despite a mottled scar that ran the length of his right cheek. The pigment was gone in the area of the scar, leaving a pinkish-white crevice in his face, which pulled the right eye's lower lid somewhat down, causing a slight drooping. But he had glorious white teeth, which flashed constantly as he played—the sweat pouring down his face of indeterminate age. His agility extended to using all four hands and feet with equal dexterity. He was totally spontaneous and free, and she felt absolutely no resistance from him to her presence.

Nor was there resistance from the latecomer, Reuben, who flew through the door shortly after she arrived. He was tall, thin, and breathless. Apologizing for being late, he immediately assumed the keyboard position. Klaus apparently had been filling in, and easily returned to guitar. Reuben seemed hardly to notice her. In fact, he seemed too stoned to notice anything much. He nodded briefly and commenced to vigorously flexing his incredibly long fingers. Except for his uncombed hair, and eyes which seemed never to settle on any one area, giving him the appearance of slight madness, he looked the epitome of a European gentleman from another century—poised, graceful, elegant—in slacks and a white gauze shirt with billowing sleeves.

Rather like a Byronic gentleman, not yet fully dressed, she thought. She noticed though that his skin was uneven, both in color and texture. This made him look ill, and she wondered if this were the case.

Other than the fact that all were about the same age, there was no justification that Grace could see for any of these people to be friends. Perhaps it was the music that brought them together. Or perhaps merely the mountain. Whatever their reasons, she felt excluded—both because of the complete mystery of the others' identities and because of their musical prowess. Her inherent inability to improvise vocally—for fear of hitting a wrong note or failing in harmony—and her inability to play any of the instruments of this loosely-formed rock group, seemed to exclude her from participation.

Wine flowed, music heightened, tension ebbed. Klaus encouraged her to join in, but she demurred, not trusting her voice, thereby fearing to try. Instead she clapped and smiled, aching inside because she was left out.

She listened for clues as they spoke, like a child trying to guess the rules of a game his pals have conspired to exclude him from. But they spoke only of berry harvests, of cabinet-making, of plans for winter, and nothing of their origins. During a break for a delicious Swiss snack called Rösti, she jokingly asked what they called themselves.

Fritz paused between bites, again chewing the inside of his cheeks, answering from beneath the shadowy brows. "Die Ernuchtern." And then he laughed. Grace laughed, too, hoping his laughter was inclusive, and not derisive. *The disillusioned,* she thought. *Appropriate for me, too.*

That evening came to a head abruptly, however, when she casually tried to converse with Ursula, trying to join their game a little. She asked Ursula what she did before she came here. There was absolute silence in the room. The others looked to Klaus as if to take a cue. He hesitated and then looked to the floor, as if tacitly signaling permission for what was to come, like a father letting go as a child steps into the street to fight for the first time.

The wine-subsided tension returned; the music-induced mellowness hardened. Fritz sprang into action first, speaking for Ursula. "What did *you* do?"

Grace had no way of knowing whether he was baiting her or was merely curious. Her mind flashed suddenly on the image of Keith in a courtroom before a jury. She erased it, however, and gave him the benefit of the doubt, explaining that she was an American actress. He asked if she found it worthwhile. And she answered that she had, until recently, and that she hoped to again.

"Hope to what?" he challenged. The others were silent. She felt like bolting, but didn't know why.

"To make a difference," she said, collecting her thoughts, a modicum of confidence returning. Then she added, "To perhaps bring someone to a greater awareness." Reuben's mad eyes twinkled now from behind the electric piano. Was it kinship? She hoped so, venturing further, "And perhaps, in time, to help create a better world."

"That's impossible," he pressed and moved closer now. Klaus looked up as if to try to tell her something. But she could not understand. Grace felt a deep sense of antagonism directed toward her, but could not be sure whether it was her imagination. Perhaps he was merely engaging in graduate level dialectics—forcing her to take a role.

Grace had always hated impassioned argumentation, even when she had been a graduate student, so she reconciled herself to bear with it as he continued. "The purpose of art is to reflect life, not to change it."

Now she reacted. She couldn't help herself. Like a mother defending her young, Grace knew she could not let that smug remark stand unchallenged. "Art is, or rather should be, not a mirror image of life as it is, but a guide to what it should be. The artist, with his vision of life, can teach others about themselves and about the possibilities. He can light the way—show the possible—spur people to act and, in their actions, create the future. It must be that. Otherwise it is only entertainment."

As she finished, she was flushed and out of breath. Except for the moisture under her arms, which she hoped no one saw, she otherwise appeared to be regaining control. She felt her cheeks flush and scolded herself for arguing so violently, escalating the scene from a mere debate into an argument. The replay within her mind told her that Fritz had merely expressed an opinion, and she had reacted as if he had uttered a condemnation—not of art but of her. And the thought crossed her mind that she was defending not art, but herself, her life, and her work.

Fritz, however, seemed unflappable, smirking as he continued, victorious in having shaken her composure. Smelling blood, he closed in. "Only political actions can change life. Songs, plays, they only describe the times. They reinforce the times. The decision to change is linked with action. And action is politics."

"But the music of our generation shows the contrary. Look at the '60s, at the Beatles. Surely John Lennon believes it's possible to change the world, and to do so through music—to make people listen, think, and then act."

"John *may* have thought that, but he has it figured differently now. Isn't that right, Klaus?" Fritz turned to Klaus for affirmation. Klaus said that it was true. He spoke as if he knew Lennon.

"John sees it as a merry-go-round," Klaus interjected. "He knows now that there's another source to change."

Fritz took over now, having elicited the answer he wanted from Klaus. "Exactly! There was a time when change was possible—perhaps. We were there. We lived it. But we lost that chance. Before the sell-outs, before the penance for crimes committed against a decadent system." He was looking at Ursula now, and she seemed passive, dull somehow. Then he turned back to Grace. "Before your man Jerry Rubin chose a career on Wall Street, it was possible. And what were you doing then?"

Truth, long outrun, was overtaking her now. Bared antagonism was palpable. Honest confrontation was now inevitable. There could be no more polite hiding, no more evasions. She felt relieved somehow, and answered a long-standing allegation.

"When flower children decorated Height-Ashbury? When communal love-ins dotted the roads from Wisconsin to Los Angeles? When friends burned their draft cards? When protestors seized buildings? When sitting spoke louder than words? Is that what you mean? You want to know where I was?" She paused only long enough to catch her breath. "I was being solid, stable, invulnerable. It fell to me to uphold the American Dream against perceived destruction." Tears welled up, belying her pride.

She felt like some masquerader whose identity had been revealed. Her admission ticket to this elite crowd was revoked. Despite her personal changes and evolution, she was still excluded from their company as if she were the enemy. After all this time, still their enemy—defending something she didn't particularly wish to defend, but which she felt obligated not to abandon.

Unlike her stoical past, where she would have presented an unflappable stiff upper lip, and disdainfully abstained altogether from the possibility of verbal combat, this time she had spoken. It had cost her. Speaking had taken all of her reserve strength, and she had not even succeeded in stopping up her water-filled eyes. Taking advantage of the eerie silence in the room as each band member tried to assess the damage from the unexpected skirmish—like soldiers timidly gaining their feet after an ambush, quietly checking to see if they're still alive— she fled the room to the wood pile outside.

How long she stood outside she didn't know. She heard only a lonely cricket. He was close by, probably in the wood itself. As he clicked uninhibitedly, she remembered the crashing of glass through a window in her British Drama of the 19th Century class at the University of Wisconsin. A chair hurled by a protestor crashed into the room, landing at her feet and spraying glass all over. She had sat paralyzed, neither joining nor condemning. She heard the words of one of her students in a play she was directing for her MA degree challenge her. "How can you just ignore this? The world is on fire, men are dying, and you blithely sit here conducting a rehearsal!" Again she had sat silent, refusing to let the revolution disrupt her schedule.

Wasn't it her duty to keep it going? To hold it together somehow? The closest she had come to the War prior to that time was at her college when she saw the Dean of Women's son become famous for his self-immolation on the Capitol steps. But after all, that was on television. And even as George had carried Mrs. M out—for the police had failed to notify the nearest of kin, dooming her to watch her only son go up in flames in living color on Walter Cronkite—it hadn't seemed real somehow. She wondered now if it had seemed real to George that night as he waited on tables. He went down in a helicopter two years later, surviving only two weeks after reporting for duty. He had the distinction of being the only one from that small college with its Air Force ROTC to be killed in Vietnam. It was real then.

This night felt like a premonition of autumn. The feel of balm was exchanged for chill, the caressing air for nipping air.

"Fritz feels you don't belong here." Klaus spoke without a trace of apology. "He feels you don't know who you are."

"Does he?" she said, reacting numbly.

"Mostly. He's trying. But he's threatened by you because you pretend to know."

"He feels I'm a fraud?" she asked.

He nodded and then added, "But I would say you're more like a wounded animal." He sat beside her on the split wood, looking at her downcast eyes. She noticed her lace trim was caught again but did nothing this time to free it.

"Do you know what they say about wounded animals?" he asked.

"Yes, they go off to die."

"Not always to die," he reassured her. "Often to lick wounds, to rest, and to heal. Then *maybe* they can return to the world. Like Deliverance. That's why I helped him, you know. It's funny, but his coming to me for help seemed *natural*—my human interference seemed *natural*. He turned to her as if to see what her reactions were. "They are all healing wounds, too," he added, nodding toward the room where his friends waited.

"For ten years?" she asked in disbelief.

"For however long it takes."

"Is Fritz wounded?" she asked sincerely.

"Most definitely." He spoke as if it were impossible to even assess the depths of Fritz's wounds. "That's another reason why he doesn't trust you. He feels you don't belong with the rest of us. You're not wounded. But I convinced him that you may be more wounded than the others even."

"Oh really?" she challenged—an edge of sarcasm cutting in. *Really, this man is presumptuous,* she thought, as she stood up and delicately extricated the lace from the perils of splinters.

"You may not know it, Grace, or you may suspect."

She turned her head away quickly to avoid his gaze. For surely he could see in the night. "Your life, your parents' upbringing, your world demanded that you brave it through, that you maintain a solid front, and that, at all costs, you set an example."

She said nothing at first. He was seeing clearly enough. Then she asked, "Was that wrong?"

"No." He shook his head from side to side and there was regret, almost wistfulness, in that no. "But wounded you are. Your wound is to have been forced to stand outside of your own time, and you are bleeding inside now—your soul is bleeding."

Some moments later, she answered, "Are you healing, too?"

He didn't even hesitate a second. "Yes."

"From what?"

There was no answer. He still did not trust her. He was still the mystery. So she tried another door in her attempt to unlock his secrets. "Where are you healing?"

"A private place—farther up."

She noted how easily some answers came and yet how resistant others were.

"Will you take me there?"

"It's a difficult journey," he warned.

She laughed and said, "I guessed as much."

He then asked if she really thought she could make it. She said she could, and he acquiesced. When she asked how long it would take, he said, "That depends entirely upon you."

CHAPTER NINE

S he was in near total darkness, surrounded by sentinels whose sheer faces were visible only by silvery moonlight. The path was dark and slippery with moss as it ascended steeply into dark crevices. That sense of being pursued was with her, the certainty that someone was overtaking her as she climbed the precipitous path. And where was Klaus? Suddenly she heard the whispered voice once again. But this time it was ahead of her, just out of sight in a gorge. She dropped back, trapped and unable to descend the treacherous green road alone, yet afraid to call out and thereby reveal her fear. How had he overtaken her? Who waited for her ahead? She geared up, determined to face him here and, as she stepped forward to challenge him in the shadows, she awoke.

Breathless, she sat up short and looked quickly around the room to see if she were being chased. The familiar oak wardrobe, tatami mat, and the hazy sunrise brought her back to reality. Her heart still palpitated as it must have in the dream from the fear of being overtaken by that Dark Stranger. Astonishing as it might seem, she knew by her body's reaction that the dream had seemed so real to her that her body and its adrenalin had responded as if to a genuine threat. *How deceptively real our dreams can be,* she reflected as she rose and dressed.

Whether because of her slow withdrawal from the dream or because of the gray, misty morning, she felt physically subdued. The muted colors of the morning were perfect coordinates for the muted colors of her life. Where was the ebullience? The brilliance? She was overcome once again with feelings of failure, of not being what others had expected her to be, and the feelings of failure reminded her of a conversation she had overheard on the bus to the airport before leaving for Zurich.

Actually she had been eavesdropping deliberately—something that, as an actress, she was prone to doing. She excused herself by proclaiming it to be one of her ways of researching human nature. On that day, the man who was roundish, in his late thirties, with a balding head, had told his plain, unadorned companion, in a noticeably Brooklyn dialect, that he had had no money with which to vacation this year and that he was forced to spend his two weeks at home. His words haunted her now as Grace remembered the distinct sound of surprise in his voice when he said, "I work very hard and this year I had no money to go on vacation with. I feel like such a failure."

The companion had of course tried to reassure him he was not, but Grace had felt an intense moment of sharing, knowing that he, too, was haunted by the ghost of what he should have been. She had felt a comradeship with him, however fleeting, and today he was on her mind.

Despite Robert's love and her success in the eyes of others, she felt fatigue of age—almost a fatigue of battle. The "campaign" was in its 34th year, and her once-optimistic joie de vivre was only a phrase to her now. Her joy in each day's advance was dampened.

She sat thus, inert on the edge of the bed, dreading this journey she had agreed to. "Agreed to!" she laughed to herself. *Christ, I petitioned it.* Just as she contemplated backing out, Klaus knocked and entered. *He's fresh and disgustingly alert,* she thought, as she looked at his flashing eyes and the evenness of his face. They exchanged amenities.

"Is it hard to get where we're going?" she asked, fearing she already knew the answer.

"It can be," he responded, as he motioned for her to get up so that he could check her gear.

"It would help if it were sunnier," she complained, looking out the window at the blanket of autumn clouds that covered the lake below.

"The trip wouldn't be necessary if it were." And as he completed the check list in his mind, he added, "Okay. You look prepared for most weather. Are you wearing a t-shirt under all this?"

She said that she was. Grace frowned at herself in the mirror, observing that her breasts were now sitting midway between her shoulders and her waist. She couldn't believe her breasts were sagging. She was flat chested. She had no breasts. But there they were, two inches lower than last year, for sure! That was depressing.

Klaus asked if she had packed her knapsack exactly as he had told her. She said that she had. Then he noticed she was not wearing a belt. Opening a drawer near the hat rack, he pulled out a hand-tooled leather belt and offered it to her. She took it numbly, convinced now that her sagging breasts must be the reason he had never made a move on her.

Then Klaus suggested they each pick a chapeau. Shaking her head in disbelief at the role of scoutmaster he was so enthusiastically playing, she selected his green Tyrolean hat and placed it impishly on her head with a jaunty tilt. She then presented herself as ready.

Once on their way, she kept a pretty good pace going, despite the layers of clothing she was wearing at his instruction, and despite the knapsack over her back. Because it was a mild, early autumn day, pervasively gray and misty, which maintained a coolness and obscured the surroundings, she was able to keep up with masculine strides with relative ease. Actually she noted they were merely traversing the ridge on an established path above and around Brunnen. Klaus was leading, with Grace a few paces behind. She therefore paid little heed to any signs or directions.

Only when they passed Morschach did she realize that they headed east and were directly above the hotel where they had met so long ago. Looking down, the fog obscured any trace of the gigantic grand dame—presumably empty once again of its crippled occupants. She thought of the old gardener and his dog, and tried to visualize his day stacking deck chairs, securing doors, and boarding up windows. Perhaps it was a few weeks early, but the cool nip in the late August air reminded her of autumn, and she pursued the daydream.

Several hours later, her calf muscles were popping, alternately tensing and then releasing as if snapped. She requested a rest, and they stopped for lunch, which consisted of a salty jerky, the contents of which she had no intention of inquiring into, a jar of blueberry compote, a dark whole grain bread, and water—pure and cold from the descending streams. The woods around them were dense, noisy with sounds of the day, and pungent with the aromas of living greenery first nipped by the cool air of autumn.

"We'll turn up there," Klaus said, as he pointed with his walking stick to the base of a mountain several miles farther east. "Kaiserstock." As if trying to start a conversation he asked, "Would you like to digress a bit and pick some wild blackberries? There's quite an undergrowth of them in the cedars just downslope."

Rather morosely, dramatizing for effect, she said no, that she would rather sit on the log and rest her legs.

"I had the dream again," she added, as if to justify her stony silences.

"I know." That was all Klaus said as he rose and packed their limited lunch materials back into his sack, first cleaning the blade of his Swiss Army knife in the soil.

Whether his presumed clairvoyance annoyed her, or his seeming insensitivity to her moroseness did, was unclear to her then. What she knew she felt was an ever-increasing resentment toward his stiff indifference. She asked herself how he dared to presume to know her mind and to understand her feelings. Instead of speaking, however, she dutifully fell in behind him as they trudged east. That didn't suppress her feelings though. As each sure step was taken on the increasingly rocky terrain, her resentment festered more and more. She became even more sure of his insolence, and more and more convinced of his insensitivity.

Finally, she put him to the test. She stopped dead in her tracks, smugly calculating how far he would advance before he even noticed her absence. He took but one step, spun around, and challenged her. "What's wrong?"

"I'm depressed," she spat out. He squinted as if to see her more clearly and his lips puckered as he blew air out.

"Am I walking too fast?" he asked, in that patronizing tone of voice adults use when addressing a child. No matter that she might be behaving like a child, to be treated as one was just too much. She stamped her foot, then flung off her shoulder straps, dropping her bag to the ground rudely, and said, "The day is too gray. I can't travel on a day like this."

"Why not?"

"Because I can't see the mountains. It's like the day I arrived here. Like my dreams." Then as mercurially as she had dropped the bag, she reached down, retrieved it, and put it back on, perfunctorily shutting off any further self-indulgence. *I'll show him,* she told herself. *I committed to do this and by God, do it I will!*

"Never mind. Never mind," she heard herself bark in her officious voice that even she could not abide. "It's appropriate that this should be a gray autumn day. After all, I'm in the autumn of my life, am I not?"

"What are you talking about?" He laughed. "You're a very young woman!"

"Yes. But I have a theory that the seasons of one's life are more a representation of faith than of age. If you were to ask me, Klaus, about spring, I remember triple-dip ice cream cones in a college town in western Pennsylvania. I remember May Day celebrations and job interviews. I remember fraternity serenades. I remember believing. Today all I know is gray—gray dreams, gray nerves, gray skies." She was striding along now, past him and on ahead of him. Shouting over her shoulder she said, "I want to go back to when my dreams were blue and green, colorful."

"You can't." His voice seemed distant at first, but gaining on her both in insistency and volume. "They never were this way. You only perceived them as blue and green."

That was the last straw. What had earlier been merely pride or competition, creating in its exercise a mild separation between them, had escalated over the past few hours to a genuine combativeness. That combativeness generated an antagonism, which she could no longer repress. It surfaced suddenly and vituperatively.

"You're so God-damned right, aren't you? You know everything." She stopped and turned to him. "Well, my friend, you never put it to the test. You don't know what it's like to believe and have it disappear. So don't patronize me!" Almost the instant she spoke she regretted it. For he was silent, uncharacteristically so, and he stepped backwards as if off-balance, unconsciously raising his right hand to his forehead as if to deflect something. When he lowered his arm, his face had changed. He was biting his lip repeatedly, as if an idea were struggling to escape his lips and was being repeatedly barred by his teeth. His eyes were icy blue. Even at this distance of ten paces, she felt a cooling between them. His anger was clear, and made clearer by the insistent tapping of his walking stick on a granite boulder. Their friendship—never exactly solid—seemed at an end.

"This is our turning point, Grace," he said rigidly, as he looked up a path below the mountain in front of them. He stood silent—his words spoken calmly like one resigned. She regretted having challenged him so irrationally, thereby belittling his way of life. As she looked at him now, as she turned her mind's eye upon herself, she knew that she was not really angry with Klaus, but rather, jealous—of his companions and, more significantly, of his serenity. She had wanted to hurt him. Apparently she had succeeded.

Grace was not prepared to apologize yet. It was too early. That could wait until she understood better what she would want to say, so she, too, maintained a silence. The crevice they were skirting became a canyon.

Klaus began to climb into the boulders, cutting a path upward at the base of the mountain near what she soon realized, as she emerged from under trees into unshielded terrain, was the timberline. He spoke to her as if from a distance. "You should put on your gloves now." She did as he instructed.

Finding her footing was difficult, but not impossible. The gloves afforded friction, and she soon began to trust his judgment, and her legs. Surprisingly, though, they did not seem to be climbing the mountain, something for which she was grateful. For a moment that morning, upon seeing his pick, ropes, and pulleys, she had doubted his veracity when he said the trip was "more one of penetration than elevation." But now, it was true, they seemed to be entering the mountain rather than scaling it.

Shortly, they were on a narrow path that wound its way along a gorge. It was strewn with moderate-sized rock, presumably from a slide. She had no way of knowing how deep the gorge was, for the trees and undergrowth commenced perhaps ten meters below them. Because of their density, she was certain it was treacherously narrow, and she began to envision one false step spilling her over the side, only to be wedged in a crevice cut deep in the side of the Kaiserstock by centuries of ice and spring rains.

How long they edged along the sheer, granite-flanked path was hard for her to calculate. It took all her concentration to keep her eyes on the path and off the precipice. Klaus traversed it fairly easily, but cautiously, and he halted periodically to give her a rest.

"Lift your eyes up to the sky a bit, Grace," he would coach. "Give them a chance to refocus—get a different perspective." He cautioned, "Otherwise you'll tighten up."

An appropriate time for him to admonish me, she thought. For in fact she was almost hypnotized by the repetition of her steps. The severity of her concentration had disassociated her just enough that she was no longer conscious of the path behind or the route ahead of her—but rather only of the sound of her cleats, one after another negotiating the obstacles.

As she looked up and squinted from the reflection of light off the virgin rock, she breathed, "Oh my God."

"What is it?"

She pointed for him to look in front of her about one hundred meters where their path came to a dead end at the foot of gigantic, and nearly vertical, boulders. They seemed to provide a steep, sheer, and insurmountable barrier to their path. The gorge widened at that juncture, and she could hear water running, presumably into the gorge, replenishing the lake below. There was no path on the other side of the gorge, and surely no way to reach it even if it did exist, short of leaping across the abyss. That was something she had no intention of doing. After all, she was an amateur at all this.

"I'm afraid we've reached a dead end," she said, surprised that her voice sounded disappointed. She guessed that deep down she had hoped there would be more after all.

Klaus laughed. "No dead end. Just a detour," he challenged reservedly.

"Oh no, you." She warned him, stopping dead. "There's no way you're getting me to go over that wall of granite. You know I'm not a climber."

"There's no need to really climb, Grace. It's an illusion."

Now Grace *knew* she had no depth perception, but even she could estimate the height of the boulders. Besides that, it was clear that the difficult and sheer, rocky slope of the mountain peak itself lay right behind them. Even looking up, she could see that the snow line of the peak was only a short elevation above them, and that the slope was no doubt steep and hostile.

"It gives the illusion of a dead end, but it is traversable." And raising his hand before she could interrupt, he continued. "Few know of it. Most, like you, assume that what you see is what *is*." And he motioned for her to follow.

They continued along the precipice to the foot of the boulders, which by now towered over them. But sure enough, for those who came right to the base of the mountain, there was a surprise. Running to the left at a right angle to them was a ledge, which joined the boulders a few yards along and seemed to leave a narrow opening between the side of the cliff and the rocks which were jammed there, having rolled to a stop during some ancient violent cascade.

"What's there?" she asked grudgingly, beginning to trust him once again.

"A path—to a lake."

"No," she stared in disbelief. "How did you know?"

"In climbing one learns, hopefully, that the mountain often presents contradictions. What appears to be the wrong place to climb may in fact be an illusion—a disguise for an entrance."

"Very mystical, but how did you know? Surely other mountain climbers missed it."

"Yes. Because they didn't listen to the water. The volume suggested to me a run-off, perhaps a reservoir of glacial water and," he smiled now, as if proud of his next observation, "I noticed, while relaxing my eyes by looking up, the top of a pine tree. Just the top two branches actually."

"And?" She didn't follow.

"And that means that the proximity of these boulders to the face of the peak itself is also an illusion. There is forest behind this impasse. And not—how do you say it—'scrub growth' either."

She couldn't help but smile and nod her head at this turn of events. When she was a child she used to love to discover cool hidden places. Today, that child-like quality surfaced again. *I ought to be apprehensive,* she told herself. But all she felt now was a surge of exhaustion. Klaus, this time, recognized the signs of fatigue and spoke encouragingly, but still somewhat distantly. "You did very well today, Grace. We came a long way."

Then he led her to the left to a large, hidden indentation—almost like a cave—which would serve as their campsite for the evening. *Nothing can reach us here,* she thought, as she slumped against the wall, relieving herself of the backpack. *Not even the wind.*

Speaking of relieving herself, she spent the next few minutes trying vainly to devise a plan that would afford her privacy without calling attention to herself. There was no suitable plan regrettably, and she finally surrendered her modesty, with some consternation at his lack of foresight. *After all, he planned everything else!*

A few hours later, for the first time in her life, she slept out under the stars, after lying awake for two hours worrying about what might be crawling under her blanket.

Before the morning sun had even begun to penetrate their little niche, Klaus woke Grace and encouraged her to rise, eat some cheese and bread, and exercise her legs. Working with her, he exercised the knees to limber them up, rotated the ankles to make them more flexible, and guided her through a series of leg stretches for calves and thighs. She suspected that this was to overcome the incredible stiffness she felt from sleeping on the ground. He must have guessed she had arthritis in her right knee, inherited from her mother. That was a personal fact she had successfully concealed until today.

She also suspected that this actually meant today's activity was going to be arduous. She didn't become concerned until he began to instruct her on which clothes to layer over each other, for removal at appropriate times. Not even that registered, however, until he removed from his pack a rope secured to pulleys and began to secure the rope around his waist. As he approached her to secure her belt to his lifeline, she looked at him, much as one imagines a prisoner looking at his jailor for some hint of his fate.

"What's that for?" she asked nonchalantly, hoping he would assume the hiccup in her voice was due to early-morning un-expectorated phlegm.

"Just in case," he responded equally nonchalantly, but with no noticeable glitch in his voice.

Then, shortly after sunrise, they left the narrow path and began to scale the boulders whose cannonball-pile arrangement obscured whatever it was he knew to be behind the barrier.

The going was more tiring than hazardous. Klaus was in the lead, securing each new footing and thus providing a pattern for her to copycat. They rarely spoke; did not touch. In fact, he seemed indifferent to her—rather coldly and aloofly letting her go it alone—his only outward sign of concern being the mute lifeline, which bound them. *Small wonder,* she thought, *after my irascible behavior yesterday.*

Catching her breath, she surreptitiously glanced behind her to see a portion of the lake below. The vantage point was awesome, but what surprised her was the hint of the gradual changing of colors in the forest below. When she was in it, she had seen none of it, but here, above it all, she saw the intimations of what was to come in a few weeks. The air had that fresh, crisp feeling and the smell of life flourishing before it surrenders to winter. Today was only a harbinger of that season to be—only a waft. And perhaps the change of colors was only a hallucination, for the hues were only subtly changing to mauves and purples before bursting resplendent into the fireworks of autumnal color. Despite the nip in the air, the sun was warming the rocks intensely. And with each new part of the climb, as she consciously instructed her leg muscles to lift or her knees not to lock or buckle, she grew hotter and hotter. The heretofore-secret-arthritis was causing constant, but tolerable, pain and great trepidation for the knee's reliability. Shedding her sweater, she stopped only long enough to secure it in her pack. Not long after, she removed her long-sleeved blouse, thereby shedding her clothes as she climbed into September.

She was wearing only jeans and a short-sleeved, yellow Western shirt now. Klaus was ahead of her and, for a time, the way evened out enough to relax the calf muscles and thereby provide her the opportunity to reflect a little on him.

The mid-morning heat apparently did not distress him, as he was still wearing his plaid flannel shirt. *Although, he has rolled up his sleeves,* she noted. He had removed his cap and had tied, instead, a bandanna as a sweat band around his forehead. Perspiration shimmered only on his forehead. The grace with which he maneuvered the rocks suggested not only that he climbed often, but also that his long, slender legs were strong and muscular beyond their appearance. She guessed that the agile man who led her was probably a remarkable skier. She had always thought him strong. Today, he was graceful. The sun, climbing higher in the sky overhead, was reflected in his hair, making it actually sparkle with blonde highlights. His face, never rugged, looked fresh and stimulated by the exertion.

Because Klaus did not pressure her, but rather let her climb at her own pace, the rate of the climb was rather slow, but decidedly safe. She began to relax a little, and smiled as she noticed how he squatted when waiting for her to catch up. He did not offer her a hand at any time, but he would from time to time encourage her with careful instructions like, "Don't bounce down onto your knee there.

LEE KESSLER

The tendons don't like it. Control…easy does it. Good girl." That was all. Today, she didn't mind.

Knowing that Klaus felt she was doing well—certainly revealing a stamina even she didn't know she had—she couldn't bring herself to tell him that the more clothing she took off, the heavier she felt. Despite the clear air, the brilliant light, and a lessening burden, she felt more oppressed with each step. Sweater gone, shirt gone—now jeans—baring her to her shorts. And yet her breathing was more labored, partly due to the climbing and partly due to the now easily-identifiable anxiety attack. *Surely*, she told herself, *here at the top of the world, Depression could not follow. Surely, here, in the beauty of the world I can escape it.*

She had come to Brunnen hoping to find peace of mind and rejuvenation. Instead, she had continued to feel the anxiety and the paralysis that had haunted her in New York. He had followed her somehow.

And at this moment, with her total concentration focused on the rocky path at her feet, she released hope and optimism. They floated out over Brunnen. The vacuum created was apparently filled by Depression, and a cynical doubt that she would ever feel right again. She had fought the battle a long time—staving off Despair, and to an extent, she knew now, reality. Where was the profound certainty she had in the future the night she and Keith had first driven into Los Angeles after a three-day drive from New York—he to commence law school, and she to support them, and eventually to begin acting? Where was the certainty of the direction of her acting, the fame she had pursued, the projects she wished to create?

Klaus was watching her. Their eyes met for a moment, and she knew that he knew. Whoever he was—who seemed to know so much, who had waited for her, and who now particularly kept his distance—he knew.

She had shed her jeans and felt that she was dropping instead the charade of feeling well, of coping. She was disappointed in herself that she seemed to be capitulating, and yet relieved somehow, almost grateful. She felt as if she were slowly hemorrhaging inside. Would the

- 160 -

emotional storms brewing inside overwhelm her, drowning her here on a granite slab 4,000 feet above a tranquil lake? She had chosen to come here—been driven actually by forces she didn't understand. And somehow this man was part of it.

"How do you feel?" he asked.

"Lousy, thanks." That much was at least honest. But she could not bring herself to admit to him the guilt she felt now. For in releasing the firm appearance of coping, of carrying on no matter what, she had opened the floodgates of self-recrimination. Knowing that she had been given so much in her life—a keen intelligence, a fierce ambition, been educated well and easily, supported by loving parents, and provided with enough money to insure basics and certainly some luxuries like travel and houses—she felt that she should have been able to hold up. Others less fortunate might understandably have succumbed to the pressures of the vacillations of politics and economics, but she should have stood fast, she knew.

After all, she told herself in a monolog as she and Klaus commenced walking, *I'm only divorced. Millions have had to face that, and most far worse than mine. True, I've had setbacks. Yet surely all other actors suffer the same—most far worse than I—with no work or even prospects of work. Let alone the millions of people in all walks of life who year after year struggle to find work and to keep what work they find.*

Of course there was the painful failure to have secured the recognition she desired. But standing on this mountain, she could almost see a planet of billions of people with that identical disappointment. If she thought she had worried about house payments and apartment rents, how many were there whose life was a day-to-day struggle to secure even adequate living quarters? If they survived—who had so few of the advantages—then she should have. *I should have been stronger.*

The noon sun was debilitating now, and Grace persuaded Klaus to stop. He seemed content to let her sit with her feelings and her internal dialogue with Depression. She thought she noticed him smile as she unlaced her shoes to let her aching feet breathe. It was then that she decided it was time to know something about this stranger who knew so much about her.

"I enjoy your music," she began, hoping again to coax an answer. "Were you a musician?"

"Not really," he said quickly and seemed to shrink as if afraid to answer. At the same time, shaking the hair away from his forehead, he added, "I knew a lot of musicians." His voice was so distant and non-committal. He was not unfriendly, but his reticence convinced her that he was indeed afraid to answer, and he therefore spoke evasively. His objectivity and seeming lack of interest in her were confusing for a man who said he had waited thirteen years.

Perhaps he is still angry with me from yesterday, she reminded herself. He tried to run his hand through his hair but was blocked by his headband. Then, she noticed perspiration around his lips as his eyes scanned the horizon, and she felt certain that he was afraid—not of the cliffs above, but of something else. She was sure of it now. *But what is it he fears?* That preoccupation absorbed her attention just long enough to lift the pall that had overtaken her. *After all, he at least answered. Perhaps I can elicit more.*

"I used to play trombone," she offered, with a natural poignancy. "But I gave it up."

"It's just as well," he said. Although Grace had made the same assessment of herself years earlier, this tendency of his to candidly express himself, with no attempt to assuage her feelings, vexed her. And moreover, it implied he was ahead of her in her own story. She had the worst urge to yell at him, but at least he was conversing, so she swallowed her vexation.

"You heard me play?" she asked artificially.

"Yes, I heard your Lucerne concert," he responded rather cryptically, munching on a tiny chocolate bar.

"Well?"

"You had spirit, good technique, and God knows, discipline…" He trailed off, as if there had been more to say, and he had changed his mind.

"But?" she persisted.

"But…you played rather like you read a book."

She was dumbfounded—not so much because he was critical of her when she had expected support—but more because of this almost unfathomable analogy. He must have seen her screw up her face for he continued unprompted. "You lacked trust in yourself, the music, and your instrument."

"Is that all? she asked sarcastically, and then before he could respond, she rationalized, "I always trusted the music and the instrument, just not my ability to express the music."

"No, Grace, it goes farther than that. You didn't trust yourself to let go, to find what was there. Remember you have to know the ending beforehand. I doubt if you ever probed what was there within the music, between the notes, or ever really pushed your instrument to explore the outer reaches of its range."

"But I was never trained in improvisation, like you," she said, defending herself. "I didn't learn how, so I had to rely on what was there, written."

He spoke sternly then. "The only thing preventing you from improvising is you: you judging, you fearing, you refusing to let go and to reach out."

"And come up empty," she said regretfully, finishing the sentence for him.

"The field of creative energy rarely yields an empty response. That's Fear's reasoning."

She conceded that, and redeemed herself with, "That's why I left music for acting."

"Isn't your acting the same?" he challenged.

"You've never seen me act," she said too loudly. "You have no right to judge."

"You read books, you play music, you run from city to city. I think I know you. I think I know how you act—and how you live." The argument was escalating now, and the dry, crackling autumn wind seemed to first kindle and then fuel it. Grace rose and, despite one shoeless foot, paced over him as he looked at her expectantly.

"You have the audacity to speak to me with an arrogant assumption about my ability," she yelled. "I have listened to you interpret me and my behavior smugly for weeks, but this is the limit. As it so happens, my inabilities in some areas have heightened my abilities in others. I know, Klaus, that you like to think you know everything there is to know about me, as if..." she kneaded her fingertips together as if searching for the right word, "as if you were some kind of 'diviner,' but you're not. I've let go of more in my lifetime than most have been asked to let go of. And my acting has grown and changed as a result. It has loosened. It is strong in its vulnerability now, warmer."

But even as she argued with an unflinching Klaus, she knew the bilious taste of desperation. As she justified her acting strides, her mind's eye flashed images of an actor's preparation, of knowing the ending and constructing the role to reach the ending, of planning beats and actions, of choosing one emotion over another, of technique and discipline—but not of inspiration. As if an abundance of these others could camouflage the deficiency of the one.

That which she coveted more than anything was as out of reach for her as an actress as it was for her as a musician—and perhaps as a human being. The more clearly she recognized this, the more intensely she fought Klaus. Her defense was an offense. And the more strident her offense, the more transparent her defense, until eventually she stopped. Her mouth was dry, her stomach nauseous. She licked her lips desperately to try to restore moisture.

"All I'm saying is that your acting has something to do with your life."

For that there was no rebuttal, and she surrendered to the security of the rock below.

"I know." She brushed her hair back behind her ear and looked clearly at Klaus's unchanged face. Taking deep breaths to ease the nausea, she continued. "I know. I must go forward. But I don't know how. I feel so helpless." Pausing for a moment, she laughed and said, "Ridiculous actually. All my intellect, my education, my scrapbooks full of accomplishments—and no answer."

"Grace, you can't treat life like a book. You're just not given the luxury of a writer who can remain stuck until he rewrites the ending to suit his wishes."

"But I don't want to be a book, the ending to which I do not know!"

Klaus exhaled loudly, shook his head repeatedly, muttering to himself and then to the sky like a teacher who's giving up for the day, hoping a good night's rest will allow some assimilation of the lesson. He spoke tiredly as he rose. "We have to go on."

The only sounds for the remainder of the afternoon were their cleats along the rocks, their breathing, and a more than occasional groan from Grace as the effects of the climb took their toll.

Occasionally, the point of ascent over a rock was too steep to traverse unassisted. Klaus would—using a pick with a long, sturdy handle—secure a position, eventually reaching the top. Then, using the rope fastened to her waist, he would hoist her up. She merely had to walk forward with her feet as if stepping up the side. It was then she fully appreciated the considerable strength he had. For one so slender, he was remarkably strong, and despite her natural fear of heights, she felt no great fear—a little nervousness perhaps—and, decidedly, an almost total numbness.

At last, just before sunset, they ceased climbing and just as he had pointed out from down below, there were trees again. Most were pines, they being the only things hearty enough to sustain a position just below the steep wall to the summit of the Kaiserstock. But there was still a bit of grass, and what other small trees were in the area now had crisping leaves, just turning brown at the edges, crackling in the breeze. They were directly over the crevice they had been following yesterday, and somewhat west of it. From their vantage point, she could now see water running out of the boulders and down into the gorge. She asked where the source was. He said they would see that tomorrow.

They set up camp in the pine needles amid the grove. It was cool now, with an edge toward chilly, and she redressed herself, adding a heavy sweater. Klaus and she had not spoken since the argument except to answer an occasional question, and she watched him now as he cooked a venison and egg dinner. Grace, although she had grown up in deer hunting country of upstate New York, had never tasted venison. Her brothers had a distaste for killing deer, and her mother had refused to cook it even if it were a gift. So, this was a new experience, and one she did not relish. The cooking aroma was too pungent, and her own great affection for the large-eyed, exquisitely-colored animal made it hard to swallow.

She tasted only a little, so as not to offend Klaus any further, and then ate her eggs. But by now the aching fatigue of the day's climb, the painful tightening of muscles in the cold, and the depression cloud that dulled her senses all combined to leave her practically inert on her blanket, her pack folded as a pillow.

Klaus propped himself up against a tree and pulled out his flute. At first she thought the evocative melody was an old English folk tune, but the intervals and occasional surprise glissandos made her feel as if the music were from another world. She asked if the tune were English. He said it wasn't. He seemed to be playing a structured piece from memory, but she couldn't be sure. Perhaps he was improvising in homage to another time. Whatever, the melody was haunting—not the lilting, soaring, Mozart flute that seemed to have been written to speak to the soul, cascading as water from a mountain. No, this flute melody was one for the soul, but this time introspective. It probed, it searched, it evoked another time. Its only accompaniment was the hoot of an owl overhead. She considered these to be creatures of the night—possessors of the spirit of darkness—for they could see where all others were blind. Occasionally, too, there was the unceremonious dropping of a pine cone to punctuate the music. Klaus ended the song on a low note that seemed to hang in the air forever. Even the wind, the owl, and the trees seemed to hold their breath for the last waves of the note to escape.

He began another, more plaintive song. Grace lay in the darkness. Tears were flowing. The music seemed to viscerally move her, as if playing her. She did not weep. She merely felt warm, huge tears spontaneously forming and flowing to the music, and, as if she were caught in a time warp, she recalled another time. She saw herself pulling her turquoise knee socks on in the dressing room of her high school swimming pool as her father's voice came grimly over the loudspeaker to announce that, "The President of the United States has been shot in Dallas, Texas." She felt once again the vise-like pressure in her chest she had felt that afternoon standing in her physics lab, like her fellow students, unable to perform experiments as they waited for the inevitable. She remembered her vow to change the world to make such a future recurrence impossible.

She saw herself with Keith in the underground city of Philadelphia on a debate tournament as they became aware of a foreboding silence in the black people who passed them—the hostile stares, the suspicious eyes. And the worried voice of a black man in a suit who had come up to say, "The King is dead. Get out of here as quickly as you can. You must fear for your lives." Then came the slow, dawning realization as to which King he meant. She remembered that, although she had paid only marginal attention to Civil Rights or to Martin Luther King except to study his "I Have A Dream" speech in Speech class, she had regretted his death and worried that it would trigger violence. She had done nothing more, however.

She saw herself lying in Keith's arms on his dormitory cot during Senior week before she graduated. They had stolen a night of total foreplay—more to break the rules of her strict "girls" dorm, as they called it then, than anything else. The radio music was interrupted to announce the shooting of Robert Kennedy and to describe his wounds. She had never liked his popular, scrappy style, but as she listened to the nature of his wounds, she prayed for his death that he might not linger long in torment.

She saw herself speechless at the University of Wisconsin as she entered the dean of her department's office on her first day there, to discover his secretary nonchalantly breast-feeding her baby while answering the phones. Pregnant single women, bared breasts, couples unashamedly making love on campus between classes, constant vocal political debates, loud protests, and love beads were all new to her then. She remembered now only that she had gone out of her way to avoid confrontation with any of those elements. She saw herself standing on top of Bascom Hill, looking down at National Guardsmen, their tanks, and jeeps as they went into formation to contain the open rebellion. She had stood above it all, and was not involved in the "War at Home." She had not participated. Someday, she knew, she would have to—just once.

Then, however, she had continued her studies, received her A's, completing her Master's Degree amidst now-vague disruption and protesting. She had proudly and disdainfully avoided their raucous music and ear-shattering amplifiers. Nothing had diverted her from what she was sure was her true course, her duty—not even cut-off jeans, Indian saris, or tie dying! She knew that if any one of those floundering contemporaries had looked at her, she would have been able to provide guidance, a way back.

She was no longer that person, however. That Grace, with her considerable joy and optimism, seemed to be from another life. The woman here on a Swiss mountain more than a decade later seemed to be living in another life altogether. How had that happened? What had happened in the intervening years to create this divorced, floundering actress who maintained residences in New York and Los Angeles, but who was now off on some mysterious excursion with a complete stranger?

Trying to recall the intervening decade, she found that by free-associating, her mind always returned to some moment in the late '60s. She could not seem to conjure up any vital, significant memories of the '70s. The ramifications of that began to sink in. Grace ceased free-associating and instead directed herself to recall specific times with Keith in law school, or the purchase of their first home, or her first acting job. The images returned grudgingly, but their visceral impact upon her was as different from the previous memories as a ghost is to flesh. They were hollow memories—sketchy and hazy—holding only facts, but no emotion. All were vacuous, and they evoked no emotion upon recollection. She asked herself, *What was it then, during this lost decade, that has altered me so substantially?*

Try as she would—spurred on by the flowing flute as Klaus trilled the end to another melody—she could remember no history of the '70s, except Watergate. And that was only because she had five years later played a role in the TV version of John Dean's "Blind Ambition."

She remembered her recent astonishment upon reading *The Right Stuff*, whose author she had never before heard of, to find that there had been more than one mission to the moon. Where had the decade gone? What had preoccupied her so that she remembered nothing of President Ford's term, except his reelection bid in which she had been his spokeswoman in a controversial anti-Reagan commercial? Neither did she remember now-President Carter's endeavors except his spicy mother and the occasional headlines about the urinary indiscretions of his brother.

Attempting to shake the sense of disorientation, which was overcoming her, she interrupted Klaus's flute by asking what he was playing. He answered, "Hara nu oni. It's modern Japanese," then put the flute away.

Listening to him breathe for a while in the stillness, she felt the need to reach out to someone, so she broke the barrier of silence between them. "Your music was beautiful. But it made me think of my life. All I can remember is the '60s, nothing of the '70s. Why is that, do you think?"

"Perhaps you were most involved then."

"No, just the opposite, Klaus, and that's what I can't understand. I was never part of that generation. I went out of my way to avoid the confusion of those people."

He did not respond. After a while she whispered hoarsely, "Klaus, it's scary. I can't remember my most recent past. Despite all of my adult life occurring in that time, I can't remember anything past 1970. I'm afraid."

His voice was supportive and calm. "Of what?"

"I feel trapped."

"Perhaps..." he hesitated for a moment before continuing. "Perhaps your life stopped at that point, and you've been living a false life since. You're trapped because you took a false exit and are now searching for the true one."

"Or I've been thinking perhaps the '70s took me to something I didn't want." She felt the stirrings of cramps within her stomach as she considered the ramifications of such a rejection of an entire decade.

Tremendous fear gripped her throat as she moaned, "I got off the track somewhere."

Only the owl answered her. *But why can't I go into the '80s?* she asked herself. *Why am I here—away from my home, Robert, my dear Mutti? Why am I on a mountain, stuck in the past—so afraid that there is no life for me down there?*

Then something occurred to her. What if she reached where they were going and found that the fear did not subside, that there was no escape for her? Even at this height, that the planet finally imposed its limits upon her? Without knowing why, she knew that this place Klaus was leading her to was her last hope, and that she must go there.

"Are we nearly there?" she whispered, trying to conceal her gripping forebodings.

"We are there. You just can't see it in the dark."

The dawn was no surprise to her. Any inordinately splendid colors it may have provided were lost to Grace, for she had been waiting so diligently for the first light of day that all she recognized was darkness and its opposite. When the light appeared, she was ready within minutes, packed and gratified not to have to listen to the conversation of owls.

Klaus was awake, but strangely silent and uninvolved. He sat separate, almost like a guide whose job was obviated by the journey's end. He seemed afraid. Grace asked herself cursorily what his silence portended, but allowed insufficient time to really digest the signals.

In truth, this morning she didn't really care what might be bothering him. Their whole relationship, if one could call it that, was so full of the unspoken—swollen with tension and strained by cross-purposes—that now did not seem to be the time to even explore the man. *After all*, she told herself, *hasn't he brought me to this place for me to experience something unknown? What does it matter that I requested it? He'll understand*, she told herself.

Restless, unable to wait, she followed his finger as he pointed to the edge of the woods, and she left. The path, obscured by underbrush and cushioned by thousands of pine needles, was short, and Grace emerged suddenly into what she expected to be a meadow. Instead, below her by a few meters down a grassy slope was a small, jewel-like lake, completely surrounded by the cliffs of the summit, and by the pine forest with its complementary spruce. Almost completely oval, a gentle slope led down to it all around, save in one area where the water lapped flush against boulder and no doubt through there somehow to the noisy cascades she had seen the day before.

A few scattered, but brilliantly colored, wildflowers brightened the slope, decorating the lake area with color—as if it needed any. For it shone like a brilliant emerald, with the unclouded water reflecting the verdant scenery around, providing occasional glints of light as breezes stirred the water, disrupting the mirror-like reflections.

It's perfect, she thought. *Like a shimmering, luminous eye.* As she stood at the edge, looking in, she was certain she could see into the earth, and that there was a friendly fire within. The deepening shades of green told her it was very deep, and she felt the chilling sensation that she was indeed looking into the eye of the earth.

At that moment—alone—she knew she *had* arrived. Tension long-stored flowed from her as if the water claimed it, only to send it over the cliff to Brunnen below. Years, long accumulating, dissolved and were shed. With each deep breath of life-restoring air, she grew younger and younger. Fatigue and lethargy diminished, and with each passing moment, she felt the gap between herself and her inner self diminishing—as if by shedding from without, and by surfacing from within, the two would soon merge. The merger was welcome. She was welcome here. Fears of what she would find vanished.

"Was it worth the wait?" His voice penetrated slowly.

"There *is* no place else, is there?" she asked, without looking at him, her eyes embracing the lucid water.

"For me, no. For you, I do not know."

"This is your place?" she asked.

"Yes," he responded, almost sadly. She turned to face him and he added, "The true Brunnen, right?"

"Have you ever brought anyone here?"

"Once. But no one quite so rooted in the future."

That started it. He had done it again—stupidly marring her serenity with veiled criticism. Feeling secure with her eye into the earth, she knew that it was time to confront him. Lady-like behavior didn't seem to be called for now. They were evenly matched now, and she knew that she must challenge and prevail if she were to overcome his intimations of superiority. The gauntlet was thrown, and she had chosen her spot.

Her inner self had now surfaced and spoken angrily at Klaus with, for the first time in her life, no self-imposed restraining. "You live in the future, too, you hypocrite. Suppose I hadn't come back? You would have spent your whole life waiting for the future!"

Responding to the challenge, his eyes flashed as if had picked up the gauntlet and knew, too, that the battle that had been brewing since her arrival was at long last commencing. Like two territorial animals, they faced each other.

"No, Grace, I lived my life. I worked. I played. I loved. All you have shown me is irrefutable proof that a person can have one instant when he sees his true self and can act on that. I came in contact with myself on that balcony and knew enough, unlike you, to stay here."

Seeing that she was confused, he pressed his advantage. "I don't know what you want from me. Or what you think I want from you. What boy-girl games you're playing. But all I have ever intended is that if you returned—*if*, mind you—perhaps I could repay you for my life. For you gave me my life, albeit inadvertently."

"I didn't see you there, Klaus," she interjected energetically.

"I know," he answered. "Maybe you weren't talking to me that day, but I thought you were, and you gave me the courage and vision to see my life for what it had become, and what it could be. I hoped only to join forces with you if you returned, or to repay you, or to support you at a moment when you might flounder. But since you returned, your..." he angrily groped for the word, "your narcissism, or whatever you call it, has treated me as if I were the competition. You have perpetually and arrogantly resisted advice, and constantly looked at me with suspicion."

Before she could deny anything, he overrode it. "I've seen you make mental notes on my flaws, Grace! I've seen your eyes diminish me."

This time she only blinked at the accuracy of his challenge. This angered him further, and he grasped both arms and shook her. "What is it you fear I could do to you, Grace?"

The recently surfaced nerves of her inner self were throbbing now. She wished she could run, but there was no place left to escape to. She wished that she could retreat, but whatever veneer of well-mannered lady had not been shattered by exposed nerve endings had just been annihilated by the rawness of his outburst. She dared not divert her eyes, for there was still danger.

"What are you afraid I could do to you?" he repeated.

Her voice was calm, though somewhat throaty. "The same thing I can do to you."

"What do you mean?"

"Take this place."

"I don't understand."

"You could take this place from me," she answered.

This stunned Klaus, and he let go of her, backing up, shaking his head and holding both palms to his forehead, as if in pain.

"My God, Grace," he cried out, "you have so far to go." As he spoke, he looked at her as if seeing her for the first time. "Don't you see that this is *our* place? No one can ever take it from you now!" Then he added quietly, "Unless you let it go."

What happened next occurred too quickly for her to separate it. In later days, she would look back and piece together a patchwork memory of the overlaid actions and words. She saw the mosaic, saw her body try to run and his swift arm stop her. She heard her gut-wrenching scream. It pierced the air, echoing from the walls of the mountain, and, as the sound bounced around, it overlapped her hoarse, almost voiceless question: "What do you want from me?"

His reply was unforgettable—lost to all but her ear as her body's strength abandoned her, and she collapsed against his chest. He had demanded, "I want you to tell me. I want to know what you are really afraid of?" This time, she answered.

The weight of the bursting answer caused them to sink to the ground, he supporting her. Her voice, wetted only by tears and racked by sobs, was first dry, barely audible, but then became more stable.

"I no longer believe in the future!" She paused a moment to gulp in enough air to continue. "Always, no matter what happened, I at least believed in the future. I had a vision of what it would be for me. You know?"

Instead of speaking, he rocked her, wrapping her forehead with his palm, holding her head against his chest as she wept. "It's belief in the future that makes it possible to live now, to commit to a relationship, to sacrifice, to accept less than you want—for now. But I see that I'm now living in what used to be 'my future.' I've arrived at the spot I always dreamed of, and none of it has come true. I don't have what I dreamed of, don't you see? It's not what I thought it would be. Not what I was told it would be."

As the flood of tears subsided slowly, her eyes blurred less, and she was content to rock back and forth as feelings continued to surface. After a while, staring only at the white button on the pocket of his red shirt, she said, "And now I have no desire to dream. I fear that I will only spend my life perpetuating delusions. I should settle for now, in comparison to the blind hope of a future that will never materialize—except in the inevitability of old-age."

"Are you unhappy with today?"

Grace stiffened, amazed that he could not see the obvious. *Hasn't he been listening to what I said?*

"Thrilled with it, can't you tell?" Then, less sarcastically, she mollified him. "None of what I *dreamed* is possible, Klaus, don't you understand?"

"It was all possible, back then, before the dream died," he said softly, as if repeating something to himself.

"Yes! Yes, that's it," she added, trying to connect with his thoughts. "Only now I feel as if there were two Graces—two different people. The new one doubts, all the time now."

Klaus said nothing. He merely stroked her hair, and she felt his body relax, as if he, too, had been holding onto something that he had let go of. The tension between them dissipated, and she knew now that for the first time he was listening.

"I believed, and I almost laugh now to think of it, that I could affect the future. Not only could, but should. No matter that I always felt left out of my own time, never part of it. Stupid, I know," she laughed. "But I believed it had fallen to me to lead the others. I listened as little as possible to the protestors, avoided all drug users, and tolerated quietly the loud, complaining brats of my generation. And I justified my avoidance by telling myself I was projecting into the future, creating a path for them and me. It was okay that I was left out. I was not meant to be at one with them."

She stopped here and looked now to the lake, the water gently lapping a few feet from them. It was easier to breathe now, as if something inside had been pushing against a door for a long time, and had finally been freed by the sudden opening of that door. Even the self-recrimination was not painful now.

"But the Future, at least the future I now know, revealed nothing but corruption, greed, and self-centeredness. Do you know that I was the last kid on the block to stop believing in Nixon?" She laughed as she looked up at Klaus, expecting a response, but finding instead only a quizzical look. He must not have understood the reference, so she tried to explain. "Nixon? Watergate?"

He nodded and added, "Yes. Yes, of course. But what else?"

"What do you mean?"

"What corruption for you personally?" he pressed.

I have to hand it to him, she thought. *He has a gift for distillation!*

"Aah…" She struggled. "The last few years of my life have been spent in total preoccupation with myself. Now I can justify some of it by claiming to have at least portrayed courageous women, to have set a good example. But the truth is that almost every waking moment is now spent on my career. What job am I getting next? How much money? Is it a good career move? How should I look? Am I aging ? Do I have my father's neck? And now, preoccupation with how do I pay for my house, my car, my apartment?

"You see, I feel that when the American Dream turned into a nightmare, it frightened everyone so much that they fled into themselves, as if turning concentration onto themselves—as if improving themselves—would somehow restore the Dream. We all fell for it, not realizing that the self-improvement, self-analysis, self-awareness ideas were still rooted in the pursuit of the old Dream. The belief spread that we'd gotten off the track—a whole generation of us—and that, if we really looked at ourselves, the Dream would be returned and we would find the happiness we deserve. But I fear that that is still all predicated on old thought patterns. There can be no new life if it's based on old patterns. The game doesn't seem to be to create a new self, but rather to use the self-awareness only as a tool to restore the old self's faith and ideas."

She stopped, as if listening to an echo of her own words, then defiantly went on. "I don't care how many women euphorically march forth from their disintegrating families and say that they have 'found' themselves and are doing what they want to do. What they want is still hopelessly defined by the old visions and expectations. Women today think freedom is not being controlled by some man. So they react against men. But that's not freedom—not true freedom. I just know. And what happens when they discover that? That even on their own—successful as entities by themselves—the disillusionment still creeps in, and they're left holding hollow victories."

"Is that how you see it now? Your independence as a hollow victory?" he asked without moving.

"Yes. I feel cheated. My ten year pursuits of the self were wild goose chases."

"But, Grace, aren't you still in that pursuit?"

She laughed once. "Probably. I'm probably trapped in it, powerless to break the futility of it. For instance, I still regret that Keith and I are no longer together. Not for each other, because I don't love him anymore—I can barely remember him. But he's a good man. There's regret that two people who loved each other once have had to go separate paths, that their paths were not converging, that their beginning dream was not possible."

"Convergence may only be an illusion, Grace. What if the human animal is never intended to spiritually converge, and all attempts at it have been a failed effort to conform to an unrealistic, artificial vision?"

"Then I would have been pursuing a myth," she said, laughing once again, adding, "It's just that possibility that I fear."

They were silent for a while before she found the strength to speak again. "I just wish I could get back, Klaus."

"Where?"

"Even though I was left out there, I was happy in the '60s. I really believed we could make a difference then. We knew we could. In that much I was a part of my time. Now, there seems to be nothing—no cause greater than myself. It's wrong somehow."

"I think the crucible is harder now, Grace. I've thought often about this. The challenge now is, as you said, to see if you can go the distance. You know, my sweet friend, when you have a cause to die for, life is always worth living. It is dearer. But the songs to inspire in that 'terrible time' were too early by a decade. The real time of despair, when there was freedom without responsibility, when there was no cause but self-interest, no rallying post, was a time of more subtle jeopardy. We are not what we thought we were. And in our time of *peace*, we have turned the war upon ourselves."

"We?" she asked, afraid to look at him.

"You and I," he answered quietly, as he lifted her head to look at him. "I wrote those songs, Grace." There were tears in his eyes. "Whether you belong or not, you are your generation."

"I don't think I can go the distance, Klaus. I don't think I can go on without a dream."

Slowly brushing her hair away from her eyes, he held her face gently, looking into her eyes. "Make now your dream—only *now*."

Unable to escape his gaze, she told him that she couldn't do that, that she felt she must be part of a larger context, and that if she could only move forward once again, she might find herself. He listened to her speak, and then with a gentle self-assuredness said, "Your forward movement will only lead you here."

"If only I knew."

"You must trust."

"I can't. Not without moving forward first. I don't know the end, you see?"

For several moments, he continued to look at her as if searching for something. Then slowly, his hand slipped to her shoulder, one finger caressing the shoulder blade. He looked at it for an endless minute, and then seemed to draw himself up for one final effort.

"Let it go, Grace. The 'end' is when you no longer need the future, when you're fulfilled in the present—with this lake, the mountains, your friends."

She looked down at his slender hand. It didn't appear to be the hand of a combatant, nor anymore the hand of a recluse. Neither was there fear or uncertainty in his voice as he leaned toward her to whisper, "Let it go."

She turned her head to kiss his hand softly with gratitude, and his lips found hers almost immediately. As assuredly as he had spoken, his arm enfolded her and guided her to the blanket of grass. As his eyes penetrated her, his hand slipped inside her blouse, warm against her breast. Moments later, she felt no doubt as the hardness of his body joined them together.

As she came in waves as brilliant as the autumn sun filtering through his hair, she breathed, "You hold some key to my wholeness. It has been withheld for so many years, and now I have it. You have given it to me somehow."

"I knew you would come back."

"And you're afraid of...?" she asked.

"Only that you will leave."

"Is that *all?*"

He did not answer.

CHAPTER TEN

It felt like the second day of her second life, as there was beauty and rejuvenation all around her. Even the trees bore no marks of the encroaching autumn, and their eventual withering in a life and death struggle. At least Grace thought it was the second day. She had lost track of time, as if she had shed her past life and the limitations placed upon it.

Now, as she lay in the grass by the inner lake counting clouds as they slipped by, even the spruce seemed the work of an impressionist painter. Its large, round fronds, stacked in a pyramid of needle balls, were so fluffy that it seemed to be in collusion with the cumulonimbus clouds overhead.

Grace thought for a fleeting moment that she could stay here forever. Klaus lay beside her, his hand stroking her side just below the curve of the breast. He rested his head on her breast, and then laughed quietly at some private joke.

"What?" she asked, caressing his hair.

"I was just marveling," he answered.

"At what?"

"Your body. It's so smooth and soft. Who would ever guess?"

"Thanks a lot!" She pretended to be perturbed.

"No. No. Not that you would be beautiful and soft, but what's inside." Looking up at her, he stroked her forehead and, looking into her eyes, said, "You've such a sad knowledge in your eyes, Grace."

"Only when I'm relaxed. Then I see it all clearly," she said rather too soberly, and then laughed at her own sobriety. The combativeness that had existed between them was since dissolved into pleasure and reunion.

And a reunion it was. Grace had known passion before. She thought she had known joy. She believed her relationship with Robert had been blessed with sexual freedom, but she was experiencing with Klaus a total union, and it was not just the reunion of two spirits who had wandered thousands of miles apart for a decade, striving to rejoin one another. It was almost as if, when he made love to her and merged his body with hers, their union put her truly and for the first time in touch with herself.

Klaus had said that there is one moment when each person knows who he is, when he can become no wiser. He holds it all at that instant. As his lips touched hers, as his body joined hers, and as their life juices blended, she understood. She felt a part of him, and yet totally herself. They were one.

Now, he even talked to her as if talking to himself. His old reserve was gone. He confided more easily in her. His mystery was nonetheless there, but she felt she had experienced the truth of the man—even if she still knew none of the facts. Somehow the absence of facts did not frighten her—for the moment anyway. She was grateful, and she talked to him as if talking to herself—her wiser self. For, in one of those miraculous connections that sometimes happens between two people, Klaus knew all that she spoke of. He challenged and, in challenging, bridged the gaps in her thoughts. They reinforced each other and reveled in her shimmering emotions as he tapped into them, one by one, as if finding her true self.

She joked, "Was it worth waiting for?"

He merely nodded and then, almost seriously, as she playfully extended her right leg straight up into the air, toes pointing toward the sun, she quipped, "Are you the one I've been looking for all my life?"

"I hope so," he answered, as he ran his hand straight up her extended leg.

"What brought *you* to Brunnen?" she asked quite abruptly.

"Disillusionment."

"Is that all?" she teased. He failed to take the bait.

"Klaus, tell me, how did you get the money for the hotel at your age?"

"I was a songwriter." He answered easily and then, seeing her frown slightly, he added, "Many were produced. At twenty I had come by a fairly substantial amount of money. I still do."

Sensing that he was more comfortable now talking about himself, she hoped he would tell her more, so she began to ask what she wanted to know. "Would I know your songs?"

"You might," he responded, and then offered, "I'll play some for you sometime."

"I'd like that." She kissed him, and then returned to her line of questioning. "But why did you convert the hotel to a hotel for cripples?"

"It seemed appropriate."

Grace laughed, thinking he must be joking, but his eyes told her he was not. She regrouped, saying, "I don't understand."

Klaus hesitated for a moment. "You asked me why I came here. I should tell you the story."

"Please."

He sat up, looking for a moment toward the lake. Then he said, "A friend of mine bought a car—an 1874 vintage carriage actually—the red, blue, and orange Rolls-Royce had come first." She looked puzzled, but he just continued, and Grace concentrated on retaining as much as she could. "The *London Daily Express* called that a 'cross between a psychedelic nightmare and an autumn garden on wheels.' But it was nothing compared to John's carriage—all yellow with flowers and four white horses." Klaus was looking now straight up into the trees, as if looking at the image he was painting, extracting portions to describe to her. "It was meant to be a toy for his son. It cost over $10,000 American. And I knew then that I had to leave...for a while anyway." He paused. "As it turns out, I never went back."

"Why not?"

He did not answer, so she tried another approach.

"You said 'John's carriage?'"

"Yes. John Lennon."

This surprised her, something she scarcely disguised, though he didn't seem to notice. She began to try to put pieces of the puzzle together. "Did you continue writing songs?"

"For a while. Then I stopped," he said regretfully.

"Do you want to talk about it?" she asked gently.

"Not yet." And she let it drop, for she felt as if she had touched a nerve, and one which was still causing him pain. Sensing that it was not reserve, but rather pain, which provoked his silence, she backed off.

The rest of the day was spent playing. For Grace, the inner feeling of being on the run had disappeared. No hyperventilation pursued her, no cramping, and most of all, no sadness. Today, alone with Klaus, she felt no concern over her daily life in the U.S. One thought about her probably long-overdue Visa statement fleeted through her mind and was immediately chased out subconsciously. She felt no guilt for this takeover of her conscious thoughts by an easier, more generous subconscious. *My peace of mind is worth the price of a smidgen of guilt,* she told herself in preparation for what she expected to be inevitable. But no guilt came.

Surprisingly, her inability to think about Robert and his proposal, her home, or her financial affairs left no trace of guilt—at least none that she recognized. *After all,* she reminded herself, *a deeply rooted mysterious feeling has led me to this place.* It had led her 8,000 miles in the last two months alone. *I am meant to be here,* she told herself. Here she would stay.

Sitting later on the boulder, under which flowed the stream to the lake below, she looked down on the path they had traversed. It seemed more dangerous somehow than she remembered when they had climbed, as if she had come quite a treacherous distance. Her life lay far below, almost in the past now, and without knowing it, she said, "It's gone." Her voice startled even her.

"What's gone?" Klaus asked, surprised by her non-sequitur.

Grace groped for her train of thought but could not find it. "I don't know. It's funny. I was thinking what a remote place this is. But I don't know what I was saying."

"Yes." He seemed to understand and then, as if to reassure her, he answered, "Very few come here, I'm sure."

"Have you ever encountered anyone here?" she asked. He said no and she asked, more rhetorically than interestedly, "I wonder why that is? How did you ever find it?"

"There are places where only the lost dare to go." Then Klaus surprised her by laughing, as if embarrassed by his own revelation. He dropped the subject suddenly. She, too, let it go. Perhaps an hour later, as the sun was directly overhead now, warming her head and livening all body surfaces, she felt mellow enough to continue the talk they'd begun that first day here. "Klaus, sitting here looking down on the beautiful Lake Lucerne, so distant, so serene, and then turning to this lucid one behind us, I see things."

He asked her what, and she said simply, "That I'm not what I should have been."

"How so?"

"I feel I have..." then she corrected herself. "Excuse me, *had* the potential to be so much more. I'm not what people think I am." She stopped for a moment to try to put order into the gushing thoughts. "I never expected to be divorced like everyone else. Never expected to work at a field where I'm forever chasing after the next job—grateful for a day here and there, living on dreams of a big break. I feel cheated."

"How so?"

"I missed my past—skipped through it really—in order to get to this future, and all I find now are days requiring stamina." Using her right hand to massage away the pressure behind her forehead, she added, "And I can't seem to go over the top." She turned to him in pain once again. Long-buried feelings surfaced, and she felt her mouth stretch with the pain, baring her teeth and causing her to wince and take in a quick breath of air. "I've got to get over the top, or no one will ever know how hard I struggled. Only the bright glare of recognition validates the struggle, I know now."

"Very few, as you put it, get over the top, Grace. We all dream. Many are unappreciated and unacknowledged. But does that mean their struggle is any less significant?"

"According to the rules of that world down there, yes," she retorted, angrily spitting the words out, her once graceful hand suddenly chopping the air stridently. "The struggle isn't enough, down there. All that matters is the winning. If you can get into the light, then you're a winner. All others are failures."

"Grace." He said her name as if trying to pull her back from some precipice. "You're not down there anymore. You're above that game now. It's what you came here to learn." Then, seeing that she was trying to listen, he added, "Do you know the theory of approaching light speed?"

"I know what light speed is, but I don't know if I understand what you mean," she responded, her curiosity aroused by Klaus's intensity. For he was on his knees now beside her, focusing totally on her—almost like a coach briefing an athlete—staying close to infuse either ideas or emotion into the willing ear.

"We've assume, trying to override Einstein, that man can reach the speed of light. We speculate what would happen at light speed and beyond, and we've tried to engineer technology to achieve just such a feat. It's all illusion, however. It is impossible to reach light speed, only to come infinitely close to it."

"I don't understand the point," she responded, stretching her legs.

"There is no 'coming over the top,' Grace. One comes infinitely close, but never reaches it. It is always, for everyone, merely a struggle to come as close as possible. And all are worthy."

"All right, say I accept that, which I'm not sure I do," she qualified firmly. "How on earth does that help me right now?"

Here, Klaus smiled, as if about to call out *checkmate*. "It doesn't. Except that, because of time dilation, where time slows down close to the speed of light, the traveler is left younger than those left behind. No one ever truly comes over the top, but those who struggle, as you put it, or travel close to the speed of light, as I put it, remain young. The others wither and age. The game turns against them, you see."

She averted her eyes from his intense gaze, trying to digest the implications of this, hoping he would not press too hard. He apparently sensed this, for he sat back almost immediately.

"You're telling me to drop the pattern that says that unless I become famous no one will know how fine an actress I am, or how diligently I worked?" she challenged.

"You should not need that validation. Your youthfulness is your affirmation. But, in any case, that is not what I was referring to."

"I'm afraid I don't understand right now."

"You will."

She must have let several hours go by before commenting again. His words occupied her thoughts, settling in forcefully, pushing all others out. She heard his self-assured, "The game turns against them, you see," over and over. But each time she came close to relinquishing her belief in the need to reach the summit of achievement and secure recognition, she returned to the certainty that in order to change anything in politics, society, or in personal lives even, one had to first attain recognition, to have the spotlight thrown on him and thereby influence those who viewed him.

These thoughts fought a mighty battle with one another during those waning hours of the afternoon. Rather than continue the exhausting debate, however, she finally, and admittedly arbitrarily, concluded that she still needed, in fact was obligated, to use her gifts to do what she could. But only by achieving fame, and the often maligned Hollywood word "clout," could she change anything.

Crawling into his arms by a late afternoon fire, she whispered, "I know you're trying, Klaus. I am listening. But I feel that I must use my talents to change what I can. I can make this world a better place. I know it."

"You cannot change anything, Grace," he said, contradicting her. "Except yourself. You can neither alter the past, nor dictate the future. But you can live now, in the present, and create a Grace here and now that will transform the future. You and others like you."

"You?"

"Yes. And anyone who puts serenity and purpose into his own life, whose justice transcends ambition, whose generosity transcends manipulation. If our individual present is in order, our collective future will be."

She smiled and kissed him, thinking he looked sad somehow. "It's a beautiful sentiment, Klaus. But I don't know how to do it." Then, as she looked into his eyes, she thought she must have been mistaken in seeing sadness there. If she had, it had transmuted quietly into a look of supreme surety. He sat up slightly.

"Just live in the present, Grace."

"Aah, a redundancy," she joked, trying to break the connection, and thereby avoid these clichés. But he resisted.

"Are you unhappy with today?" he challenged.

"You asked that once before."

"Are you unhappy today? Right here, now, with me?"

"Of course not," she answered. "I'm sublimely happy today." And as she gazed out over the mirror-still waters, she added, "It's perfect."

"Everything you've done in your life, Grace, has brought you to this moment. It would never have happened if we'd stayed together on that balcony thirteen years ago. You had to live what you have lived, and I what I have, to have found this moment to be what it is."

"Yes."

"You say you're unhappy with your life now. But let me ask you, if there were no past, if there were no dreams that have been shattered over the years, if there were no goals, once established as yet not achieved, to nag you, would you be unhappy with today?"

She could not speak now. There was a tremor in the innermost recesses of her mind. Ancient instinct told her she was on a precipice. Was that precipice danger, or merely change? She felt close—so close—and knew that something was changing inside now. Her mind's eye saw clearly now—and turned to him for the answer—just as she herself did.

"As a young girl, you dreamed of a future. Your mother dreamed one for you. Your friends, your college dreamed a future for you—or at least embellished your own dream. When you began to live your life, however, your choices created in reality a different future. It is not lesser, merely different. And I think that if you really look at your present future, and cease comparing it to your dream future, you would be serene. You created something other than your dream, Grace, that's all."

"But without dreams, how can I go on?"

"If you must dream, let go of expectation." Again, there was a tremor deep within, more profound this time. It widened the fault and a voice, long silenced, erupted. It told her he was right. She must listen. Her conscious thoughts wanted to resist these ideas, but that tiny insistent voice, activated by the earthquake of the soul, prevailed. But, like a college student secure in his laissez-faire economics background, listening to a new Marxist professor shattering his premises, one by one, she felt that something was being taken away from her. She was being asked to part with something upon which she'd anchored her life, and her mind valiantly resisted.

Nonetheless, she heard it all. Perhaps it was his certainty, perhaps his love. But she heard.

"The future, Grace, can't be what you thought it would be. It was predicated on, what is it you Americans call it?" He answered his own question before she could even try. "The American Dream. In the '60s there was a new awareness for all of us—an expansion of this dream to create human consciousness. There was also accompanying rebellion. And whether you participated or not, you *were* there. You were one of the children of Camelot—you were a child of Arthur. So am I. Your President's influence spread far beyond America. In status quo or in rebellion, we believed mostly in man and his capacity for humanity. But then your war brought new awareness, rebellion, and deeper challenges. But we still believed in the feasibility of it all. That government—good responsive government—could blaze a glorious future. Then one by one they died—the ones who dreamed. I let go then and came here. I saw only rampant, cancerous disillusionment as the dream disintegrated. More accurately, it revealed itself to be a nightmare—a dark end to a tunnel.

"I watched it. Not only was world harmony not possible, not only was political honor not possible, but home and family were not. And the Brotherhood of Man may not be possible. Hard work yielding money and a good job became a ghost of previous decades, haunting today's young. And material objects came to own their owners, enslaving them in perpetual struggles to make payments on the objects, which were once considered a God-given right.

"I say let that moribund dream die, Grace. It's not worth your tears. Live today—what you actually have created. Here there is peace. Look about you into the sequence of life. You can almost breathe the harmony. There is birth and death here. And renewal. Breathe it in, Grace. Go forward."

He spoke so transcendently. She took his hand, as if that act would overcome her desire to run. Deep inside, she knew that he was right. But to remain meant relinquishing, and relinquishing meant courage.

She sighed. "I don't know if I have the strength."

His answer was swift, and he looked deep into her eyes, as if to see her innermost response.

"You will. Your wounds will heal here, and strength will come. For this is what I meant that night when I spoke of your wounds. You are part of a wounded generation, Grace. Some, like those friends who went to Vietnam, made the passage from childhood to manhood, when all perceptions alter and one sees the world irrevocably from a new point of view. Old concerns are gone. He is imbued with a keen sense of the present, and of the reality. He goes forward from that point. For a soldier, the past fantasy dies quickly when the staggering reality of mortality affords him the rite of passage. However wounded or scarred, he is forevermore no longer a child. His passage occurs in a single moment.

"Others of us in Camelot were protected in adolescence, secure in our dreams, oblivious of the passage out of childhood. Instinctively haunted by the knowledge that you must become an adult, Grace, you root around in the past searching for something to make the rite of passage to adulthood easier. You are only now growing up. Your maturity has been retarded, and thereby made more painful. Your dreams die harder and more painfully than if they had been seized from you by a sniper in the jungle near Da Nang."

He caressed her hand, holding it firmly. "You are not alone. Your entire generation, who smugly, or in relief, avoided the war and its subsequent passages, has been slowly bleeding inside as the dreams decayed little by little, and reality appeared more and more clearly."

"Is that why I can't get out of the '60s?"

Klaus nodded. "I think so. Something in you knows that the transition should have occurred there. And you're searching, hoping to find some clue for your future in the ruins of memories and faded dreams."

"What can I do?"

"You cannot return to the past, hoping to affect the future. You can only hope that your time spent perusing the past may clarify the present, and that your present clarity will create the future."

Grace said nothing in return. She trusted him on this, and knew somehow that this girl, considered the ultimate woman by so many in her life, had just now made the passage. She had just now become a woman. The little girl was gone.

And with the birth of the woman came a new perspective on the life around her. In the late afternoon light, in the autumn of the year, the symbolic season of death had commenced—but accompanied by so much life activity as to give the lie to it. Before her eyes, leaves were tinctured in variegated colors, their brightness decorating the hills. The squirrels scampered feverishly, noisily instructing one another as they carried nuts quickly to their storage holes for the coming months. A fox dragged a fallen branch behind him to the mouth of a small cave near the boulders, and most probably furnished his home for the winter. Overhead, geese awkwardly moved into formation to continue their flight to a more seasonable climate. And the cool, crisp air titillated the skin, its chilliness confirming life's reaction.

All forces of survival, she thought, *as the present Nature prepares for the future.*

Not long after that, they left the "true Brunnen," as Klaus called it, to return to its namesake below. This time, however, Klaus followed her down the mountain.

That was three weeks ago. Tonight, as a blazing red sun left an afterglow of purple and orange as it set, she stood on the path near the ridge. Tonight was a music night, and the gang was to gather for their weekly jam session. The memory of that last session haunted her tonight as she stood in jeans, her satin blouse, and a shawl loosely protecting her shoulders.

There was unfinished business, she knew. Her stomach was cramping with fear, but it had to be done before the session. She had left the chalet without telling Klaus where she was going, and she had stopped now, she told herself, only to melt the lead in her legs. She would get herself moving soon. She knew she could—soon. *I owe it to him,* she coached herself, and then said out loud to no one but the flaming sun, "Screw it, I owe it to myself."

The next thing she knew, she was standing outside the way station, wishing to God they weren't home. The lights within the restaurant told her Lady Luck was not with her on that, however. The night air seemed cold, and her knuckles stung as she knocked—very softly. She waited a beat and was about to leave when Fritz opened the door. She said nothing. Nor did he. After a few awkward seconds, Ursula's voice demanded, "Who is it, Fritz?" and he stepped aside, motioning for Grace to enter.

Fritz merely dropped back into the room. *Probably to get close to Ursula,* she thought, closing the door behind her. There they stood— all three of them silent—in a room she couldn't even take time to observe. Her heart was pounding in fear, and she knew that if she once took her eyes off her objective she would lose her nerve altogether. Her mind raced like a word processor experimenting with phrases and sentences, trying to find a combination appropriate to begin with. She had no way of speeding up the process and was preoccupied instead by wetness under her arms.

Just then the "African" came out of what was probably the kitchen. Seeing her, he smiled and started to speak, but he, too, was almost immediately frozen by the chill in the room. Fritz finally broke it. "I see you survived," he said flatly.

There was hint of regret in the subtext she was sure, but it was a start. *No turning back now,* she thought.

She heard herself stutter, "Yes. Yes. Yes." That variation in line readings went on for what seemed like an eternity before her word processor supplied her with the meager attempt at conversation. "Yes, Klaus says I'm going to be quite a climber." She smiled. There was only more, dense silence. Fritz looked at her cream satin blouse and, recognizing it from that other night, said,

"I see some things don't change."

That did it. The word processor clicked off. Her mind cleared. Her heart stopped pounding, and she began what she had come to say. "Fritz, that's enough. I know you don't like me..." and, seeing that the "African" was about to interrupt, she waved him away, saying, "Please, let me finish." Then, turning to Fritz and Ursula, she continued, calmly. "That doesn't matter. What does matter is that you're here on this mountain for a reason. I don't know what it is—for either of you—but I believe it's important to you. I don't know anything about you. I will never ask, if you don't want me to know. You have my word. But likewise, I'm here for a reason. I didn't know that when I arrived, but I surely do now. And it's important to me to be here. You couldn't know that. You don't know me. But it is important. And I will say this. That what you feel you need to know, I will tell you."

"Why?" Ursula asked, with no particular edge of antagonism.

"Because wherever we may have come from, for whatever reasons, we are here now. Our paths have crossed. I know we're different. I know you don't approve of me, Fritz. I don't know why. I can guess. I don't know anything about you. If I did maybe I wouldn't approve of you either. I don't know. But what I want to say is that I can make space for you. I ask that you do the same for me." She had spoken sincerely, apparently, for there was a noticeable relaxation of tension in the room.

Or is that just my perception? she wondered.

Fritz looked to Ursula, who had never taken her eyes off Grace during the whole scene. She was studying her, looking for something, and was apparently satisfied, because she signaled to Fritz with her eyes and a nod of her head. It was almost as if she were giving him permission, and this role-reversal confused Grace momentarily.

Then Fritz asked, "Why did you come here?"

"To finish what was unfinished. I was afraid, but I had to come." Then she smiled slightly and added, "I didn't want tonight's music to be like last time."

Throughout it all the "African" had remained still and silent, but at this admission, he broke into a grin, almost leaped to her, and clapped her soundly on her shoulder. "All right," he purred, caressing those words as if they alone could express his approval of the breakthrough. His gesture gave her courage.

"And something else," Grace added, with a need to confess.

"What?" This time Ursula spoke.

"I don't know any way to finesse this, so I'll just risk it. I was hoping that…" She paused to wet her lips. "That, if we made peace, you might tell me about Klaus."

"Ooh, man," the African whistled through pursed lips. "Lady, that's a delicate question, don't you know." His voice tripped lightly and rapidly over each syllable.

"I'm sorry. I shouldn't have asked like that, but I know so little. I thought perhaps you could share." Seeing that they did not seem hostile, she continued. "He told me he wrote songs."

"Aye, that he did—a long time ago."

"I thought, since you all play, that you might have all been together then."

"No, Lady, no." The African took over. "Just me and Klaus. Fritz and Ursula are latecomers. And Reuben, too."

Again Fritz looked to Ursula for a moment, and then spoke. "Klaus managed a group called the New Searchers in Wales. Ever hear of them?"

"My God, yes. They were a big act in the '60s. I never listened to their music that much, but my first roommate played their albums often. She liked Jerry and the Pacemakers, all those people."

"Well, Klaus wrote their songs and managed them for a while," he offered.

Turning to the African, she asked, "Were you with them then?"

"Yes." At that point, he signaled by his watch that they were late, and started out the door. Fritz and Ursula grabbed sweaters and followed, motioning Grace out ahead.

She ran a few steps to stop the African. "I'm not trying to pry. I believe Klaus trusts me, but it's such a mystery. If I could at least know how you know each other, perhaps I could understand. Klaus may have told you that we met on a balcony."

They all nodded, so she continued, now almost in tears. "Well, it seems to have been a terribly important moment in his life. He says that it changed him, but the whole event is a mystery to me. I hoped that if you knew him then that you could help me. I need to understand, and I know so little."

It was Ursula who, with a flick of the eyes, again gave the cue. Fritz spoke first. "I can't tell you about Klaus, Grace. His facts you should hear from him." Seeing the sadness in her eyes as she nodded her head in mute resignation, he must have felt some need to communicate more. Guilt? Pity? Respect? She would probably never know. Maybe he didn't even know. But what he did stunned her. He said, "I can tell you mine though. Let's walk."

As they all walked carefully along the ridge path, stopping more often than normal to observe the show of colors of the sunset, Fritz looked at her several times, and then began to explain his presence on the mountain. She listened.

"I'm American. Or was American. An attorney, practicing criminal defense in San Francisco. I loved the Law, and I chose that because I wanted to commit my life to the preservation of the individual's rights within our court system—to provide Due Process and Justice to anyone, regardless of color or income."

He paused a moment and spat unexpectedly on the ground. That made Grace momentarily nervous, but he continued. "That proved to be difficult. But I was good. I wanted to be the best. And I *believed* in the American Judicial System. It is beautiful. At the core, in its concept, the system is pure. It can protect both the individual and the whole as well. And it is—and this always moved me—blind. It knows no color, no religion, no age, no money."

He spoke eloquently, and for an instant she could envision him self-assured, with his hair trimmed, persuading a jury. The hollow sadness of his voice undermined that image, however, as he continued. "It's in the application of the system, however, that the fuck-ups occur—human screw-ups, ignorance, prejudice. An inept lawyer virtually assures a man a place in a cell block. Being black, or poor, or stupid means probably an inept lawyer. To be poor meant to go to jail. I didn't think it was right. I wanted an accused's wealth or race to not matter. And I wanted judges to be forced to be responsible only to Justice. I fought the battles. I think I made things better." Then he laughed, and that irony that she had heard in his voice when he sang before was evident again. "I acquired quite a reputation."

"What happened?" she asked timidly, still feeling and judging like an outsider.

"In 1973, I was accused of malpractice."

"Did you win?"

"No. My client had bombed a U.S. Army Center on Bank Street. She was caught at the scene. She was guilty, and I counseled her to plead guilty—to take responsibility for what she had done. After all, she'd done it to make a statement."

He seemed tense now, but he continued. "I *believed* in the idea of equal justice under the law. She had done it. She knew what she was doing, and why she felt compelled to do it. She chose to do it anyway." He seemed to expect a response, but Grace didn't know what to say. "Anyway," he continued, "I advised her as I would have advised any other client—even if she'd been black and poor. She'd done it. I told her to pay the price, that there didn't seem to be any mitigating circumstances in the eyes of the Law. So, I advised her to plead guilty and hope the court would be lenient. She did, and was sentenced to three to five years."

"And you?"

"Six months later, she recanted her plea. Her family hired a new lawyer, and I was charged with malpractice—for encouraging a guilty person to plead guilty. A later court ruled that, in fact, I was inept and that she had been denied Due Process. I didn't try to get poor blacks off, regardless of the offense. I just tried to insure Justice for them. And I didn't want all wealthy whites to go to jail either. It wasn't a matter of color for me. It was purely a matter of consistent application of the principles. Do you understand?" he asked—more to find out if she believed him. She said that she did.

"I believed in Justice *only!* I wasn't really interested in political causes. But Justice doesn't mean getting a guilty person off, does it?"

This last question was directed to Ursula, who focused her eyes directly on the ground, standing motionless. Grace felt waves of confusion around Fritz. She saw clearly now that he had had a vision. It had been shattered, and he was still piecing it together. And now, for the first time, she had an intimation of what Klaus meant when he had told her they were all wounded. She no longer resented Fritz—nor feared him. He was merely his own defense attorney now. She reached out and touched his arm and said, "Thank you."

That seemed to bring him back momentarily, and recovering his more formidable presence, he said, "Well, I asked myself what was the point? And I quit. A malaise seemed to follow me everywhere for months, always reminding me that I had been played for a sucker. Nothing I believed in was what I thought it was. So, I came to Brunnen to ski, met Klaus near Morschach, and the malaise somehow disappeared. I never left."

"Why not?" she asked.

"It may still be down there waiting."

"I was released from prison in 1974 and came here shortly after," Ursula spontaneously interjected, briefly looking up to meet Grace's eyes to see if she understood. She did, or thought she did. Seeing the confusion in her eyes, Ursula anticipated her by saying, "The answer to that question is yes. I was Fritz's client. My parents encouraged me to travel after my release. I was paroled early for good behavior." Then she added as an afterthought, "What a joke. I'd been traveling all my life. Only they wouldn't see. To this day, they still can't accept the fact that I was underground from nineteen 'til the time of my arrest."

The realization that Ursula might have been part of the Weather Underground doused Grace like ice water, causing an emotional chill to race up and down her spine. She was face to face with what she had defined as the enemy when she had stared at the rubble of the bombed Math Research Center at Madison. She stood opposite all that she had opposed in the past, and all she could think of was what a proper joke that was. Then she thought perhaps she had misheard. After all, she liked Ursula. *And she's so frail,* she thought. Grace said nothing, however, swallowing hard instead.

"So I traveled. Looking. Only it was all gone by then. It had been a labor of love. We wanted peace—world peace—and an end to an unjust slaughter. Even if it took revolution to de-corrupt a government, it would be a beginning." She laughed, her voice almost rasping. "I even had the opportunity to be a martyr to my cause. But I fucked that up. I copped a plea. Instead of securing the forum of a trial to expose our cause—to generate headlines daily for the SDS—I was afraid of jail, deep down, so I copped a plea. And that wasn't all. I was still scared even after I was sentenced. So I recanted. I told myself it was because I'd been conned by my lawyer, told myself that I would make restitution to my comrades by going to trial. But I *knew,* you see. It was just my own gutlessness. They had said they'd see me at the barricades—we all pledged that—and I had failed them. Fuck."

Ursula stopped now, removed her glasses and rubbed her eyes before continuing. "But by then it was over. Do you know, Grace, that even after Watergate no one really cared? They lost it somewhere. I was in jail, and they lost it. I got out to rejoin them once the country could clearly see the vile forces that had been governing. Surely, I thought, everyone would understand now. They would listen to our voices now!

- 196 -

We wouldn't even need violence to shake them to consciousness. But it was gone. Everyone had gone underground—into himself. And then they began to pop up here and there—dressed in grown-up suits, ready to rejoin the System. Bullshit!"

The cold fire of anger in Ursula's eyes told Grace that her self-hatred was still consuming her. Disillusionment burned iron, leaving anemia in its wake. She tried to imagine what Ursula must have looked like then—before her paling.

But Ursula continued. "I came to Switzerland and was stranded in Brunnen waiting for the Gotthard Pass to open up. I ran into Fritz. It's funny, isn't it—to come that far? I felt I owed him an apology. I stayed."

"To apologize?" Grace asked.

"No. To alter the only world left over which I had any influence—myself."

"And you're married?" They nodded. Then they all laughed, as only those who have awakened to find themselves steeped in irony can laugh.

"And you?" she asked, turning to the African. He jumped up from his favorite squatting position, dusting off his pants with the fury of one who is trying to brush off hot embers.

"Me? Ohhhhhhh, lady," he began, with an *oh* that descended a scale. "My story's a simple one, you know. These two are the crazy ones here!" He laughed and winked his good eye, his voice lilting across the words like a West Indian, or perhaps just an Indian. She did not know dialects that well, and despite his nickname, Grace would have guessed him to be from Bombay. He smiled constantly—all words were sent out from behind those gleaming teeth, which created the illusion of a permanent grin.

"I'm just a poor musician. Emigrated from Rhodesia to Wales in '63 and joined up with a band. A few good lads. I'm a good drummer, don't you know?" He winked again and zealously pantomimed a snare roll and cymbals, then confided as if for her ears only. "Tribal, you know?"

Grace liked this man, frenetic energy and all. He was so guileless, so full of joy and abiding tolerance.

"Is that where you met Klaus?"

"Ohhhhh yes, lady," he cooed, protracting the *oh* this time as if it were an aria. "He was just writing songs for the lads at first. Then later, when he got out of knickers himself, he managed the group. That's when we hit big." Then he stopped.

"And?" she coaxed.

"And what, lady?"

"What happened?"

"Oh, I left the group." He laughed again. As he skipped forward a few steps, she sensed evasion. He must have known she was on to him, for he turned, motioning for her to join him, and then added, "Had to," he said, never relaxing his broad grin.

"Is that why you came here?"

"Oh, no, lady, I came here to help a friend, don't you know?"

"When?"

"1970. After the accident."

"What accident?"

"For that, dear lady, you must ask Klaus," he quipped, and bolted on ahead. Fritz and Ursula hesitated an awkward moment and then, apparently deciding there was nothing more to be said, also walked on. Grace followed.

After all, she reassured herself, as she watched the trio hurry to their music, *they have told me what they could. True, each abbreviated— almost as if the one incident defined each of their lives,* she thought. She wondered whether each of us could distill the sum of our life's experiences into one incident that encompassed or altered it all?

Then, too, she reminded herself, *further discussion will surely lead to confrontation.* No doubt she was not what they had once respected in their youth, but each had seemed prepared, if not to understand, at least to accept. It was a start.

But once again the mystery recycled to Klaus. She hoped he would tell her in his own time, for she knew now that was the only way to unlock the secret. She was powerless to unravel it any other way.

She joined the jam session. A short time later, she joined in one of the songs, timidly at first—fearful of her voice's accuracy of pitch.

Then, as the music of a spiritual ballad from her college days embraced her, too, Klaus smiled and turned the second verse over to her. Lyrics long forgotten, returned. It was easy.

October arrived with a decisive warning of the cold to come. Ample fires were required nightly to warm the cabin. But the days were glorious, possessing a wonderful contradiction of sun's warmth cutting the crisp chill of Nature. Today everything crackled—logs burning, dried leaves falling underfoot, the earth in the early morning frost, nuts harvested and stored for winter, and the wind charging unobstructed across the ridge, testing the strength of perennial shrubs and trees.

The town below was all but deserted. Local residents closed their summer tourist businesses and settled in for their months of holiday. Some left altogether for milder climates, only to return with the geese. All others began to stock up for the skiers whose search for diamond slopes would begin in November.

For Grace, the brisk health of autumn exhilarated her. She had learned to live with Klaus's mystery and to trust that, whatever his reasons were for withholding his past life from her, they must be compelling and were to be respected. She hadn't forgotten her old chemistry lesson. Some things do stick. Her exhilaration was complicated somewhat by occasional, mild depressions. These recurrences frustrated her, but, in contrast to the past sensations of darkness and fear of the dark, she was comforted by the knowledge at least of *what* it was she feared— the Future, that once shimmering dream. She could understand her paralysis now, even if she still remained paralyzed.

Standing on the ridge spot where she had sat that first day so many light years ago, she tried to count how long she'd been on the mountain. She had no desire to go down below. True, she told herself, the village was beautiful below, but small. The emerald–colored lake was placid, but contained. Here, above it all, she could see so clearly that she didn't care to go below and risk losing her perspective.

The longer she stayed here, the less obligation she felt to anyone. She'd received a few letters from parents and friends, and had started to answer. Except for the confusion and sadness in her Mutti's letters, Grace felt no regrets.

She was letting go, and each of the characters in her life seemed to accept that. She felt much lighter now than she had upon her arrival five months earlier, but she felt more distant—at times almost remote—as if there were two worlds, one within the other. She felt as if she were now a permanent inhabitant of the innermost one. She could barely remember the other. It was difficult now to remember the color of gray-blue she'd so carefully selected for her living room. It had been a bold choice, she remembered, one which her friends felt wouldn't work. But it had, and her living room had become a showplace.

She could remember her mother's round, bright face but could no longer hear her voice. She could remember the shape of Keith's body, but not his face. To her surprise, she had forgotten his address. Robert? She remembered Robert. At least she remembered his laugh, but not how he felt. She looked down at her thighs—visible in shorts worn now on one of those last days before the winter wools would replace shorts—and wondered if those little whitish dents were cellulite. *Subtle shifts of the breasts and subtle indentations on thighs and bottom are the calling cards of age.* She wondered whether Klaus noticed—or cared.

Returning slowly in the late afternoon's dusk, she found the letter on the table. Perhaps Fritz had brought it while she was out. Klaus was not below. He was not out back, nor on the ridge. He must have seen it, too.

The familiar handwriting looked strained somehow. *It's just my imagination,* she told herself. *Or perhaps it is I who am strained.* A surge of stage fright swept up and down her body before departing. She sat on the bed and read it. The letter was mercifully brief.

"Dearest Grace,

Thank you for sending me your address, so that I could write without worrying about losing you in the mail. I spoke to your parents yesterday and promised them I would write to you. Or call. But then, of course, I realized you have no phone.

"I love you, Grace. I miss you terribly. I try daily to understand why you've left. And I ask myself what it was that I did or said to force so violent a reaction. And I come up empty.

"Searching my heart, though, I feel I must speak my mind and tell you what I want. Although I love you dearly, more than anyone in my life, I will not wait forever. You are obviously working through something very important to you. I admire your convictions. But I, too, have reached a fork in the road. It is time for me to make a choice and go forward—if not with you, then hopefully with someone else. I've spent enough of my life avoiding life. I'm ready now to face it.

"Please understand that this is said without anger. It is not my intent to serve you ultimatums. I've always hated them and know you, too, would resist any such manipulation. But you should know my honest feelings and understand the possible consequences of your actions. After all, you've always known how much I fear being left.

Robert"

"PS: Your house is fine. The geraniums are just blossoming. Please answer me."

She must have been sitting on the bed for several hours. It was long dark, and the muscles in her legs were cramped from sitting cross-legged. Since there was barely a moon tonight, the room was in near-total darkness. Only a slim, silver shaft pierced the window pane, cutting a narrow path to the foot of the bed, there ending its illumination. She rose, tentatively stretching the tightened inner thighs, crossing to light the lantern and start her evening fire. In the distance she heard the faint, deep, plaintive sounds of a flute. It seemed to speak for all three of them.

She answered Robert. Perhaps she would have written soon in any case. She preferred to think she would have. Whatever, the answer was clear to her now.

"Dearest Robert,

Forgive my not writing sooner. You deserve better. But only now am I seeing clearly enough to know just what to say to you. So here goes, my dear friend. First, let me say that although I have some regrets in doing so, I am sending my attorney authorization to sell my house. It has taken me a long time I know—painful for you in its uncertainty—to decide upon the future. But I am very clearly not ready to return to the house. I may never be. And it seems pointless to hold onto it. So it will be sold.

"Now, the difficult part. This means that I am not ready to return to America yet. I understand completely your feelings and your need to continue your life. I'm honored that you have remained my faithful lover and supporter as long as you have. But you must live your life, Robert. You deserve the best.

"If I were able to return, it would be different I know. But I cannot return. What I can do, though, is finally tell you why. I am at least prepared now to share with you my transformation, my state of mind—or whatever you choose to call it.

"This last year, Robert—not because of you, but probably because of my age and the changes in my life—I have been forced to really examine who I am and where I'm going, and *what* it all means. You may ask why I didn't ask those questions ten years ago. And that's precisely the problem. Because I did not, I'm a stranger in my own time now. I feel like an outcast from my own generation. My God, I'm just *now* reading John Cheever!

"I think I was born going on thirty—always so mature, such a perfect little lady, so wise for my years, so free of the anxieties and heartaches that afflicted my peers. I avoided rebellion responsibly and prepared to settle comfortably into middle age. Only now, I see the dreadful trap I stepped into. The price for blithely escaping the process of growing up is premature age. And I feel I'm too young to settle for middle age. I'm no more ready for security, no risk, or predictable family commitments than if I were seventeen again.

"And, in seeing this, I see also that I cannot work in a field just for money—where there's no humanity, no treatment of individuals as people, but rather as lighting equipment to be turned on and off at will until they burn out. I know now that I truly love actors, and me among them. My eyes fill with tears as I think of the strength I have seen in what I regard now as one of the world's most underestimated classes of people. Time and time again, like you, I have seen friends get up when knocked down. And with hope—somehow surviving all doubts and abuse—as if that were all part of the job. All hoping to give a little piece of joy to someone else. All bravely trying to conceal their fear of the unknown and, worse yet, of the unspeakable possibility that Chance might just not smile on them after all, and thereby pass them by.

"You asked if I were angry at anything you had said or done. My love, nothing could be further from the truth. I love and admire your insight and your determination to vanquish your own demons, and to fit into the entertainment industry. It is not you I am rejecting but rather the world you live in that I can no longer participate in. I have fought my last battle in my personal War of Honor. Curiously, I'm sure I'm right for me. I feel no guilt about not providing a model for others to follow. I feel no shame in quitting. If this that I'm experiencing is defeat, it is not so difficult to take as I had imagined. After all, my love, I gave it my best shot. To be one's best for even one moment is all one can hope for, right?

"My best is not what I had hoped for. It is, however, what it is. This is what I have learned here. I do not, however, have a clue what to do with this insight. As I said, the future is a mystery. And you know how I have trouble with mysteries! But I'm trying. And every day I feel stronger.

"What I want to tell you is that I loved you dearly. And I know my love was good for you. I still love you, you monkey. I probably always will. But I cannot be with you. I have met someone here who is helping me to see clearly. I cannot say I love him. I do not know how I feel. But he is patient with me, and I am learning from him. Enough to stay away, you ask? Who knows? Perhaps. So, go your own way. Be happy. And have no regrets. Grace"

Just as she was sealing the envelope, a draft of air sucked at the roaring flames, causing them to sputter for a moment.

"Klaus?" she asked. There was no answer, and she turned then to the door. The flickering fire caused his face to alternate between shadow and illumination, and the reddish glow seemed to intensify his presence in the doorway.

His eyes were questioning, like one who knows the answer but fears to hear it. His chest heaved quickly as he asked, "Are you going?" and then it was suspended motionless as she softly answered, "No." He exhaled an aching moan as he closed his eyes, leaning against the door. She ran into his arms, feeling him tremble as he received her. He kissed her hair possessively and said, "It's time."

CHAPTER ELEVEN

❧❦❧

"You told me I didn't know what it was like to believe and then have it disappear," Klaus began.

She winced, remembering a less charitable conversation a few weeks earlier, one she hoped he'd forgotten or overlooked. Apparently he had not. She kissed him, taking his head in her hands as they lay in bed. "I didn't mean it. Truth is I think I've always sensed a giant ache in you. It's in your voice, if I really listen."

He laughed a bitter, ironic laugh, and then confessed, "I'm not who I appear to be."

"Oh? Who are you then, really?"

But Klaus only smiled and said, "That I can't tell you." Before she could ask why, he added, "But you'll know someday."

"Promise?" she teased, hoping her smile concealed her disappointment.

"I promise."

"Okay." She yielded with some evident frustration—a fact she knew he took note of.

"Thank you."

Then he told her of having gone to Oxford to study comparative religions, and of having spent his sixteenth birthday gift from his parents touring West England and Wales.

"You went to Oxford at sixteen?" she asked, barely concealing her amazement.

"Yes. Anyway," he pushed the story along, "I fell in with a group of musicians in Wales."

"The New Searchers?"

"Yes." He hesitated, looking puzzled. "How did you know?"

"Fritz told me."

"Oh." She saw his mind calculating behind those blue eyes, apparently satisfied for the moment. "Well, I liked their music. It was different—economical, and controversial. Kids danced and moved, you know? Well, we were talking, and I said I'd like to try a lyric for them. It's funny. I think they were just humoring me at first. But I did it anyway. They loved it, and I started writing songs for them. They were nice guys, but naïve, you know. As things turned out, I ended up their manager."

"Had you ever done that before?"

"Mein Gott, nein. Nobody had. All we knew was that we liked your Elvis Presley. We all wanted in. I felt the world was changing and that the combined powers of poetry and music would be the instruments of change—poetry that distills life to the truth, music that explodes viscerally. And I began—not so much to reach the mind or the heart—but rather the viscera, and thereby the essence of the human condition. It was exciting. So we ran the circuit, becoming friends with a couple of guys from Liverpool." He stopped for a moment and laughed once.

"What?"

"I was just thinking how blind we all were then. But their new manager, Brian, was breaking through for them. They were on the verge. The rest you probably know."

For a moment she thought he must be kidding her. Then she remembered their conversation about John and his psychedelic car. "You're talking about the Beatles, aren't you?"

"Yes." He seemed surprised. "I thought you knew."

"No."

"We were friends." At this point, Grace sat up, something inside telling her she must pay very close attention to this.

"Go on," she encouraged.

"Well, they became, what is it you Americans call it? Superstars?"

"Uh huh."

"And our band did well—especially in England. Germany, too, most of Europe in fact. But never in America." He paused for a moment, seemed to be looking at something, then shook it off, whatever it was, and continued. "In London, we picked up a young drummer, a Rhodesian. I'll never forget. He had the fastest hands and feet I'd ever seen. He could play anything. After a couple of years, we had a prominent London booking agent. We were told he was the best."

"When was this?" she interrupted.

"1967. I was pretty useless by that time as a manager. We had become a fairly big business, and with the phenomenal success of the Beatles by then, London was hot to export any British talent available. The world was buying."

"I remember."

There was not a trace of wistfulness in Klaus's voice as he continued. "So I took a hiatus. The excessive money was beginning to confuse me."

"Why?"

"Power. That's all. We had begun with a desire to speak to our generation, to use our minds, our voices to reach them—to be the vanguard." At that, they both laughed in ironic recognition. He continued. "And the money seemed to obscure that purpose." He spoke as if this were still a discovery for him. "I was writing songs for money now, Grace. A lot of money. Then John bought that carriage, and for the first time I smelled hypocrisy. I could smell the cruel power of greed. I began to wonder whether I were helping or using, and I felt trapped—caged by my own vision. You see, there's a peculiar love-hate relationship between rock stars and their fans, Grace. The love is so great that they will tear you apart to get near you. More frighteningly, to get you to do what they want. Capricious." He seemed to caress that judgment. "What's worse though, they will tear each other apart to get to you. John felt a responsibility for that."

"I don't understand."

"There were casualties at one Beatles concert. You know the story—kids smoking pot, caught up in the territorial imperative."

"What?" she asked.

"Their belief in their divine right to their space before their idol. Any intruder will be fought. Anyway, fighting broke out at one gig, and some kids were injured in the press of the mob. John felt responsible. Worse, he was disillusioned by the realization that few are really capable of respect for their brothers. Most just selfishly push for more. I had a lot of trouble with this, too. I was preaching one thing in my songs, yet somehow encouraging them to do something else. You can't have peace on earth punching the next guy out so that you can get close enough to hear me talk about brotherhood." He suddenly flinched, as if he'd had a muscle spasm in his chest.

"Are you all right?"

"Yes, yes, I'm fine."

"It's funny, Klaus, but I never went to a big rock concert…never wanted to. I just never wanted to be around those people. Lying in the grass, smoking dope, pushing and shoving. There was nothing for me there. I sensed that hypocrisy, too, and I can understand your disillusionment."

"Can you?" he asked quietly, looking at her for a long moment. "Be careful of patronization, Grace." But before she could collect her thoughts enough to grasp why he seemed to disapprove of what she thought was a compatible reaction to that generation, he said, "I can't blame my peers for preferring to climb trees in order to listen to music, to sit on trash bins or astride fences, or to lie stoned in the grass in the warm sun. There was war, Grace. Whether they felt there were forces greater than them acting on them, which were controlling their fate, or—for those who believed in duty and country—whether they felt an *obligation* to forces greater than themselves, there was an acute awareness that this might be the last time they could be happy. The last chance to lie in the sun as a golden youth, to drink wine with friends, to make love to a girl, and listen to music written about, and played to, them as equals—and not as subordinates who would be used later as cannon fodder. We did not control them. We let them be. We did not patronize. We let them have their last idyllic, glowing, imperfect moments in the sun. And they loved us, and they hated us. And I imagine, if I'm truly honest with myself, I loved—and hated—them."

Grace could not speak. In the past, she might have felt defensive, as if he had been chastising her, but she didn't feel that now. *Thank God,* she told herself. He was sharing. He knew something she didn't, and at that instant, she had the self-esteem to take his gift. She passed a silent kiss on her fingertips from her lips to his and said only, "What happened?"

"I came to Brunnen to rest for a few days and think." He winked. "And I met this plumpish girl with magnificent eyes on a balcony, muttering something about 'soul place' and 'not wanting to leave.'" He reached for her hand. "She turned me to stone that day. But she was wrong. She left. I stayed and bought a hotel. But I did continue writing. Somehow I felt better just being here. I told myself that, as long as I was here writing the most topical lyrics I could, I was performing some kind of service for my people. Let my partners take the complicated adulation of the fans, the cars, the determined groupies, the accouterments, if you will. I would still have my integrity, I told myself. And it worked. I assuaged my conscience successfully for three years—until the riot."

"What riot?"

He seemed not to hear. "The 'African' prefers to call it 'the accident,' but I don't view it as an accident. Not fate. This was premeditated—a collision course created by the Business." He tightened his grasp of her hand and said "business" almost as if it tasted bilious. Klaus seemed far away now. He ran his hands through his hair several times.

Whatever it is, he is still wrestling this ghost, she thought. She wondered for a moment if any one of us ever really rids ourselves of ghosts. Then he laughed—twice—and returned to her.

"There were race demonstrations in London, in sympathy with your riots in Detroit. The white backlash was startling, however. Empires die hard, Grace. Our band was the only successful group in the country with a black musician, our drummer. The facts are confusing, but a riot erupted at a concert in protest to one of our satires—a light number about a roaring drunk priest who haunts his hypocritical parishioners. That's the irony. It was meant to make them laugh at tyranny. When it was over, Banu—that's his given name—had been cut below his right eye, down his cheek, the full length of his face, and his right wrist was broken. It's never been the same. And you've seen his face."

"Yes." She knew there was nothing she could say to assuage his disillusionment, so she encouraged him to continue by asking, "So the band went on without him?"

"Yes, with a temporary drummer. Banu's wrist healed. He exercised like hell. His eye…it healed. But by this time our booking agent decided he shouldn't return."

"Why?"

"Business, Grace. Pure business. The band was becoming a 'major,' showing signs of making it over the top. He felt we couldn't risk further riots or sustain any cancellations of bookings. If the owners feared a riot, they might back out of their contracts, and we wouldn't get the exposure we needed. After all, we were British, needing white support. Banu was a liability. The other three decided they had to split up the group and go on without him."

"And you?"

"I was in Switzerland. I yielded. He was the best man I knew, Grace, the only truly good, genuine man. He just wanted to play music. He made me smile just watching him play."

"He still is that man, Klaus."

He looked at her, wrinkled his brow, and then rubbed his hand across his forehead as if to erase the pain. "Thank you," he said in apology. "That's my wound talking. A man who has sacrificed his belief in human rights to peddle his songs can be moribund sometimes, Grace. Anyway, trying to save myself, I severed connection with the group. Then I came up here. Banu heard I'd freaked out and came to help me. But then, they started coming every month."

"What?" she asked, having no idea what he was talking about.

"The perpetual proof of my hypocrisy."

"What?" she pressed again.

"Royalties." For a moment, there was silence. "I had resigned from the crime, depositing myself up here to do penance, but it was not to be an easy penance. My past achievements were to be honored, regularly. You see, people liked my songs. I poked fun. Yes, I provoked. But I also wrote about the human spirit, about freedom, about change, about love. And even after the group disbanded, musicians played my songs. But I was too ill then, and I saw it only as a constant testimony to my crime. Banu tried to reassure me. But eventually I won. I converted the hotel to a sanitarium for cripples—literal and figurative—the literal down below, the figurative up here."

"And just what are figurative cripples?" she challenged.

"You and me, love—the cripples of disillusionment. And Fritz, Ursula, Reuben and his drugs, and eventually Banu holding still to his belief that love and talent were enough. He has his own wound to heal. Once I got past mine, he had time for himself."

Grace didn't quite know how she felt. Thoughts were slow in coming. At last she knew. The mystery was over now. And she knew why, for years, she had been drawn to this place, like a poor pilgrim to its mountain cathedral. Their paths were meant to converge. Klaus looked exhausted, but relieved, as if the story were one he had long wanted to confide. She felt so very close to him that her heart hurt.

"What happened to your friends, the New Searchers?" she asked finally.

"They were famous for a while, but they were eclipsed by the Beatles. Not long after, their agent went into Real Estate in South Africa and they disbanded."

She looked up quietly, searching his face for any clue that he was joking, as the touch of irony seemed too perfect to be true. But he was not, and that struck her as comical She began to giggle.

"South Africa?"

"Ja, Ja." His lips quivered, too.

And then they both laughed, the kind of laugh that comes from within, from a sudden awareness when irony meets absurdity. For the next several minutes, it came in waves. Finally, as they both had spent themselves and were reclining, Klaus sighed deeply, becoming serious once again.

"The money got to them, too, you know?"

"Who?"

"The Beatles." Neither said anything for a while, and finally Klaus added, "Except Johnny. He's all right now." Then, almost as if to reassure himself, he added, "I think. It took him a while, but he's found himself and the meaning of his life. He was here for a time."

"Here on the mountain?"

"Yes, about four years ago. We played a little music together, reminisced about politics, the times of change, our fevered visions, our present inertia. He said he didn't know how he could go forward since he didn't know where he was. Sound familiar?"

Grace groaned.

"We talked of self-fulfillment and the peace that follows. He left looking for it. I heard he even had to get into Primal Scream. But I think he's all right now. He's listening to his own drummer now. He's made it."

"Have you?"

Any hesitation was negligible. "I think so. At least I'm in the home stretch anyway. I know now that my songs won't change the world. Protesting won't. Riots won't. My best self may, if I can attain that state. If I live a life of today, loving what is, and not what might have been, I will have a chance to create tomorrow—a tomorrow of peace with what is, of respect for what will be, and of appreciation of what has been. You see, if I can create an environment for myself of love, generosity, compassion, and awareness, then those very things will be nurtured and grow here, and will flourish almost exponentially. That, and only that, can create what I dreamed of so many years ago. I firmly believe that. The key is here on the mountain. Below, it gets confused and muddied. You see, Grace, here I clearly see that I cannot change the future. I can only create today. Let it create the future."

"I just wonder which one of us is the dreamer now," she mused. But before thistly doubt could take root, she kissed him, caressing his forehead and heart until he fell asleep.

Exactly when it was she had accepted her "Outpatient Clinic" was unclear to her. Sitting here now in her pink silk shirt, jeans, and mauve mohair sweater recently mailed by her mother, she looked around the room of her self-sufficiency and smiled as her eyes came to the dressing table Klaus had built for her. It had a large, rectangular, hand-carved wooden frame. The drawers in the small table were lined with cloth to protect her laces and satins—a much appreciated gesture from Klaus. It had been his way of saying that he was accepting her as she was, and that there was nothing fundamentally irreconcilable between her feminine preferences in clothes and the rustic, self-sufficient environment he had carved out for himself.

In fact, she thought, *he seems to enjoy my pastels and delicate fabrics, seems proud that his environs could embrace even these. Not unlike a flower blooming in a desert garden...* so she prided herself.

The three short blasts of the alpine horn, the pause, and the repetition of the three blasts were a signal from Fritz to them that a visitor was approaching. Klaus didn't seem to be around, so she went to the door to see who was looking for him.

The sight of her parents coming toward her, gingerly escorted along the hardening path by Fritz, struck terror in her for a moment. She could feel the color flee—first from her face, dissolving in a downward retreat to the floor—and she felt a rush of panic. Hiding wouldn't work. After all, where could she retreat to? Besides, there was no time. Before she could even get her thoughts together they were there.

Grace greeted them and told them she was surprised to see them. Her father said she should be. She thanked Fritz for delivering them safely, looked at him for reassurance, but saw him shrug instead, politely excusing himself. Just then Klaus climbed up the ladder from below asking whom the horn had signaled. He was wearing only jeans and had not combed his hair yet. Grace saw only his bare chest as she introduced him to her Mutti and Vati, as she called them—a carryback to her college years when she studied German and liked the German endearing form for mom and dad. Her Mutti looked like a frightened rabbit at this particular moment, her eyes darting back and forth from Vati to Grace to Klaus, as if she were about to bolt for cover. Her father was, as usual, unflappable and coldly courteous. She could just imagine what was going on behind those gray eyes. Long ago, she had discovered that her father's eyes, which were normally pale blue, became more and more gray in direct proportion to the degree of his anger. Today they were pale gray. But he was too skilled a concealer to let it show beyond the eyes. Klaus of course knew it all though. As if he were taking cues from this prepossessing man, he grabbed a shirt, repeated his pleasure in meeting them, and said he was going berrying, mumbling something about the last of the crop before winter. Then he was gone.

A fine conspirator he would make, she thought. *Abandoning me in the thick of things!* She told herself she would address that issue with him later, presuming of course that she survived this.

Right then, however, her mother sat down after some difficulty in locating what seemed like a prescribed sitting area. The large, free-form, all-purpose room confused her, and her darting eyes exposed someone perpetually afraid, who didn't know what to expect, and who was therefore looking for familiar surroundings. Her full, pink face, however, was adorably cherubic, as it always had been. She settled into a chair by the dining table, which she pulled into the room a bit, threw her hands up in the air beside her head and grinned, as she always had upon seeing her darling daughter. Grace thought her mother was more stooped, and, as they embraced, her round, soft Mutti held her tight and close for a long time. She was desperate for affection, Grace knew. She smiled as she looked at this aging woman who resembled a somewhat frightened fairy Godmother.

Her father, in contrast, had a decided look of disapproval on his face. *Or is it fear?* she suddenly asked herself. Grace sensed that he, too, wanted a long embrace. That familiar "harrumphing" cough, which sounded like a man coughing up his feelings, drew her attention. She gave him a cursory squeeze. It was all that she felt. His eyes flickered for a moment and then settled. There was a distance between them. *No point in denying it,* she told herself. Perhaps his disappointment in this was what caused him to take the offensive. *After all,* she reminded herself, *the fear of vulnerability breeds aggression, as if the offense could camouflage the fear.*

"Why didn't you notify me you were coming?" she asked, offering her dad a chair. He chose to stand instead and began pacing the room.

"You're ruining your life," he answered.

She said to herself, *This is how it's going to be is it?* It had begun.

Grace sat on the edge of the bed, realizing too late that it was unmade—certain that it afforded him enough evidence of her dissipation. But it was too late to move without drawing further attention to it.

Looking at her father, she saw that he was tall but stooped, and his neck had double folds of aging flesh falling vertically from under his chin down into his collar. *A skinny neck, rather like a gobbler's,* she thought. And like an aging dictator whose wobbly stance belies his once-formidable presence, he proceeded to conduct the disciplinary scene he had presided over so often in the past.

"I said nothing about your changing majors, young lady," he sputtered, pacing all the while. "You could have been a great surgeon, like your brother."

"He's an alcoholic, Dad," she interrupted.

"What the hell does that have to do with anything?" he fired back. "He's a great surgeon."

"Yes, he is. And paid his price for it."

"I don't know what you're talking about, and I don't want to get into that. Now I didn't say anything when you didn't have a baby with Keith. Your mother and I thought you needed the responsibility, isn't that right, Ruth?" He turned to his wife but continued before she could even focus her thoughts, much less speak. "But we said nothing."

"We didn't even say anything when you left your personnel manager's job and became an actress," he huffed.

"I thought you were proud of me," she challenged quietly.

"I was. I am. But acting is dangerous, hanging around with kooks, and now look!" He paused for a moment to harrumph and to catch his breath, perhaps to regroup. "I didn't say anything when you divorced.

You asked for our love and understanding, and we gave it. You seemed so certain about what you were doing that we thought you were okay."

Her mother sat silent, her eyes following him closely.

"But now here you are on some mountain, God knows where, selling your house and living with some...some..." he licked his lips, as if testing some unpleasant taste to identify it, "foreigner." Shaking his head from side to side and steadying himself by placing his hand against the fireplace, he pressed on. "Where did you go wrong? How did you lose your senses and...your values?" he demanded, waving his arms about, as if to encompass the room, offering it as proof of her folly. When he stopped, he was visibly shaken and crying, as he was prone to doing recently.

The silence was dense. The tension-packed molecules in the air could scarcely bump against one another, let alone move freely. "I don't know if you can understand," she said, hearing her voice bash against the intransigent molecules. Hoping the sound would carry, she passed the turning point. "But I'm happy here. I've found myself here."

"That's rubbish," he spat out and coughed again. "Just some psychological garbage you've picked up along the way." His voice was strong again, and then the reverberations commenced. You have a responsibility to live life, Grace, not hide from it."

Aha, the trump card—responsibility, she thought and smiled slightly.

He continued. "It was bad enough when you took up with an Irishman, but at least he was a nice man."

Her mother seemed to want to speak to this. All she uttered, however, was, "Clifton, I don't..." before he overrode, thereby causing her to stop mid-sentence, relegated to mumbling something indistinguishable to herself.

"But this, this...whatever his name is..."

"Klaus. She interceded dutifully.

"We know what he is. A hermit, for Christ's sake. We're lucky he's not a black man."

And then, almost as if on cue, the African bounded through the door, excitedly asking for Klaus, and then embarrassedly excusing his interruption. Grace introduced him to her parents and sent him to the woods. As he left, he turned to her Mutti and cooed in his mellifluous, lilting dialect, "Goodbye, beautiful lady." Her Mutti grinned. Whether she blushed, or was just flushed from her climb, was hard to tell, for Grace's Mutti always reacted well to her friends. If someone were friendly, she responded indiscriminately. If her mind harbored prejudice, her spirit surely did not. Her actions surpassed her thoughts. She loved. And for that Grace loved her dearly. For never standing up to Clifton, however, for always letting that burden fall to Grace, she was angry.

Too late for change now, though, she instructed herself.

Her father had been cool and had not taken his eyes off the scar below Banu's eye. The African undoubtedly had sensed it and had chosen wisely to escape. She knew she would have to apologize later. But before that, Clifton started up again, bellowing, "You see, Ruth, it's as I said. She's learned nothing from us. She's become a kook! I'm ashamed to say, she's not the daughter we created."

The essence of a turning point is that, once passed, there is no retreat. Everything after that moment is changed. The turning point closes the door on all that's gone before. Something in Grace recognized that the time had come. The time for silence, for private thoughts, had passed. She had to speak now, or forever remain silent. There would be repercussions, she knew. She had reached the turning point. It had come to this.

"You're wrong, Vati. I am what you created, just not what you dictated. The time has passed for me to try to please you anymore. I have to live for myself now, for what I want. And not just for what will avoid causing you pain or embarrassment. I'm sorry if I'm not what you wanted, but Vati, bear with me, and know that I love you. Enough to say this." She swallowed twice and took a deep breath, praying that the air molecules could support her heaviness. He looked wary; her mother looked truly frightened.

She began. "Vati, you only love those who agree with you. The price of your affection, from everyone, is agreement—total agreement. You have no tolerance for anything short of that. I'm not doing what you would do, so you disapprove. Anything outside the realm of your limited experience frightens you and therefore is condemned by you. You don't know about it, therefore it shouldn't be." He harrumphed, but did not move.

"Or I may be doing what you secretly desire to do and you're jealous."

"Ridiculous."

"Perhaps. But what I see—what I've heard all my life—is that if someone is not a parrot for your beliefs, he is stupid, mixed up, ruining his life. Let me tell you something, both of you. I nearly ruined my life trying to be everything you want me to be. I married a man who fit your ideas of the ideal husband. He fit mine, too. Only he wasn't. And it damned near killed him to try to play the role."

Like a snowball rolling, the truth was magnifying itself now. Long buried, it came up—fast, hard, and relentlessly driven by its own momentum. She saw their faces but nothing interfered with the rush of words.

"I went to a cloistered school and never knew the War was on. Perhaps the single most important event in our time, not just for my generation, but for our whole country, and I didn't even know it was on! I denied the feelings of my peers. I sat back and judged. And then wondered why I was isolated from them. I have never consciously hurt anyone—physically or emotionally—except my little girlfriend, Mary Jo, when I told her I hated her, even though I didn't. And I've never truly forgiven that lapse. She cried so. I could not get her to stop. We were never friends again.

"I have tried never to lie. I have never stolen. I have believed in the dignity of each person and hoped for a better world. I have done my part to make the world a wiser, more tolerant, hopeful place to live. I have attempted to give what wisdom and joy I possess back to others. And I have not asked for much money in return. I have never harmed another to get money. If you're ashamed of that, I'm sorry for you. If you feel you failed in your creation, again I'm sorry for you. I love you as parents, but I cannot surrender myself to your will. Ironically you gave me more courage than that." She stopped for a moment, almost out of breath in the wake of the avalanche.

"I would never have spoken, had you not come," she concluded serenely, "but it's best."

Her Vati's eyes were no longer even gray. They had paled to colorless and overflowed with tears as he blurted, "What did I ever do to that girl to make her talk to me like this?" and, motioning for Ruth to follow, said, "She doesn't care about anyone but herself. Not about us. I don't care if I never see her again. And you're not going to either, Ruth." Drawing himself up to his full 6'2" height, he left.

Her mother was flustered. Like a normally obedient dog who momentarily doesn't know quite who his master is, she stood suspended between the door and her daughter. One step toward one, and one toward the other. Her eyes, too, were rheumy.

"You have the right to see me if you want. But you must take the responsibility then, Mutti. Just once." Her mother's eyes told her she was afraid. Knowing the all-too-familiar consequences, she would never take that step. Grace knew it, and so did her mother.

"You're not ashamed of me, are you?" Grace asked.

"No. I'm just confused. I don't understand why you feel you must live here."

"Because this is my final destination, Mutti. Everything in my life led me here." Taking her hand, she caressed it and continued. "We go through life, Mutti, as through a storm. Most perish. But the lucky—and there are only a few who are—come to a place of peace and tranquility. There, everything is in perfect proportion to that around it—neither too large nor small, too strong nor weak. It affords a perfect perspective on the operation of the whole. Life and death are in perspective. Storms pass. I arrived at that place. I survived. And I cannot leave. I am once and finally free. Do you understand?" she asked, squeezing the hand she loved so dearly, searching desperately in her Mutti's eyes for a glimmer of comprehension.

"I don't know. I just don't know." Her father's commanding voice intruded through the closed door, ordering obedience of his wife. Ruth jumped a little and then said apologetically, "No."

Grace nodded acceptance as she thought of her father standing outside—too proud to return and listen, too vain to relinquish his principles, which were all he had left, too cold and alone to go to the station by himself, too afraid to go. Too lonely. And so he stood in the cold, and commanded his wife through heavy wooden doors.

Through that same door a few moments later, Grace heard him yelling at his wife as Fritz escorted them along the path. Something about "disloyalty," and her mother's cowed voice, were all she heard. Only then did she weep. It had been spoken, this non-retractable truth. She had hoped her illusive freedom would never demand this as its price. Right or wrong, the umbilical cord was severed, and it was a rather messy tying off.

"Why is the price so high?" she cried out, as she woke.

Sitting up in bed, her knees up and her elbows propped against them to support her aching head, she felt as if she had been torn apart. She was perspiring and yet cold inside.

"For what?" His voice came out of the dark.

"My freedom," she screamed, before she realized he was awake, and that she must have awakened him. "I must have been dreaming." She apologized as he gently pulled her back against his warm, reassuring body.

"About what?" he asked, gently cupping her forehead with his hand.

"A conversation I must have some day."

CHAPTER TWELVE

The berries were picked and preserved, the nuts harvested and stored, the game, such as it was, skinned and packed in ice. Although it was only November, the ground was hard, already steeling itself against the assault to come. Nature geared up in November. The winds increased, as if they enjoyed the absence of the resistant walls of leaves. The night temperature likewise dropped to gradually prepare the earth. The grass lost its smell. In fact, the autumn air surrendered its husky, full-bodied warmth and embraced now the clean, uncomplicated edge of cold. Just as in spring, the body merges with the air surrounding it, nerves reaching out for its caressing nourishment and its impending life; in autumn, the body begins a separation from the air that surrounds it—as if self-preservation warns it to withdraw from the air, whose biting edge soon can harm, warns it to separate itself from impending death, and to substitute artificial devices of warmth: a coat, a fire, a lover. The fire was already necessary now, not just for occasional warmth but for continuing insulation.

Grace had never liked November, with its premonition of death. This year was no different. Occasionally, and for no reason that she could understand, she felt afraid. Perhaps it was the shortness of the days or the grayness of what little daylight did exist. Even the lake below, which she had always seen as deep midnight blue or shimmering emerald, reflected the grayness of the mountain and its dying and dormant foliage.

She could hardly wait for snow now. Although it would virtually maroon her for the winter, especially since she did not ski, she welcomed the brightness it would undoubtedly provide. There was snow now nearly every morning, but only a little.

However, as the month advanced, several storms hit and a regular, pleasantly-deep blanket decorated the ridge and town below, lifting her gloom. The shortened days passed quickly, as Klaus protected tender plants from Winter, digging up bulbs and securing them in the darkness below the chalet's flooring. Apparently Deliverance had decided to take up winter residence under the chalet, too, where the warmth of the house itself would protect him. He scampered in and out regularly as Klaus worked there, startling Grace sometimes—his eyes glowing in the dark like an otherwise unseen apparition from Halloween.

Klaus had Grace sorting grains and seeds. Some were for planting in the spring, but most were for the birds. He felt that, since he had intervened by robbing them of a large portion of the acorns, chestnuts, and dried berries that normally would have weathered the first storm, thereby serving as proper food, it was his responsibility to provide an alternative. She loved it because it took her back to her youth, when she had carefully stocked homemade bird feeders with all kinds of seeds and suet for her "feathered friends," as she called them. She and her best friend had drawn up a club charter, which read, "We the people of the United Bird World…" that was all she could remember. That and the fact that it had occupied them for many a cold winter afternoon. *A glowing reminiscence,* she thought, as she sorted sunflower seeds.

Their nights were spent by the fire, which caused the chalet to glow to one approaching it from outside. To Grace, it seemed like a warm cocoon. It was more difficult now for the music get-togethers. Mostly because each of the others had their own work to do to get ready for winter, and also because of the increasing difficulty in traveling from one to the other. Fritz and Ursula were closest at the Luftseilbahn station, but the station and its restaurant occupied them. That and their responsibility to deliver supplies and mail to the ridge's inhabitants. It was a task made more difficult and time-consuming by the snow. She didn't mind the privacy though. Although she had made peace—more like a truce with Fritz—she sensed she and he would never be truly comfortable together. They had stood on the opposite sides of one too many past confrontations to fundamentally trust each other now. One too many judgments had intervened from both sides. Like former enemies allied now by altered circumstances, they wore their new robes uncomfortably. At least they had a mutual trust in each other's need to be on the mountain. That was a start. They were *all* convalescents, after all.

Reuben still looked, at every session, as if he were being pursued, his hair flying behind and about as if to divert the pursuer's attention—all this, despite that incredibly elegant body grace he possessed. *He might be fleeing*, she often thought, *but he is fleeing in style. Gainsborough could have done him justice,* she mused. She, however, saw only his desolate, pained eyes. He seemed to belong nowhere, and was therefore grateful to be at all welcome here. Klaus told her he was still battling the drugs that had destroyed his career, but that he was gaining ground.

Of all the motley group, she felt the greatest kinship with the African. She didn't want to think it was only because of the story Klaus had told her. She wanted to think she would have valued his particular vitality for itself, as there was no escaping his incredible gifts as a drummer. His agility and spirit had caught her attention that first night. But more recently she had come to appreciate his brilliant ability to support. He knew by instinct at just what instant the guitar, voice, or keyboard needed reinforcement. He filled the line out, always knowing just how much to support, and how much to guide. And guide he did. A pause—an uncertainty in the line of the song—and he was there, sometimes gently, sometimes aggressively. But always, with a seemingly infallible sense of proportion. He *enjoyed* his sound. How he enjoyed!

Grace had been free of dreams recently—particularly of the pursuit dream—and was feeling especially light-hearted. The mysterious presence that had pursued her across the years and continents was on hiatus. Tonight, as she listened to "Let It Be" from down below, she smiled. It had been one of her favorites. Since they played mostly British tunes unfamiliar to her, or new pieces Klaus was working on, the sounds of a familiar song from that time pleased her. She decided to join them—she and Klaus covering the vocal. She improvised very well—all except for one note, where she misjudged the interval and broke the chord. *No matter,* she told herself, *it is fun anyway.*

Klaus's voice sounded different to her tonight as he sang. It still seemed to reach beyond each note, striving for something, straining for the outer limits of his range. She had not liked his voice that much when she had first heard him sing. It was too gravelly, too strained. But tonight as she listened, she thought the natural huskiness appropriate. Then suddenly she knew that his voice was not strained. He had not pushed too far. His voice was merely pained. The recognition of the difference, and the honesty of it, enlightened her, and filled her with warmth. Banu was there for Klaus, supporting him always.

She was flushed and feverish tonight. She knew that. Grace asked Klaus if he would teach her to play guitar so that she could sing ballads and accompany herself. He said that he would.

As everyone left for the night, Klaus reached quickly for her hand, pulling her back as she started to climb upstairs. "Let's stay here," he coaxed, pulling her gently to the second fireplace directly below the main one upstairs.

"All right." They sat in front of the fire. He poured her an amaretto and then lay back against a large, Navajo cloth pillow and closed his eyes. Grace saw the copy of *Venture to the Interior* and picked it up. She opened it and read the first page. The style of poetic imagery interested her. This appeared to be a travel diary, and yet it had an air of mystery mixed in, and the grace of poetic prose. She turned the page and continued, compelled by Van der Post's account of his plane trip into the unknown territory in Africa that he was commissioned to explore. She had no idea how long she had been reading when she sensed she was being watched. As she looked up, she saw that Klaus was watching her with a very tender but very far-away look in his eyes.

"What?" she asked.

"I'm afraid I'm useless now," he joked, running his fingers through his hair, leaving a few stray hairs standing up with static. She didn't grasp his meaning. "I've been watching you read for the last ten minutes."

"And?" She still didn't follow his gist.

"And you read page two after page one. Then pages three, four…" He rotated his wrist to indicate a continuation.

The recognition of her victory over the final page was immediate. "My God, I did, didn't I?" She sat up on her knees, almost giggling. "I didn't even think. I just did it." She squealed and kissed him. "Thank you."

"You're welcome." He laughed and settled back once again, watching her gloat for a moment and then, flushed and happy, return to her reading.

The only sound was of the dry pine's popping as it burned, occasionally shooting a cinder out onto the stone hearth. She had no idea how long they stayed like that. She was mesmerized by Van der Post's narrative until Klaus asked rather cryptically, "You won't ever leave me, will you?"

Grace closed the book without looking up. She felt a twinge of fear in her stomach. Then she answered, "I love you."

"Then stay with me here."

"Right here?" she teased, not knowing exactly how serious he was about this. His answer clarified that much.

"You've come so far, Grace. You shouldn't leave. You were meant to be here." And then, as if he wanted to reinforce his assertion, he added, "You, more than anyone."

She would have preferred not to talk about this, what with the amaretto flush, and the ensuing mellow relaxation. But something she'd never seen before in Klaus's eyes made her take notice. It perplexed her because she couldn't grasp quite what it was.

"Klaus, don't you ever want to go down from the mountain?"

"No." His answer was immediate, unconsidered.

"But you seem so whole and content here. Wouldn't you go down even to share your knowledge? Perhaps to teach others what the mountain has given you?"

He didn't answer. She took that as encouragement and continued. "But Klaus, so many do not know that what they're pursuing—dying day by day for—is an illusion, that they already possess the very thing they desire. All they need do is recognize it, seize it, nurture it. You gave that to me. Don't you feel obligated to others?"

His bitter, scoffing laugh surprised her. "To very few, my love. To very few." Then seeing her frown, he pressed the lines away with his forefinger and continued. "I don't believe in the possibility of political change. Fritz, Ursula, and millions like them went that route. You've seen them, and the depths of their disillusionment. It doesn't work. It can't. It's doomed to failure because there are no political answers—only answers of the self. And the only ones capable of finding life in themselves are those who've fallen deep enough or been afraid enough to look at themselves because there's nowhere else to turn. It takes a very particular kind of desperation to appreciate yourself: life, love, nature, and that only. The ability to embrace the present—what is, and not what ought to be, or might have been—can't be taught. Let alone the ability to take the best of the past, and live in the present."

He finished and then sat facing her. "I love you, Grace. You have become part of me here. Neither one of us was whole without the other. I want you."

As she looked at his slender hands, holding hers like a daddy guiding his baby's first steps, she wanted to tell him that she wanted to go downhill occasionally. She wanted to go Christmas shopping. She wanted to see Sophie, maybe even pick up her friends in Zurich, if any wanted to visit her from Los Angeles. She loved his certainty, and him. There was no question that she was healing. The old feeling of paralysis was gone. *After all, I am singing.* She catalogued her progress to herself. *I am reading, all without fear now, and all due greatly to this beautiful man. But…what?* she asked herself. *What doubt shadows my certainty?*

His hands touched her breasts now, at first delicately and then firmly. As she lay back, transfixed by those piercing, somehow-different eyes, his hands stroked and caressed the curves of her waist and thighs. Her lips were dry. He saw that and kissed them with a promise of more. Deftly drawing her to him, her breasts rose and fell rapidly now until the pressure of his chest arrested them, and the conquering energy of his body passed through his clothes and hers into her innermost nerves. The dryness of her doubts gave way to the wetness of lovemaking.

She was on the ridge in three feet of new-fallen snow, gathering pine branches and fallen cones to make a wreath, when she heard the shots. There were five of them—in the distance. Her heart stopped that morning. Her mind listened. Then she heard them again, closer now. Then screaming and crying. Then a dazed groping as the fifth shot reached her—on instant replay.

The radio reception was bad. Each sentence was marred by static. But the tension and sadness in the voice of the announcer were evident as he read the news bulletin, interrupting a program of Swiss Christmas music.

Fritz had come recklessly running through the snow hysterically waving his portable radio above his head as if to flag Klaus. She had been too far away to hear his words, but she knew immediately that everything had changed. When she saw Klaus stumble, falling to one knee, and then get up and stagger inside, she returned as fast as she could. She arrived, breathless, in a blur of snow, only to hear the announcer repeat, "Once again, John Lennon of the Beatles has been shot to death outside his home in New York City last night at 11PM, New York time." Then he went on to say something about "violence in America," and the rest was a blur to her. Part of her mind heard the remainder of the bulletin, part of her mind tried to analyze why she felt as if she were exploding, and part watched with horror as Klaus, who was leaning alone against the wall near the door, repeated over and over to himself, "They got him. Got *even* him."

"Who would ever have known seventeen years ago," Fritz cried, his intense brow nearly covering his eyes, "that it would come down to this? If only he could have known the end."

"That sounds like something she would say," Klaus snapped to consciousness, referring to Grace. His outburst apparently startled even him, for it silenced them both.

Without knowing why, Grace began to sob uncontrollably, tears streaming down her face. She had to get out of there—away by herself. Her body was trembling, vibrating inside, and she truly believed she was going to rupture at the seams. There was a deafening screaming in her soul. She wanted to scream out loud, but felt only dry heaves, her brain pulsing, pounding relentlessly against her skull. Outside the chalet she could barely see through the blur of tears—crystallizing painfully now in the winter cold—to the blur of her thoughts. Her mind was racing as if she were a projectile in a time machine. Locked on a track, she returned to 1963 and back again at a mind blowing speed. Then again and again, each time seeing no images, only colors trailing behind her until some momentary flash of a scene from her past revealed itself and then was gone. With each swing back to the present, she was sure she would fly apart and this inner projectile would merely shoot off into space.

It was then, as she sank into a drift of diamond-studded snow at the top of the ridge, that she knew *she* had been shot. Something in her was dying, and she was exsanguinating right here, as surely as Lennon had. But why? She hadn't been a big fan of the Beatles, she told herself. She liked their earlier music up to "Let It Be," but had paid little attention to anything after that, and knew absolutely nothing about any of them personally, except that John and Yoko had been separated and then reunited. Why then did she feel she was dying now? Why had the death of a singer fragmented her?

The snow around her felt warm. The new snow falling on her from the deep gray sky now calmed her, brought her peace. She was relaxing, enough now to feel the stinging of the ice on her cheeks. The need to flail and scream had passed. The need to understand prevailed. Shockingly, as she tried to remember dates, places, people from the past, she could not. Almost as if the time machine in its frantic back and forth trajectory had obliterated her past, she found now that there was not a single memory she could take refuge in. She would have settled for anything—a quiet Sunday in her hometown in spring, a new dress, a dance, a final exam—anything. But all were gone. John Lennon had been nothing to her, yet he had been everything. He had been her past, and they had been as closely linked as if they were one. They had grown up in the same times, and his death provided her a rite of passage. Klaus had said that in war there comes a moment for each soldier when he crosses from boy to man, when he surrenders his youth and innocence, and there is no turning back. He is forever changed. Nothing is ever the same again. He is of a new age.

Grace understood that now. She felt at one with those in the human race who had entered a battle and survived, but lost something intangible during. John Lennon was a symbol of her past—her innocence and her youth. Even as he lay bleeding in a New York City courtyard, her past had been leaving her. The little girl was dead. The woman had survived.

She grieved now for that dead ideal. She would miss what she had been, and dreamed of. Ironically she had come to this mountain because she was stuck in the past. And that *past* had just disintegrated. "Traumatic amputation," she believed they had euphemistically called it in Vietnam.

Watching her footsteps now filling up with snow, she knew that in another half hour they would be completely obliterated by the new-falling snow, leaving no trace of her. She, too, would probably disappear into the landscape and return to the earth, so to speak. It was growing warmer, and more peaceful. There was absolute quiet.

Recognizing the symptoms now, she ordered herself to rise and return.

It had been five days since Lennon died, and a vigil had been set at the request of Yoko for that Sunday. At 8PM in Amsterdam, in the town square, where Europe's youth of the '60s had wandered, played guitar, and smoked dope, thousands would gather to coincide with the 2PM vigil in New York City. Grace had wanted to go, but Klaus, who had said not one word since the broadcast, had broken his silence to ask her why. She had told him she wasn't sure but she felt somehow that it might be her last chance.

"To do what?" he had asked.

"To be with *my generation*. If I have changed, then they, too, have changed. We may never stand together again as one."

"Please stay here," he had begged.

"I resisted so long, Klaus. I want to be there just once," she had pleaded.

"I need you. Please don't leave me on that day." He was shaking, and she had agreed to stay.

But since the broadcast, her brain had felt cramped, almost to the point of numbness. Words spoken long ago were attempting to surface but lay trapped inside. Almost as if she were sending herself a message, which was trapped en route, some idea was trying to express itself. She did not know what though, only that the inner struggle was exhausting her.

On the day of the service, the friends gathered at the chalet. Everyone was subdued, but each needed to touch the other, as if touching each other could confirm their humanity. *Brutality does that to the survivors,* she thought.

There were ten minutes of silence on the air in a live broadcast from New York's Central Park. The crowd at the band shell was near 200,000, and yet at precisely 2PM there was silence. Total silence. Only the occasional whump, whump of a police helicopter, or a baby crying, interrupted the palpable silence.

Then, precisely ten minutes into the vigil, it was ended by the amplified sounds of "Imagine." As John sang to his own piano about the brotherhood of man, about dreamers, and the world as one, Fritz took Grace's hand. She reached for Ursula. The circle was complete with the African, Reuben, and Klaus. They all stood now, undivided yet separate, deep in their private anguish.

"He told me one day he would write his own epitaph," Klaus reflected, breaking the circle. "I cuffed him and told him he already had." Then his voice broke, and he spoke as if John were there with him then. "Not you. By one who loved you. Surely not you." Then he bolted down below. There were a few moments of silence as each of the others looked to one another for a cue. Down below, Klaus seemed to be banging drawers in anger. Grace encouraged the others to leave and then crossed to the ladder. Before she reached it, however, she heard the lower door slam and knew that he had left.

She lay on the bed, still fully dressed, hoping the sound made by each gust of wind was Klaus returning. It was a fierce, ugly night outside, and the wind roared from one side of the chalet to the other, as if surrounding it. She was frightened enough by that assault, but even more so because Klaus was not there. He was out in it. She prayed to herself that he knew what he was doing.

For the past hour or so the notes to a poem—a refrain from her past—haunted her. But they were only fragments, and she could neither recollect what poem nor piece them together. Inside, the struggle with that buried message continued.

She could not tell when she fell asleep, but the storm was real in her dream—fierce and disorienting. She was out in it, searching for Klaus, yelling his name, and vainly listening for a response. She was approaching an angular snow pile with trepidation when the Stranger appeared. She could not see him at first. Blinded by the snow, she struggled on. She poked the pile of snow with her foot. It was not Klaus. Then she spun around to confront what was following her. There was no one there. So she staggered on, her feet guiding her through the forest and to the boulders near the inner lake—the one Klaus called the "true Brunnen." She was near the lake now, and it was dark. Someone was following her. Fear of the night, and of the stalker, gripped her. Then ahead, curtained by the blowing snow, stood the Stranger, waiting for her! He had revealed himself at last. All she had to do was pierce the curtain, and she would know who had followed her so long. She walked forward into the spiraling snow and came face to face with the Stalker. It was herself.

She woke suddenly.

Completely disoriented and shaking, the dream faded quickly from memory as she looked up into Banu's eyes. Startled, she cried out.

"Wake up, Grace." He spoke with urgency. "It's only me. But Klaus is not here. We must find him."

"Yes," she affirmed, vaguely wondering if he, too, were part of a dream. He was not.

"Hurry. Get dressed," he urged, and she knew instinctively that Klaus must be in danger.

"You should have called when he didn't return," he said, reproaching her.

"I thought he could take care of himself," she cried. "Can't he?"

"I don't know. He's wounded, too, don't you know?" he retorted, buttoning her heavy parka and securing her head with a thick, woolen cap Ursula had made. Then, seeing the fear in her eyes, he added encouragingly, "Of course he can, dear lady, I just want to find him, that's all."

He pushed her out into a crunching, sparkling day. The first intake of air caused a sharp stinging in her nostrils, and then her lungs. The ground crunched underfoot, the force of the night's wind having packed it firm enough. All trees were drooping, their boughs struggling against the weight of the new snow. Overhead, the sky was bright blue, punctuated only by a few wisps of high cirrus clouds. The entire mountain sparkled like a jeweled eye brow to the still-unfrozen lake below.

"My God," she said. "It's beautiful." But Banu was already ahead of her, rearranging his rope and pulleys. He came back to hand her a spiked pole, and to check the tying of her climbing boots.

"You look secure," he said. "Good footwear."

"Yes. Klaus got these for me."

"Where is he, dear lady?"

"I don't know," she answered, looking to the east. He understood and motioned for her to lead the way.

They had been walking several hours when she stopped, for no reason that she understood, and turned to him. All that was visible beneath his ski mask was the scarred, drooping right eye. "I want to go on alone. I think I know where he is. But I must go alone."

"But you don't…you've never climbed. Not in winter anyway," he argued.

There are times, however, when one truly knows one's limitations and capabilities. Grace *knew* that she could do this. Moreover, that she must. Banu clearly read the look in her eyes when she answered, "I can do this. You wait for us here."

After a long moment, he conceded. "But this is a dead end," he explained, looking at the icy path along a gorge, which stopped at boulders along the face of the mountain.

"It only appears to be." She laughed and knew immediately that he would not understand. "Wait here. Please?"

"All right." He shook his head as if palsied, then began to set up camp as she walked away from him along the path.

Her determination alone carried her past fear. She overcame the icy path, where one slip would have plummeted her below. Finding most of the boulders mercifully barren of snow, she climbed with great concentration and surety. She remembered the easy ones from their first journey. For one moment, as she paused to catch her breath and rest her leg muscles, she looked down at the white world below in the deep gorge. She sensed that courage is probably only fear driving one forward rather than paralyzing one, that the motivating force behind both cowardice and courage is fear—either emanating from the same seed. She pushed on and, having no one else to pull her up, she used her pick at the steepest point just as she had seen Klaus do.

At the top now, she ran quickly through the lighter snow under the pines, careful not to let low-hanging branches scrape her face. She arrived easily at the slope above the lake. There, like a green cat's eye, it sparkled, stark against the white face of the mountain surroundings.

Klaus was sitting on a rock along the water's edge, forming snow balls and idly throwing them into the water. He would watch the concentric circles emanating from his disturbance, wait for the surface to settle again, and then toss in another.

At first she smiled, both amused and relieved that he was safe. Then something began to frighten her, for his appearance, even with his back to her, worried her. He was hunched over and, had she not known who he was, she would have guessed him to be an old man, puttering at the water's edge for want of anything better to do. She braced herself to confront him, and told herself it was best to get it over with.

"Hi," she began lightly as she approached. He didn't turn.

"How did you know I would be here?" he asked, tossing yet another snowball mechanically into the water.

"I didn't. I just happened to be out for a walk. It was such a nice morning."

He laughed, causing her fear to abate somewhat.

"You made remarkable time. Did you do that by yourself?" He asked as if that weren't possible.

"Banu is with me, below the boulders. He was a little skeptical about dead ends," she joked, and then became more serious. "Actually, I didn't know if you wanted him here. The rest was much easier than before. I must be getting stronger."

He nodded and turned to look at her, as if sizing her up. "A fitting irony."

"What?" she asked, sitting beside him.

"That you would grow stronger, while I..." His voice disappeared as he looked up toward the summit.

As she watched him, she was grateful that he couldn't see the shock on her face. In only one day he was transfigured. Not only was he thin, his cheeks wind-burned and cracked enough to make his normally handsome young face appear gaunt, but he seemed frail, as if his once-hard body had lost its sweet vigor. He was pale and visibly trembling, despite which he had unzipped his parka and removed his gloves. His fingers looked blue. She put her arms around him, but he did not yield.

"John told me right here that he had acquired so much, yet felt so empty," he volunteered in explanation. "He asked me how that could be possible. He said he couldn't go forward because he didn't know which way he was facing."

She tried to reassure him. "Klaus, I think he had found peace."

"I hope. He saw clearly you know," he said, as if the two concepts were mutually exclusive, and he looked at her as if it were important she understand. "He saw that all that he had pursued—not just money, but *change,* too—was illusion. That he already possessed all that he could dream of. He had the guts to get out of the game. His new life was a solution. But they killed that."

"I know."

"A casualty by any other name would be the love of a fan," he parodied, and then muttered something about "incapable of grasping" before rambling incoherently with only an occasional word like "hypocrisy" or "capricious" making itself understood. Then mercurially he shouted, to no one in particular, "They will kill all of us, Grace, if we let them. He didn't even have a last word," he cried. "The good die young and the enlightened die mute."

"But their life, as they lived it, speaks for them. That means something, surely," she said, trying desperately to focus him. But he only laughed.

"Come. We must go back." She tried to lift him.

"I can't."

"What do you mean?"

"I can't go below," he stated flatly and finally. "John went below, but they got him. Why struggle for them? Live for yourself. Then they'll see, you'll see. You do see?" he begged.

She placated him as best she could. "Yes, Klaus, but we'll just go down to the chalet. You'll rest and get well," she urged, sensing for the first time that her lover was ill, seeing for the first time the depth of the wound he was covering. Something had snapped. Among the casualties of disillusionment on this hill, he was their rightful leader.

She wanted to cry but couldn't. For the idea, which had been nagging at her since Lennon's death, was taking shape now, apparently intensified by Klaus's trauma. It was imperative that she think clearly now. For some reason that she didn't understand she knew that his life depended upon her communicating now.

"Klaus, look at me," she commanded, as she fought off the late afternoon cold. "*Look at me.*"

He did, but his eyes were filmy. "Klaus, can you hear me?" He said that he could.

"You were right, Klaus, about my being trapped in the past because I was disappointed in the future as it had materialized. You were right about needing to live only today—each moment for what exists in the natural order of this beautiful planet. I came here obsessed with being recognized as an actress, and despairing that I might not succeed, wasting my life in the interim. You taught me that that was the test— that the meaning was in going the distance. And that I was mired in past preconceptions, in the mundanity of fame and possessions."

"I was wrong," he interrupted faintly. "Death reaches even into that 'distance,' invalidating even that."

"No. No." She shook him. "You were not wrong. At least about that," she qualified. "But you were wrong about something." She didn't know whether he was listening, but she had to try to penetrate his consciousness, which now seemed so intransigent. "Klaus, sometimes one must look to the past to renew the present. I know that now. Do you know how I know?"

Again, there was no response, so she continued rapidly. "I remembered the '60s here with you this summer, and especially this past week. True, I remembered riots, bombs, tear gas burning my eyes, mobs of shouting students, flag-draped coffins, body counts, funerals for slain leaders, and rock music to accompany the rampant doubt. All of it ugly. But do you know what? This is the most astonishing thing of all, Klaus. I was *happy* then. Yes, the '70s brought peace, of sorts. It certainly brought self-preoccupation. But I was not happy. I'm trying to tell you, Klaus, that my mistake was not in dreaming but in trying to know the ending. I see now that a dream should be a guide, not a prison. You saw that, but you went too far. You tried to deny the dream itself, and it's the dream that's essential to survival. Your wound won't heal because you're denying yourself."

He seemed to stop trembling, as if he were trying to understand, but doing so required all his physical attention. He looked at her now and didn't look away. He was listening. She knew she mustn't stop now, for without really knowing why, it was all so clear, and she was beginning to feel very restful.

"We survived the fire, Klaus—you, I, and the others. We came out of the '60s stronger. There is no need to deny or fear that strength, and especially not to pretend it was mere children's naivety. We can talk. We can guide. For me, that means dreaming, and the task will be for me to let the past renew my present, rather than cripple it. For you that means being here on the mountain, reassembling the broken spirits that come to you—making them whole enough to dream again."

"But John…."

"John was just one death," she whispered calmly. "Try again."

"I don't know. If I stay *here*," he looked around, "I can begin again. By myself. I can harm no one if I stay here at the inner lake."

"And no one can harm you, is that what you're thinking?" she challenged. "You think that *here* you're safe from those you're struggling to help?" She pursued relentlessly now. "That they can't turn against you?"

He didn't answer. Instead, he swallowed hard several times, so she continued to apply pressure. "All week long I've been hearing a song or a poem in my head—part of it anyway. But I couldn't remember the words, or lyrics, whatever. You know how bad I am about lyrics," she joked. "But on my way here, words started to come. I don't know why. But sitting here with you, watching you, and the changed look in your eyes, I remembered the words. Klaus, are you listening?" she asked, as if checking his pulse.

"Yes." He choked a bit on whatever he had been swallowing.

"Turns out, it was actually a poem. I think it was written for you. You can set it to music."

"What?" he asked, his voice faint but wavering.

She turned his head and looked into his eyes. "Shall I recite it for you?"

"Please."

She began, a little timidly at first, then more confidently as the once-crystallizing idea materialized clearly for her. *This was what had been gnawing away at the old subconscious,* she thought. This was what had been trying to push its way up since that terrible December 8 shooting.

"Do you remember the 'Keep on Keepin' On' memoir I told you I had begun long ago, and never finished?"

He nodded.

"Well, this was in it. I had forgotten. It just returned to me in bits and pieces these last few days." She paused for a moment to collect the words, or what words she could remember. "It's rough, Klaus, but this is what I remember at least."

He sat mute, simply looking at her.

"There was a time we thought each person mattered. A time when we thought we could make a difference. But past failures ring in suspicion, and future dreams engender fear. No matter what has gone, dear friend, keep on keeping on. The future matters.

"Comrades have fallen. Dreamers have gone. But for the sake of what matters, keep on keeping on. For out there in the future waits a boy with trepidation. Your legacy can reach him—if you keep on keeping on.

"No matter what is gone, dear friend, finish the run. Keep on keeping on."

And at the end, she repeated the refrain of the crude poem: "No matter what is gone, keep on keeping on. The future matters."

Her voice was clear and certain now, and Klaus's eyes were trying to focus once again. Though he still was some distance away, she knew the words were reaching him, for he unconsciously grasped her hand and clung to it. She improvised now, as she reached for his other frozen fingers.

"Never lose your dream. Without our legacy, hope for a better day dies. Keep on keeping on, sweet dreamer. Keep on keeping on."

She almost kissed the last line to him as she warmed his hands inside her parka.

He mumbled something that sounded like "synchronicity." But she didn't understand. When she asked what he meant, all he said was, "Remarkable."

She drew him close and began to lift him to his feet and, as she did, she whispered, "Even those you love will disappoint you if they stay long enough—if you stay long enough. But you must leave something for those to come. They will be blinded by their time, and we must try to show them the path." She looked for a long moment at his haunted face and then added, "Will you carry on?"

"If I can," he answered, as he looked back at the lake longingly. At the same time, however, he unconsciously buttoned his jacket and shook the circulation back into his left foot. "I could stay here, live here," he conjectured.

"Your friends are all waiting at the chalet. They need you, Klaus."

"And you?" he asked pointedly.

"I need you. Yes."

"Will you stay with me?" he asked, his now-clear eyes riveting her attention.

"I'll try," she answered simply. "Will you come below?"

"I'll try." And he did. His first steps were painful, she could see, and she supported him as best she could until his circulation returned in the legs. There was no telling how long he had sat, doubled up, numbing his arms and legs in the night's bitter cold. Slowly though, as the circulation returned, he straightened and seemed to regain his former stature. Only his pale face made him look somewhat of a ghost of himself. But his eyes were alert, almost little-boyish now, as he walked stiffly beside her. *He seems normal again, only understandably tired,* she thought, reassuring herself.

Because sunset was approaching, bringing with it its concomitant cold, she urged him on as fast as possible. The resolve that had carried her safely up the boulders must sustain the both of them on the descent. They must reach Banu by dark. *If we can get that far,* she thought, *we will be home free.*

They were at the top of the boulders now, just ready to begin the descent. Grace was a few paces in front when she heard him stop behind her. Turning to see what held him up, she saw him looking back through the trees toward the inner lake.

"What are you thinking?" she asked, hoping to get him moving.

"Just that there is one moment when each person is totally in stride, where magically dreams, energy, and purpose converge. And in that moment, he is all that he can be."

"Hmmm," she agreed, motioning for him to hurry. He looked over his shoulder at her, smiled enigmatically, then turned toward her and, using his stick to knock snow from around the cleats, prepared to descend.

At that time of day, there were no signs of life near them—not even the tracks of an animal to lead them. There was only the sound of their breathing. Grace climbed down an easy level, and was assessing which step to take next when he called out, "Have you ever seen anything like it?"

It took her a moment to realize he was referring to the sunset unfolding before them. It was indeed a spectacle. The Alps across the lake below were powerful and almost totally white. The lavender and reds of sunset, however, were tinging them opalescent. The deepening sky behind them silhouetted each peak, enhancing its drama even more. But most striking of all was the sun—an enormous, blood-red ball that was settling slowly beside the highest peaks, where it would eventually disappear behind one of the lowest. It dripped red onto the lower ridges, purpling the sky behind it. The scene was one of perfect balance—as if there were a gap in the symmetry of the mountain range, which the sun had chosen to fill with its glorious orb. Balance and beauty. And perfect harmony.

"Do you think if I searched the world I would find anything as perfect as that?" he mused. She laughed lightly. The fact that he was joking a bit now reassured her.

"A masterpiece, right?" she answered, sharing his appreciation. He did not answer. She thought nothing of it at first. But then suddenly, the familiar knot in her stomach returned.

"Klaus?" she called over her shoulder, afraid to turn. She waited, repeated his name again. Still he did not answer. "Oh to hell with it," she swore, as she gave in and turned to him. He was gone!

She would never really know the precise instant he went back, nor the precise moment when she realized she would not go back for him.

The dream had ended.

And she woke.

It's getting late, she thought. She had no way of knowing how long she had been up here, but she knew Robert would be worrying about her down below. Her time on the mountain had definitely restored her though. She felt rejuvenated and saw very clearly again. Although she suspected the knot in her stomach would still be there, with every descending foot of the aerial car, the images of her life became more vivid and more focused. Reaching the bottom, she knew she was still afraid. She breathed in deeply, with some trepidation, and then beamed, as no darkness was inhaled. It had been left on the mountain.

Robert was still on the beach where she had left him earlier that afternoon. He had removed his sweater and was using it as a pillow for his outstretched body. She noticed the sleeves of his striped shirt were rolled up, and guessed it had been a warm day. Hearing her footsteps on the pebble beach, he sat up quickly.

"I was getting worried about you," he exclaimed. He always did, she thought. "You were gone a long time," he said, reprimanding her gently.

"I know. I guess I must have fallen asleep. I'm sorry."

He looked at her warily, as if she were different somehow, or as if he didn't know what to expect from her. "Did you enjoy yourself?" he asked.

"Very much."

"You were gone so long, I thought maybe you'd met someone up there," he joked.

"You might say that, yes," she answered pensively, the dream's images still vivid in her mind.

"That's nice," he answered, and asked no more. He was groaning with the muscle stiffness from his hours on the stone beach and gathering his things more than listening. She guessed he hadn't even heard her.

"You know, I've been thinking."

"What?" she asked, handing him his sweater, certain now that she was happy to see him.

"That you'd have to have a gentle soul to live in this place."

She nodded, took his hand, pulling out her map of Austria as they walked toward the car. "I've been thinking, Robert, that maybe we should just bypass Innsbruck and go directly to Vienna. What do you say?"

He nodded.

CHAPTER THIRTEEN

❦❧❦

As if in complete simpatico with the setting sun on the mountain that day, the blood red ball of the sun off the Santa Monica bluffs sank below the horizon of the Pacific, turning the attached sky into ribbons of opal, red, yellow, pink, and amber.

It was still warm, with no breeze blowing. Throughout the afternoon, refreshments had been replenished, bathroom breaks taken, and then the manuscript rejoined just where Grace had left it. Her three interviewers were totally immersed in the story. At some point she noted that they had all stopped making notes and were just listening. *They are going to be grateful for the low-tech recording they made,* she mused. *It's too good a story to miss. And their inexperience has caused them to lose sight of the mission.*

Grace Archer was regarded by many as one of the great storytellers in modern American literature, and small wonder her story had captured their attention, too. But, she knew they would gather themselves. This part had been easier than anticipated. Truth be told, she was relieved to have finally spoken of her months of psychological residence with the mysterious inhabitants of that mountain dream, and of Klaus's impact on her. She closed the manuscript, with an affectionate stroke of its cover.

Doug exhaled. "Wow! A dream…a dream…" He fidgeted for a moment with the recorder, pretending to check to make sure he had gotten the story. Grace knew he was stalling, to buy some time to digest the revelation, and to formulate an intelligent follow-up question.

Before Alyssa could usurp that position, he asked, "Did you and Robert marry?"

Clearly he's out of his element here, Grace mused. *Handsome as he is, he's inexperienced in the ways of love and romance. Probably not the hard story journalism he had in mind!*

"No." Seeing both men were very curious about that she added, "We realized that although we cared about each other a great deal and might always remain friends, we did not have the same goals and priorities."

Not wanting to be left out, Adam's guttural voice belied his leprechaun appearance. "What did you do then? After you left the mountain?"

"I started a marketing business, which I own to this day. I found a church that fed me spiritually, and which helped me to know how to know. I met and married a businessman, and was married to him until he passed away in 2008. And, I became a writer." She smiled at the simplicity and the elegance of four short sentences that summed up her life. But she knew they would want more.

It was the final follow-up question she now dreaded. Watching Alyssa through the afternoon, Grace knew that Alyssa would not fail to ask the key one. She was a romantic. The question would not come from a man but from a woman. Waiting for her now to do so, Grace looked slightly to her left into the distance and smiled.

"Ms. Archer," Alyssa began, "I know in your manuscript, Klaus is a dream. It all was a dream. Please excuse my impertinence, but somehow I think there is more here—something you are not telling us." Alyssa paused, assessing Grace's demeanor, then continued with an instinctual question. "Did you ever see Klaus again?"

Adam and Doug were clearly startled by that question, and had that, "What the heck? Wasn't she listening to the story?" look on their faces. One could almost hear them thinking, *Didn't you get that this was a dream?!* Their embarrassment hung in the air.

Grace's breathing was momentarily interrupted. There was still time to bail out, to just leave the interview with the exotic and romantic—though tragic—story of Klaus and his Grace. For she had indeed come down alone from the mountain, and ventured forth into what had become a blazing adventure the likes of which she could never have imagined—either before the mountain, or even while on it.

Recent events of the last couple of years, however, had shaken any tranquility and quietude she harbored about that time—and memories from the past overtook her regularly. Somehow she knew though that the real climax of the entire romance had only just occurred, and that could only mean the remaining years of her life would likely also be marked by tumultuousness and life-changing discoveries. But first, she would have to rewrite the ending of the book. Truth was indeed stranger than fiction.

Taking a deep breath, and swallowing her doubts, Grace looked directly at Alyssa and dropped the bomb shell that would become the subject of TV talk show hosts interviews and commentaries, articles, you name it, for months to come.

"I have a confession to you three." They were all listening, this time with notepads ready. "Klaus was always intended to be fictional—a matter for discussion over coffee." She could almost feel Alyssa expectantly honing in.

The boys seemed oblivious to the subtlety of her statement. Their minds were spinning with myriad questions they and others would have regarding what, then, did he represent? Who did he represent? Was he another part of her? Was Klaus another voice within Grace Archer—signaling the ongoing debate one has with the part of oneself that wants to risk and go forward, and the part that wants to settle and hold on to the moments of peace they cherish?

Grace looked directly at Alyssa. "That's right. Klaus, when I lived and wrote this, was fictional." She paused for a moment, knowing full well that she was famous for writing novels whose scenarios ended up playing out in real life more true than fiction. And that was a coincidence or prophetic vision that baffled and fascinated journalists, government leaders, and entertainment industry film makers. No one knew just how she could have written suspense novels that time and time again proved almost true—without having any access to the real facts.

She sighed before continuing. "Then, I actually met 'Klaus'—on a different mountain, in a different country."

The two boys' jaws were dropped, but Alyssa, clearly the romantic of the group was totally into it. "Oh, my, God! I knew it! You are serious?"

"Yes, my young friend, I am." She paused for all of them to take a breath. "It was in the winter of 2013, and for three months I stayed on the mountain with him. But, in the spring, I came down from the mountain. I had to. And my journey continued to us meeting here today."

Alyssa almost feared the answer she knew she was about to receive on her obligatory next question. "And 'Klaus,' did he come down from the mountain?"

"No. He stayed." There it was: fact and fiction, novel and memoir, fantasy and reality all intertwined into a story that defied imagination. "A vision from 1967, revisited in 1980, waited for me in 2013." And *that* is the truth of it.

ACKNOWLEDGMENTS

I want to especially thank Stephen and Kim Winters for their wisdom. Their simple reminder that this is my testimony assuaged the fears I had of letting this story be known. You are much appreciated.

My editor, Stephanee Killen of Integrative Ink, once again added her talents and insights into making the book a clearer communication than it originally was. Linda Gipson of Gipson Studios created a soulful and aesthetic cover, which evokes the mystery and gentleness of the story. Both of you are a joy to work with.

And very especially I want to thank the test readers who took their valuable time to read the rough manuscript and communicate their experiences with it: "Sam" Warner—who is one of the most thoughtful, insightful writers in America today—I thank you. Your depth of understanding humbles me.

Eileen Batson, my publicist, I thank you for not only reading the book but also sharing your personal experiences in reading it.

Rich Whiteside, Kim Winters, Safiyah Banks, Gayle Bax, Anthony Ziccardi, Tammy Newell all provided insight and encouragement.

ABOUT THE AUTHOR

Lee Kessler is a television actress, screenwriter, playwright, and stage director. Her career in Hollywood and New York spans 40 years, and includes dozens of guest starring roles in episodic TV, mini-series, and movies-of-the-week. She had reoccurring roles in the series *Hill Street Blues* and *Matlock, and was submitted for Emmy nominations twice for her starring roles in the movie* Collision Course, and the ABC special, *Which Mother Is Mine?* She co-starred with Peter O'Toole in the movie *Creator.*

Lee became the first actress in the world authorized to portray the legendary diarist Anais Nin when her play, *"Anais Nin—The Paris Years,"* was produced in New York and Los Angeles, with a subsequent tour on the West Coast. She also directed the West Coast premiere of A. R. Gurney's "Who Killed Richard Cory?"

Since the publication of her Amazon best-selling suspense novels *White King and the Doctor, White King Rising,* and *White King and the Battle of America: The Endgame,* Lee has made numerous radio and TV appearances discussing the books' relevance to the events we have all experienced in the first decades of the new Millennium, and has spoken often at book signings and private readings in New York and Los Angeles.

She has a passionate commitment to the youth of today, known as Generation Y, and speaks to them often about their role in keeping America free. Further, she challenges them to make the journey from being the "Trophy Generation," which is their current mantle, to the "Hero Generation," which she believes they are destined to become.

CPSIA information can be obtained
at www.ICGtesting.com
Printed in the USA
FSOW01n0210230218
44620FS